It had been so long

Nick smiled and fingered the knot in his tie. Abby was playing jazz again, finally. He used to hear her doing that in the days when she occasionally smiled her shy smile and wasn't quite so thin.

She was looking forward to a night on the town. His hand shook, and he studied his fingers with disbelief. Old Dorset, Mr. Cool, shaking like a high-school senior going to his prom.

He hoped she'd like the restaurant. It was one of the best places in Seattle. He wanted to give Abby wonderful things. And wonderful food, things to make her feel good and be healthy, seemed a good place to start. He'd bought flowers, too, long-stemmed pink roses. Later he'd find a way to give her the rest of what she should have. He'd find a way to be with her...all the time....

ABOUT THE AUTHOR

Before turning to writing full-time five years
ago, Stella Cameron edited medical texts.
Her dream then, and even as a child, was to
become a writer. Stella enjoys creating
characters who take on situations people
normally wouldn't tackle—like Nick Dorset
caring for a pregnant neighbor in *No
Stranger*. Stella herself has been a coach at
several births, which for her have been
moving experiences.

Books by Stella Cameron

HARLEQUIN AMERICAN ROMANCE
153–SHADOWS

HARLEQUIN SUPERROMANCE
185–MOONTIDE

HARLEQUIN INTRIGUE
50–ALL THAT SPARKLES

No
Stranger
Stella Cameron

Harlequin Books

TORONTO • NEW YORK • LONDON
AMSTERDAM • PARIS • SYDNEY • HAMBURG
STOCKHOLM • ATHENS • TOKYO • MILAN

For Dennis and Marikae Moraski,
who shared a miracle.
For Donna Clifford, who shared her knowledge.
And for Andrew Perlbachs—a gentle man.

Published April 1987

First printing February 1987

ISBN 0-373-16195-6

Chapter One

"What love life?" Nick laughed. He leaned against the window frame and twined the telephone cord through his fingers.

"Don't fence with me, Nick Dorset. Who are you seeing? We all refuse to believe you've turned into a saint. I'm your sister, remember? I know you."

Some things never changed. "Sure you know me, Janet. Boy, do you know me." He enjoyed the calls from his sister in Omaha. The banter was always so comfortably predictable. Janet, two years older than himself and ecstatic over marriage and motherhood, felt it her duty to nag him into similar bliss.

"Are you listening to me?" Janet demanded his attention.

"Sure, sis. I always listen to you. And I know everyone in the family thinks it's time I settled down and had ten kids. Unfortunately, no one's offered to fill the bill."

"You mean you never give anyone the chance to offer, or accept, either." Janet's high silvery voice sputtered along the line. Nick was twenty-nine, she persisted. He'd had his flings. He was established. If he had to settle in a dreary, wet place like Seattle, at least he could have the comfort of a wife to share his home and to come back to from all those awful planes he piloted. Didn't he ever think of giving up flying? They'd all thought he would be tired of playing airplanes by the time he got out of the air force.

"Mmm. Nope. Not yet, Janet. I enjoy commercial flying even more than the service. Faraway places with strange-sounding names and all that. The only thing I'd like better would be my own planes—my own business. But that'll come in time." Absently he twisted the rod to open the vertical slats of the wood blinds. Instantly the gray light of an October afternoon made fuzzy lines on the opposite wall. He'd lived on Seattle's east side for six months, and the area's moody grandeur never bored him. "By the way," he added, "Seattle isn't dreary, kiddo. Wet, but never dreary. I'll have to get you out here sometime."

"Don't change the subject, Nick. You left a trail of disappointed hearts behind you here. There *has* to be a woman in your life. You just aren't talking."

He sobered. This sister, physically so like him, also had an uncanny habit of picking up emotional vibes he'd hardly acknowledged. "Rein in that imagination, Janet." The muscles in his broad back had tightened unconsciously and he shrugged, trying to relax. "How's wonder kid and Crete?" *What kind of name is Crete?* He smiled despite himself. Janet's husband might have an unlikely name, but he was a decent sort, and Nick thoroughly enjoyed him.

"Great." Her voice became warmer. "Oh, Nick, it's so good to have someone to share everything with. And Penny's gorgeous. Her ballet teacher says..."

Nick tuned out. He'd have several minutes in neutral before he was forced to add anything to the exchange. Two-year-old Penny was a subject on which Janet could expound indefinitely and without prompting. He let the words pour over him. He could see Janet, tall and well built, her tawny eyes flashing animation while she repeatedly pushed back her wavy brown hair. He realized one of his hands was buried in his hair right now and shook his head slightly. As teenagers, they'd often been mistaken for twins.

A vehicle door slammed outside. He edged around the bay window to sit on the arm of a dining chair. From there he had a clear view of the corner outside his condominium building. His unit, on the third floor, overlooked three converging streets.

"I know you'd love to watch her," Janet was saying.

"You bet I would," he agreed, narrowing his eyes to see who was loading a chest of drawers into a U-Haul truck parked directly in front of the Lake Vista condos. "You'll have to let me sit in on a lesson next time I get home. But isn't she a little young for ballet?"

"The best dancers start at two. Her teacher told me that Nureyev and Gallina..."

Russian ballet dancers, or any ballet dancers, weren't high on Nick's list of fascinating topics. The scene he was witnessing held far more interest.

Surely that was John Winston from next door. The guy was in some hurry. With the help of a man whom Nick didn't recognize, Winston bundled pieces of furniture carelessly into the truck.

A silence in his right ear snapped his concentration. "What'd you say, Janet? There's a lot of noise on this line." John Winston and his buddy were shoving a rolled carpet in now. Every few seconds, John glanced over is shoulder.

"Say it again, Janet. I can't hear you." His own lack of attention wasn't helping.

Winston had stopped, holding an end table at waist height. Rubber squealed, and an old brown Pinto slowed to a halt a few feet from him. A tall woman got out, and Nick took a deep breath. The familiar jolt hit somewhere deep inside him. Abby...John Winston's *wife* Abby, he reminded himself. Her brother, Michael Harris, flew for the same airline as Nick. Michael had given him the lead on this condominium.

Nick rolled onto the balls of his feet to peer down on John and Abby Winston. John had gone into action again, shoving the table into the other man's hands, grabbing a cardboard carton. When Abby grasped his shoulder, he shrugged free and turned his face from her. She just stood there then, both hands shoved deep into the pockets of that baggy black coat she always wore. There was an ethereal quality about her, an intriguing air of deep preoccupation. She was an artist of some kind, store display design, Michael had said—whatever that meant.

Janet was asking if they should hang up.

"Right," Nick managed. Her voice really was fading in and out. He didn't feel like talking anymore. "Okay, I'll call you in a few days, and maybe we'll get a better connection. Give my love to Mom and Dad and everyone. Hug Penny for me. I should get a couple of days layover back there sometime next month.... No, I don't think it'll be Thanksgiving, but as long as we see each other... Yes. Love you, too. Bye."

He reached to hook the receiver into its wall cradle. This could turn into a long day if he didn't come up with something to occupy himself. If it weren't for the fog, he'd be on his way to Honolulu, but Seatac International was socked in.

An ember spat from the fireplace. Nick hurried to retrieve it from the hearth and piled another log on the flames. He sat on his haunches, thinking, as he so often did, about John and Abby Winston. They'd proved to be disconcerting neighbors. It struck Nick that he hadn't seen John for weeks. The guy must have been on a trip. A merchant seaman, a big, handsome man, he always had a hearty greeting when they passed. He had that gift for meaningless banality that made Nick vaguely uncomfortable. Particularly when he was often forced, only minutes later, to listen to John's raised and angry voice through an adjoining wall. No audible reply ever came, and in contrast to her husband, Abby Winston had little to say in the hall or the parking lot. Invariably she muttered something indistinct before dropping her shadowy gaze. But she was beautiful. Very, very beautiful.

Nick returned to his vantage point at the window. Something odd was in progress with these people. John's job took him away regularly, sometimes for long periods, but with a U-Haul truck? No sea trip would require transporting dressers and rugs—and a grandfather clock? And why the rush? They must be moving out. The sinking feeling in his stomach was easily identifiable: disappointment. And he couldn't pretend it would be John he'd miss. He frowned. Maybe some of what Janet had said was right, and he was jealously guarding his bachelor status. Burying himself in an adolescent infatuation with a married woman who scarcely knew he was alive was a pretty safe way to stay unattached.

John threw a paper cylinder into the truck cab and hurried back into the building. Nick heard his running footsteps on the stairs and the thud of the door across the hall. The man who'd been helping load nodded to Abby and climbed into the passenger seat of the truck.

Minutes passed. Abby stood, the toes of her boots overlapping the curb, rocking slowly back and forth. The breeze that swirled the fog into shifting wisps flattened her short black curls to one side of her head. She was thin, too thin. The coat also flapped dispiritedly, first wrapping her slender back tightly, then billowing wide. Nick imagined her eyes, huge and gray, thickly lashed; the fine, upsweeping brows. Oh, Abby Winston was very beautiful all right, and very out of reach.

Footsteps sounded on the stairs again, going down this time, leaping, two, three steps at once. John Winston wanted to be gone. The woman at the curb didn't turn as her husband passed her, a kit bag over his shoulder, a large suitcase in his other hand. He hesitated a few inches from her, shrugged, threw his baggage into the truck, and latched the back handles.

Then she moved. Nerves leaped all over Nick's body. Her hands hovered close to John Winston's sleeve for seconds before she touched him, and he turned. Nothing. No expression on those masculine but almost too pretty features and in the eyes that Nick knew were blue. Fair curls blew this way and that from beneath a watchman's cap while the man stood like a carving, waiting. For what?

Abby drew fractionally closer, gripped both of John's arms, and in profile Nick saw her lips move. The man only shook his head and broke contact.

Instinctively Nick opened the window a few inches, knowing at the same time he was too far away to hear anything that was said.

John raised his hand and Nick did hear something. "Goodbye," John Winston's shout came. "Good luck."

And now he was smiling broadly, backing away, running around to climb into the driver's seat and gunning the engine to life.

Abby's hand was also raised. The truck swung in an arc and headed west, toward the freeway. Her pale fingers remained uplifted, gradually splaying, before she dropped her arm.

At last she turned, and Nick found he couldn't breathe. She hunched, looking closely at something he couldn't make out. Her feet scuffing, she came close to the building until he had to crane to keep her in sight. Immediately below his window, she stopped, and he saw what held her interest. With the thumb and index finger of her right hand, she turned her wedding ring in slow circles. Her bowed head hid her face.

The breeze increased to a whining wind, rattling the windows. Unlikely hailstones fell in smattering handfuls against the panes. Fog and wind and hail—only in Seattle, Nick acknowledged wryly. She'd lifted her head now. She must be cold, and the hail would hurt her face.

Good, she was coming in. He stood. It wouldn't do for her to realize he'd been watching. *Oh, my God.* He leaned his forehead on the cold glass. Those haunting gray eyes were flat, unseeing, and she continued to turn the ring, around and around.

In his mind, he saw again the closed gaze John Winston had given his wife. The nonchalant wave, the empty words "Goodbye. Good luck." The running, wanting to be gone.

Abby had clutched her collar tight to her neck. Nick saw the pinched set of her normally soft, full mouth. She'd just said goodbye to her husband. And, without any proof more tangible than his own gut feeling, Nick knew it was a last parting.

John Winston wouldn't come back.

Chapter Two

"You're uptight as hell. Are you going to make this easy on both of us and tell me what's wrong?" Marie Prince spoke with her usual harsh bluntness.

Abby wasn't in the mood for a woman-to-woman confidence session. She ignored her friend and looked around the living room. This place needed attention. Immediately. Michael was supposed to drop in on his way from the airport. If she didn't figure out a way to camouflage the gaps in the decor left by John's departure, her brother would ask questions she wasn't ready to answer. She pulled a potted areca palm beside the couch to fill a space vacated by an end table and assessed the effect. Now an empty spot glared where the grandfather clock had stood with the palm beside it.

"I'm not going to go away, Abby, so you might as well break radio silence."

"What?" Good Lord, she was losing it. For a few seconds she'd almost forgotten Marie was there, draped over the one remaining armchair. "Sorry, Marie. Guess I was thinking about something."

"That'll do for a start." Marie flipped her long honey-colored hair behind her shoulder and arranged her body more comfortably. "Why are you pacing like a caged cat?

And rearranging furniture? Not typical, my friend, not at all like our dreamy girl.''

"I'm not—'' Why was she shouting? She never shouted. "I'm not a dreamy girl, Marie. I'm twenty-seven. Too old to be any kind of girl. And I'm not uptight. Michael's coming for lunch, and I was deciding what I could fix him, that's all. Don't you have to get back to work?'' Sometimes Abby wondered why she and Marie had remained friends for so many years. They were completely different. Maybe that was the attraction. Marie was direct, always let you know exactly where you stood. Abby couldn't overcome her reticence and knew she never would.

"I've got time yet.'' Marie watched her narrowly, calculating. "John's been gone again for two weeks?''

Abby sank wearily onto the couch. "I don't remember telling you that.''

"You don't seem to remember much these days.''

She let the wise remark pass. "Yes, John's been gone again for two weeks.'' Two weeks since she'd had to accept that he meant to finish what he'd started.

"What did he say when you told him about your job? That must have rattled him. You were always so into display design.''

Every inch of Abby's skin turned clammy. "I don't know what you're talking about.'' There was no way Marie could know about that.

"I tried to reach you at the store. They said you left on the fifteenth of October. I called and called you here. No answer. That's why I came over. Where have you been keeping yourself? The jerk who fired you wouldn't give me any more information.''

Unfamiliar anger started a slow burn in Abby. "Connie Reese isn't a jerk. I hope you didn't give her a bad time. She couldn't tell you where I've been because she wouldn't know. And I wasn't fired. I quit after falling off a ladder. Under the circumstances, I thought I should find a job where I could keep both feet on the ground for a while."

Marie crossed her legs and leaned back. "You were probably right." Her green eyes flickered over Abby. "How are you feeling now?"

"Great." She didn't want to discuss all this. She wished Marie would leave. "Do you still like working for the secretarial agency?"

"Sure. It's a living." Her long pink nails danced, typist style, back and forth on her jean-clad knee. "And I like variety. At least I know I'll be with a new set of faces every few days."

Abby tapped her fingertips together. Whatever happened, her family mustn't get wind of the mess she was in, not yet. Yet she needed someone, a sympathetic ear.

"Abby, you didn't say what John thought about the job change. I expect he understood, didn't he? When is he coming home?"

Questions, questions. Marie had been in the condo fifteen minutes, and already Abby felt battered, exhausted by the incessant questions. "John doesn't know I quit. He walked—he left before I could tell him. I'm not sure when he'll be back. This could be another long trip." She'd better keep her own counsel, after all. Less danger of complications. Fortunately she hadn't revealed where she'd found work. "Marie, I'd love to talk with you all morning, but I'd better get on. I want to whip up some lunch for Michael."

Marie pouted theatrically. "Michael, Michael. Always Michael. Always *has* been Michael first with you. Why can't I stay for lunch, too? That brother of yours was a crummy kid, but he sure grew into some hunk, and—'' She caught Abby's eye and held up a hand. ''All right, all right. I get the message. I'm leaving.''

Abby was instantly contrite. ''I'm sorry. It's just that you and Michael rubbed each other the wrong way from the day you called him an undersized runt. Doing that to a fourteen-year-old boy in front of his first girlfriend was a good way to make an enemy for a long time.''

''He asked for it.'' Marie laughed. ''He said I was fat in front of half the football team. My pride has never recovered.''

Abby couldn't help grinning. ''I think you two could have been great friends if you didn't hate each other so much. You have such a wonderful gift in common—elephant memories.'' She looked away, remembering how uncomplicated childhood had been. ''Don't go just yet, Marie. Michael won't be here for an hour or so.''

''*Is* there something you're not telling me?'' Marie asked tentatively. ''Are you in some sort of trouble?''

The temptation to unload the accumulated bitterness soured Abby's mouth. She rubbed her face with both hands.

''Hey, hey. Don't get upset, please. You know what a chicken I am around a crisis.''

True, Abby thought and looked up, a bright smile fixed in place.

Marie came to sit beside her. ''What's happened?'' She looped an arm awkwardly around Abby's shoulders.

''A lot,'' Abby said and remembered what she really liked about this sultry woman, had liked since they were grade-school kids together. Marie, so determinedly tough, hid her own pile of disappointments behind a brittle wit, but only to protect a kind heart that had gotten her into trouble too many times. A pretty face and sexy figure had brought her very little real happiness.

"Okay, friend. You don't want to talk about it, and I'm pushing you. Sorry. I never was Miss Tact." Marie smiled crookedly. "But I do care about you."

Abby took a long, shaky breath. "Give me a little time. I've got some things to sort out in my head, alone. There's so much I haven't faced and still don't understand, I—I just need time, that's all.'

"It isn't John, is it?"

Buzzing filled Abby's head, and little disjointed sounds. "John?" There wasn't enough air in the chilly room.

"Oh, Abby. It is John. You started to say he walked out just now, then stopped yourself. But that's what you meant, isn't it? He's left for good this time. Damn, I should have known. And now of all times."

"No, no, no." Abby shook her head. The blurring at the edges of her vision frightened her. Just like the day she'd fallen from the ladder in the store. "I'm not going over this now."

"You two never were right for each other." Marie shook her gently. "Look at me. This is awful, but it's not the end of the world. I went through a divorce and lived to tell the tale. And I didn't know anything was wrong with my marriage until I was told I wasn't wanted anymore. At least you had warning. John's been giving signals for ages. I was surprised—" She closed her mouth firmly and rested her forehead against Abby's. "I'm sorry."

Everything Marie had said was true. She and John had been on a direct path to disaster from the day they married. Now it was hard and painful to remember the first blush of their love and that careless certainty that they'd go on as they were, carefree, forever. How soon the freshness had died, been killed by John's increasing indifference and infidelity. Her head throbbed.

"What happened, Abby? Did he— Has he been— Oh, hell."

Abby met her friend's gaze steadily. "You're right: John has left me. Actually he left me before the last trip. He only came back to get his things." Surprisingly it didn't hurt so much to tell the truth. "We're getting a divorce. He filed back in September, and it will probably all be over before the end of November. I knew it was coming, but I kept hoping we'd pull things together. I wouldn't face that it was useless. People in my family don't divorce."

"Damn it, Abby. I always felt you two were really different types, and—and it had come to this in the end." She inhaled sharply. "I know how you feel about marriage, about not giving up. But you don't love him anymore, do you? Not really?"

"Don't!" Abby implored. She got up and crossed to the fireplace. Charred remnants of wood gave off a faint, acrid odor. "No." Resolutely she faced Marie. "It's true. I don't love him. I haven't for a long time, a year or more. He destroyed what we had—" She paused, pressing a finger and thumb into the corners of her eyes. "I'm trying not to lay it all on him. It takes two, isn't that what they say?"

Marie nodded mutely.

"I guess I made him feel guilty, and he couldn't handle that."

"Guilty? How do you mean?"

Abby spread her hands wearily. "Not by what I said. More because I never said anything, I think. He's only worked when he felt like it. His mother's been so good to him, sending money, thinking she was encouraging him to make something of himself. But it didn't work that way. Knowing he could always get money if he needed it seemed to make him believe he shouldn't have to settle down. But, Marie, he's thirty-two years old. *Thirty-two.* He knew he wasn't being fair. And feeling guilty made him angry, and it just kept getting worse. This past year has been awful. I was never sure he was really at sea when he said he was. I know there was— I'm sure he met— I think—'' She stopped. Some things didn't have to be said, should never be said.

The green eyes watched intently. ''You think what? Don't hold anything back now. It'll help to get it all out.''

''Please—'' Abby willed steadiness into her voice. ''My parents are my main concern right now. If they knew how things stand with me, they'd, well, first they'd be so hurt about the divorce. They'll have to know, but it doesn't have to be now, not while I'm trying to get on my feet. I've got to make myself financially secure. John and I split what we had, but it wasn't much to begin with, and with all the expenses there will be, I need a chance to build up some savings. If Mom and Dad found out, they'd try to help, and they can't afford it. So, Marie—''

Quickly Marie broke in, ''Don't say it. You don't have to. I wouldn't tell a word of this to anyone unless you said you wanted me to. But I want a promise from you in exchange.''

Abby raised a questioning brow.

''You'll talk to me regularly. I want to know exactly how you are all the time. You're going to need a friend, and I want to be that for you. Promise?''

''Oh, Marie.'' They met halfway across the room and hugged. As always, Abby felt gangly beside her diminutive friend. ''Yes. Of course. Thank you for everything." She sniffed and laughed. "I feel better already. Now if I can just keep snoopy Michael from catching on, I'll be doing fine."

"He won't." Marie wrinkled her nose. "Men don't pick up other people's vibes the way women do. No sweat. Just don't say anything. John's on a trip, so what else is new?"

No sweat. When Marie left, Abby surveyed the room again. Marie had never yet failed to say what was on her mind. She hadn't mentioned how bare the place was, so she couldn't have noticed half the furniture was missing. Michael, always rushing, flitting from subject to subject, was even less likely to realize anything was different.

She checked her watch. Michael wasn't due in at Sea-tac airport for another hour. Postflight formalities and driving here would take forty-five minutes more. Time for her to make a run to the store. The cupboard was definitely bare. She needed to watch what she spent for a while, but a few groceries would be a good investment, both to divert Michael's suspicion and to provide a couple of the balanced meals she'd neglected for too long.

THE FAMILIAR navy blue uniform and peaked cap caught her eye the instant she swung the decrepit Pinto back into her parking slot. Darn. Michael had beaten her to it, and she'd wanted to set the stage before he arrived.

She switched off the ignition, waited for the predictable rattling sound in the engine to stop and rolled down the window. "Hi, Mike," she yelled, grinning broadly. "Be right with you." It was so good to see him. He'd bent down to fold his flight bag in half. Then he straightened, and her smile faded. The uniform was the same, but it was her neighbor, Nick Dorset, and not Michael who approached her car.

Abby rubbed her chilled hands together. A panicky fluttering assailed her nerves. The man had thought she was calling to him. He must think she was a nut.

"Hi, Abby." He stooped, bringing his face close. "How's it going?"

"Fine, thanks." She fiddled with her keys and reached for her bag on the passenger seat. "Sorry I shouted like that. I thought you were Michael." In all the months Nick had lived next door, she'd never initiated a conversation. But that didn't mean she hadn't noticed him.

"I was going to stop by and see you."

"Oh?" She looked directly into his eyes, puzzled. Coming to see her? Her skin heated. There was no reason for Nick Dorset to stop and see her. He was merely being nice, trying to ease the awkwardness she must be giving off in signal waves.

"Yep. Michael asked me to talk to you." He had unusual eyes, deep-set, a kind of gold-brown. Dimples formed lines beside his full mouth. She'd never seen him so closely before.

He smiled, evidently not noticing she was tongue-tied. "He's hung up in Chicago. Iced-up wings or something. I said I'd stand in for him, keep him out of trouble with you."

"Oh," Abby said again and blushed. She must sound like an airhead, but she couldn't seem to think of anything else to say. Nor could she look away. His mouth was wide, and his teeth were strong. Abby glanced at the deep cleft in his chin, the vertical shadows his smile made beneath high cheekbones, the straight nose. A big, unnervingly handsome man, only made more appealing in the perfectly cut airline uniform. She made much of shoving her keys away. Even if she were in a position to think of another man taking an interest in her, Nick Dorset would be the last to consider Abby Winston as anything but his married neighbor, the sister of one of his colleagues.

"Mike said he hopes to get out by this afternoon. That means it'll be late this evening before he gets in. He said to tell you not to worry, and he'll call when he's at his apartment."

Abby rallied. "Thanks." She put her hand on the doorhandle, but Nick opened it first and stood back for her to climb out. "Thanks," she repeated and cringed. This was ridiculous. "I would have worried. He's not always too good about letting someone know when he's held over. We should all be used to him by now, but I guess we can't help being human." There, she sounded together now, in control. She'd also just said more to Nick than she'd ever said since he'd moved in. Somehow she'd almost been afraid to look at him too carefully before. There was an air about him, a force field that moved with him. Even with the few words they'd occasionally exchanged in passing, she'd felt a stirring of interest she couldn't afford to feel.

She opened the hatchback, expecting him to leave. He came beside her. "Let me help you with those." One long hand, tanned from Hawaiian stopovers, closed around the top of a grocery bag.

"No," Abby said too vehemently. She swallowed uncomfortably. "I mean, you have your own things to haul in. I can manage a couple of grocery bags." She laughed, and the sound was unnaturally high. "I need the exercise. Thanks for letting me know about Michael."

"You're welcome." He took a step backward, keeping his eyes on hers until Abby buried her head in the hatch. She was lonely, that's all, and reacting to the long absence of a strong man's presence in her life. John had ceased to be there for her months ago.

She juggled the two sacks and slammed the trunk shut. The bags weren't heavy, just unwieldy, and they ground the handle of her purse into her wrist.

"That much exercise no one needs." Nick's voice stopped her as she shoved through the outer doors to the building. He'd pushed his cap to the back of his head. Thick curly brown hair stuck out in all directions. "Give me those." He slung the strap of his flight bag over his shoulder and took the bags into one arm. With his free hand, he guided Abby upstairs.

She mustn't puff. The three flights were no steeper than they'd ever been, they just seemed that way each time she climbed them.

At her door she hesitated. He made no move to give up the groceries, he simply stood there, smiling amiably, waiting. Abby took a deep breath and fumbled for her door key. "You must need to get on. Set those down, please. I'm a hopeless loser of keys. This may take time." She scrabbled along the torn bottom lining of her purse.

He only broadened his smile and leaned against the wall.

"Really," she said. "Don't bother—"

"It's no bother," he cut in. His was a gravely voice with a warmth no woman would miss. "Take your time."

Her fingers closed around the elusive keys, and she unlocked the door. "There. Finally. I—" She couldn't dismiss him like a delivery boy. He was Michael's friend. "Would you like to come in? I'm dying for a cup of coffee myself. And I bought stuff for Michael's lunch. It shouldn't go to waste." Of course, he'd refuse. She was vaguely horrified she'd included lunch in the invitation.

Coffee would have been enough for conventional politeness.

"Sounds wonderful. I like cooking, but I'm always lazy when I've been out on a trip."

Abby led him inside, her heart thudding uncomfortably. She had to be crazy. What must he think of her? A woman who rarely spoke, let alone issued lunch invitations, and now she was allowing him to carry her groceries and come into her home as if they were old friends. He wouldn't know John was away. She shut out the start of the thought that John was gone permanently—not simply away. But Nick didn't know anything about them or her, and he'd think she was just being pleasant to someone Michael knew.

A thought did strike her fully, with a blowlike force. She must guard against any slip with this man, as closely as she'd intended to do with Michael. If Nick Dorset discerned anything amiss, he was likely to mention it to Michael, and the damage done would be just as great.

Nick cataloged every move Abby made. She was as edgy as a cat. He could almost see her nerves, tight as fiddle strings, a hair away from springing wildly from her control. And, oh, was that control ever tenuous.

For two weeks he'd watched and waited for some sign of exactly what was happening next door. Nothing. Running into Michael Harris in Chicago today had been the answer to a dream, an excuse to actually talk to Abby.

He carried the brown bags to the kitchen. The living room was Spartan, each piece of furniture tasteful, but widely spaced as if a lot was missing. But he knew it was. Muscles knotted along his jaw. He could not allow himself to give away that he knew something was wrong. She must be the one to tell him if she wanted to. And she wasn't likely to open up with a man she scarcely knew.

"Here?" He smiled over his shoulder at her, then set his burden on the kitchen table when she nodded. "Ah," he sighed, deliberately cheerful, dropped his bag and took off his cap. It bothered him that they were strangers. He wanted to know Abby. He wanted to know her very well.

She wore the baggy black coat and made no attempt to remove it. "Sit down." She waved toward the living room. "I'll make that coffee and rustle up something to eat." The attempt at lightness didn't quite come off.

"Let me help."

"Well. Oh, I guess." She smiled, the soft mouth parting in a way that made his eyes follow the motion. "You can make the coffee. It'll have to be instant, I'm afraid. The mugs are in the cupboard over the sink."

How many women could manage to look exotic in a worn old coat? She did. Its starkness intensified the beautiful fragile bones in her face, the big, almond-shaped eyes beneath her sweeping brows. *Had* John Winston left for good? Nick felt instantly guilty. He was actually hoping John had cut out permanently and left the field with Abby open for him. *Good God.*

"Did you find the mugs?"

He started. "Yes. Right where you said they were." All two of them, not counting a chipped one set off to one side. He filled the kettle and put it on to boil, found a jar of coffee and scooped a spoonful into each mug. Glancing sideways, he confirmed what he thought he'd already seen—she still wore the wedding ring. It slipped loosely around her knuckle. He frowned. She was thin, thinner than she used to be. And the air in her condo was arctic, which must be why she kept on her coat. She probably didn't even realize she hadn't taken it off.

"Do you like tomato soup?" Abby lifted a small can from the bag, then a package of sprouts.

"Love it." His throat tightened. Her face was drawn now, anxious while she thought he wasn't studying her. An insane longing to take her in his arms shocked him. *Whoa, buddy. Watch it.* "Here," he said, reaching to take the sprouts, "you start the soup, and I'll finish unpacking these things for you."

Her eyes turned up to his, luminous yet strangely empty. Beaten. That creep had left her, and she was struggling to hold her life together. And there was very little money around here. Nick straightened his shoulders. Abby was a tall woman, but beside her he felt huge and very masculine. Protectiveness was a foreign sensation, but she made him want to take care of her.

She hadn't moved. "You must have better things to do than unpack my groceries," she said in a small voice. "I feel like a nuisance."

Nick laughed with a heartiness he didn't feel. "A nuisance? Don't kid yourself. I was lonely and wondering what I would do with myself this afternoon. I almost invited myself to lunch. I'm the one who should feel like a pest."

Abby laughed too, softening the pale line around her mouth. "Right. You are a pest. But I'm glad you're here." She reddened and turned away to open the can.

Once she must have been spontaneous like that all the time—the way Michael was. Somehow the natural sense of humor had been ground out of her, and Nick had a good idea by whom. He reached into a sack. He'd never been easily put off from anything he really wanted. And he really wanted Abby Winston. With some patience, he might just find a way to get her. A flash of amusement rose in his mind. Ten kids might not be what either of them would ever want, but she'd certainly fill the bill very nicely as that "someone to come home to" Janet had mentioned so often.

Boy, did he have a way of getting ahead of himself. Way ahead.

Pots and bowls clattered as Abby prepared soup. Nick lined up her purchases on the table. Four loose carrots in a plastic bag. An apple. A small package of ground meat and a single, thin piece of whitefish. Cheddar cheese and a loaf of unappetizing-looking store-brand bread. Food intended for one and not much of it. She had bought two large cartons of milk.

Nick held back the million things he wanted to say. Another person's pride was sacrosanct. Abby was clearly trying to keep up appearances. She must have a chance to become comfortable with him before he tried to gain her confidence.

"Oh, good grief." She shoved the pot to the back of the stove. "I forgot the sandwiches. Cheese and sprouts okay?"

"Perfect," he said evenly. He knew perfectly well cheese and sprouts were all she had, but he'd have said yes to turnip and liver sandwiches if that's what it took to stay with her as long as possible.

He finished making coffee and carried it to the living room. He'd been inside the Winstons' condo once, when Michael first brought him over to see the one he'd actually bought himself. Nick was almost certain there'd been a glass-topped dining table in the bay window. Now the area was empty except for a pile of brightly colored cushions heaped in one corner.

Uncertain where to set down the mugs, he stood in the middle of the room. Damn, he didn't want to embarrass her. He sat on the couch. There wasn't even a coffee table anymore. What had happened here? Why would Winston feel it necessary to strip the place like this?

"Here we are." Abby carried a tray. She took what was clearly an instinctive step toward the window and stopped. For a second she seemed disoriented, and Nick almost went to her. "Uh, here we are," she echoed faintly.

Nick breathed hard. "Let's sit on the couch. We'll be comfortable." One end table remained. He put the mugs by his feet and reached to take the tray. She handed it over and watched him slide it onto the end table.

"Good idea." Her lips came together, and the eyes became vast. She stood, pressing her palms together, swaying slightly as if uncertain what to do next.

What could he say, should he say? *Has your husband left you? I know he has and that you're having a hard time; please let me help you. I'm crazy about you; I have been from the first time I saw you.* Instead he patted the couch beside him and said, "Come on. The coffee and soup are getting cold."

She crossed her arms tightly. "Are you cold? I'm not." Her chin came up, and a spark of defiance lighted her eyes. "But I can turn up the heat if you like. If you ... if you think the coffee and—" She looked down at her coat, and a hint of pink swept over her pale cheeks. Then she laughed.

Of course, the heat was turned down to conserve money, and that's why she kept on her coat. Nick experienced the closest thing to panic he remembered since his first solo flight. He was out of his depth. And far from helping Abby Winston, he was making her acutely miserable.

She almost rushed to the thermostat, rotated it sharply, much higher than it ever needed to go. In the next instant she unbuttoned her coat, fumbling, tugging until it was off and she could hang it in the closet by the door.

"There." She faced him in a loose dress of some gauzy blue stuff assembled in horizontal panels. When she crossed to stand in front of him once more, the fabric floated about her slightly. It was too light for the time of year.

"There," Nick agreed in a voice that didn't sound like his own and handed up her coffee.

She took a sip. The feverish color remained in her cheeks. "Not so bad for good old instant brew, huh?"

Nick said nothing. He clutched his own mug so tightly he could feel every groove in the pottery. Desperately, his heart jamming his throat, he tried to concentrate on her face. Not that it mattered where he looked. He'd finally discovered what any fool would have seen a long time ago.

Abby Winston was pregnant.

Chapter Three

Pregnant. Nick slammed his front door behind him and tossed his flight bag down the length of the hall. What a bloody fool. And what a bloody fool he'd almost *made* of himself. A few more minutes of ignorance, and he'd probably have been concocting some way for them to get together again. Inviting her to go somewhere, even. Thank God for small mercies. At least they'd been spared even more embarrassment.

Hell, hell, hell. He skimmed his cap after the bag and dragged off his jacket. She would have expected him to know she was pregnant. Whether or not he'd actually seen the obvious shouldn't have been a factor. Why hadn't Mike Harris mentioned the baby? Nick started for the bedroom, loosening his tie as he went. Mike hadn't mentioned the baby because he was Mike. The guy only sat still when he was driving a bird. That was probably also the one activity capable of keeping his mind on a single course for more than ten seconds.

Nick slumped on the edge of the bed. He had embarrassed her. In those few seconds after he'd glanced at her stomach, while he'd riveted his eyes on hers, he'd given the whole show away. She knew he hadn't been aware of her condition and that he was shocked. He'd gulped the coffee and the soup, forced every bite of sandwich down his throat, prattling on all the time about absolutely nothing. And Abby had pushed the spoon around her own bowl, not eating, and hadn't touched the sandwich.

Pregnant women were supposed to eat properly, weren't they? Janet had been a fanatic... *Oh, damn it.* It was none of his business. Nick stripped quickly, trying not to think, and pulled on running pants. If all else failed, there was always exercise. He'd run this mess out of his brain.

Warm-up first. Stretch. He dropped to the rug and gripped his ankles, pressed his knees to the floor with his elbows. One, two, three. Press and release. He closed his eyes, concentrated on breathing, in, out, fill from the bottom, in, out. Shoot. That son of a bitch Winston had left her alone and pregnant. He'd taken his pick of what they'd owned and gone away. Did Michael know?

Push-ups. They were the thing to fill the mind. He rolled on his stomach and stretched out. Jeez, he must be getting old, his calves felt like warped shoe leather. What had happened to the college track star of a few years ago? Up, hold, down. Ten of these were going to feel like a hundred and ten today. He'd never make his usual fifty.

How would she keep on working and care for a child? *Concentrate, Dorset.* Twelve, thirteen. He was moving more smoothly, breathing better. If Mike knew, she wouldn't look so alone and desperate. He'd never allow her to go short of money or live in a bunch of cold rooms and not have enough to eat or— The Harrises were a close family. They had to know. If they didn't it was because Abby didn't want them to, and it wasn't his place to interfere.

He flopped onto his back, clasped his neck in both hands and did a series of rapid sit-ups. Now he'd go to the track at the junior high school across the street and run until he was too tired to do anything but sleep. He grabbed a shirt and sweat jacket and left the building at a trot.

The track was a godsend. It had been one of the factors that helped make up his mind on the condo. Gravel scrunched beneath his feet, flew up in damp little clumps behind him. The air felt good, cold, whipping his skin, riffling through his hair.

None of his business. The words kept time with his thudding feet. Abby Winston was none of his business. She wasn't the only lovely woman in the world. And plenty of them were neither married nor expecting a baby. Who needed someone else's grief? Janet had been right: it was past time for him to spread out, meet people, women. Next week he was due to visit Omaha. Maybe he'd look up some of those disappointed hearts his sister never failed to mention. Yeah, maybe he'd just do that.

"ABBY, HONEY, eat one of these turnovers. Your dad made them specially because he knows how you love them."

Abby smiled at her mother and took a pastry from the proffered plate. She wasn't hungry, but she wouldn't disappoint her silent father. "Thanks, Mom." She smiled at Wilma Harris. "And you, Dad." George Harris watched and waited, unsmiling, until she took a bite. "Mmm. Dad, like I always said, no one bakes an apple turnover like you do."

The pale face rumpled into a thousand wrinkles that seemed permanently flour-lined. George had been a baker since he was sixteen, and his skin had long ago taken on a powdery quality as if the residue in the air where he worked followed him everywhere. Even his thinning hair was dull white.

By comparison, Wilma was florid, an energetic rotund woman never seen without a splash of magenta lipstick and highly rouged cheeks. Her hair, steel gray now, was still brushed up at the neck and sides into the crinkled puff she'd worn as long as Michael and Abby could remember.

"Don't I get a magic confection?" Michael stopped pacing the tiny room and hovered at Abby's elbow. "We know who's the favorite around here. I don't get special tidbits baked for me."

Abby grinned up at him and punched his ribs playfully. "Sure, Mike. No one does anything for you, including all those poor girls you keep on strings in every city you fly to."

He sat on the rug by her feet and hung his dark head. "Not true, not true. I'm maligned. Any one of them is free to go whenever they like."

Wilma laughed delightedly as she invariably did over Michael's inflated reputation as a lady-killer. Even their father grunted, shaking his thin shoulders convulsively.

"About time you settled down, son." George's voice, always a surprise since he spoke so rarely, crackled deep, yet oddly papery. "Like your sister. Your mother and I are getting into this grandkid bit. You should see the stuff she's piling up for the baby." He smiled fondly at Abby. "That little man's not going to want for anything, I can tell you."

Abby kept the corners of her mouth turned up. "Little man, Dad? If it's a little lady, doesn't she get anything?"

"Oh, George, listen to you." Wilma laughed comfortably. "In a while I'll show you the christening gown

I've started, Abby. Two yards long. All lawn and Austrian lace." A happy blush rose in her cheeks. "Cost a bit, I can tell you. But nothing's too good for that baby—our first grandchild. And it doesn't matter whether it's a boy or girl. Either can wear a gown like that. I was thinking maybe all your children could use it. Like a sort of heirloom. And Michael's, too."

All your children. Today, while they were all together, Abby had hoped to find the courage to explain what had happened with John. The baby was due in less than two months now. She couldn't pretend much longer.

"Mrs. Winston wrote to me," her mother continued. "What a lovely lady. She thinks the world of you and John. And she's so happy about the baby. She'd like to come out when it's born, but the trip from New York would probably be too much for her, and she's sensible enough to admit it. That heart of hers…" Wilma clucked sadly.

A deep breath drained Abby. She felt herself sink and shrivel. What would the news of John's defection do to her mother-in-law's heart? The sensation of being closely watched prickled over her skin, and she met Michael's piercing blue stare. He raised his brows, and she felt he could see inside her head. Quickly she looked away.

"Wilma, tell Abby the rest of what Mrs. Winston said." Her father had leaned forward in his reclining chair. "About after the baby and all."

Abby studiously avoided Michael's unwavering stare but knew he hadn't take his eyes off her. He'd guessed something. Unwittingly, by what she'd said, or not said, she'd given herself away. He might not have figured out exactly what was wrong, but he was suspicious. Nick could have alerted him. Nick had definitely guessed she had a problem—in addition to the pregnancy that had so patently surprised him. Hot blood rushed to her face at the memory. How could he not have known that? He'd looked so shocked when he realized. And he'd almost fallen over himself making a hasty retreat. She'd seen him twice in the week since that disastrous lunch. Each time he'd nodded briefly and headed for the running track, looking too spectacular in shiny clinging blue pants and muscle-hugging shirt. Damn. She wanted to go home. Instead, she said, "What did Mrs. Winston say, Mom?"

Wilma finished pouring fresh coffee all around. She sat again, slid on the pair of half glasses that hung from a chain around her neck and fished an envelope from her apron pocket. "This only came this morning. I'll read you the bit George is talking about. Mrs. Winston's as proud of you as we are. Your art and everything and the way you've settled John down. I'd have thought she was more old-fashioned than me, but she even says she's glad you've kept up with your work, and she hopes you'll go back to it when the baby's old enough."

The expensive paper rattled as she looked for a specific page. "Here it is. She says: 'I've been thinking so much about them, John, Abby and the baby. I know I can't make the journey, but I've only got one son, and I'm not going to give up the pleasure of holding his baby. As soon as Abby's up to it, I'm going to pay for them all to come to New York and stay for a few weeks. We'd probably better wait for the weather to be a bit warmer before the baby travels, but then I'm going to have them come. I think looking forward to that is all that keeps me going these days.'"

Wilma folded the letter slowly and pushed it back into her pocket. "Poor soul," she muttered. "She doesn't have the pleasure of seeing the pair of you the way we do."

Abby coughed and put a hand over her mouth.

"What is it?" Michael said, instantly on his feet. "Are you all right?"

She nodded, coughing more loudly as tears filled her eyes. Pointing to her throat, she muttered, "Just a tickle. Excuse me," and rushed from the room.

In the tiny rose-papered bathroom off a narrow hall, she locked the door and sat on the toilet cover. The too-familiar pounding had started in her temples once more. She reached to run water over her fingertips and touched her lips, her brow and jawline. Nausea hadn't been a problem since the first few weeks of her pregnancy, but now she was sure she would throw up. The apple turnover sat, a leaden lump, in the pit of her stomach.

"Abby! You okay?" It was Michael, calling through the door as he had so often when they were kids and she'd run away from his teasing to find a place to hide. "Abby, please say something. You aren't fooling me."

"Coffee went down the wrong way," she managed. "Thought I was going to choke to death. Go tell Mom and Dad I'm okay so they don't worry."

"They aren't worried. Open the door, sis," Michael whispered. "I want to talk to you."

Oh, God. Nick Dorset had let the cat out of the bag. Slowly she reached to shoot back the bolt, and Michael came in, closing the door behind him.

"Okay. We don't have long, so come clean. Is it money? I know John's at sea again, and the checks don't always get through on time. Is it that?"

She stared at him. "No, no, not really." He didn't know anything. Relief slackened her muscles.

"Oh, Abby." He dropped to his knees and hugged her, smoothing damp curls back from her face. "This isn't a good time to be alone, is it? You want John with you.

How could I have been so dumb? No experience, I guess. Forgive me for being an insensitive jerk?"

She nodded against his shoulder. "If you were, I would."

He leaned away, a sage expression on his boyishly good-looking features. "Pregnant ladies get blue for almost no reason. I know I read that in a magazine once. Must have forgotten, that's all. I'll come over more often. We can go to the movies. Yep, that's what we'll do, go to the movies."

Hopeless. She was steadily drowning in her own cowardice. But how did you tell all these happy people, all these people who thought your world was rosy, that you were getting a divorce and the whole damned sky was about to fall around your ears?

"Thanks, Mike. You're sweet. You always were."

He grinned, instantly cheerful again. "That's what all the girls say. Come on. Let's get back."

Abby laughed and let him lead her to the living room. Their parents stood side by side near the black metal fireplace, the top of George Harris's head barely reaching his wife's eyebrows.

He cleared his throat loudly. "Abby, your mother and I have been talking things over, and we want..." He paused, and Wilma elbowed him gently. "We wondered if you and John would like it if the baby was christened in New York. After all, John is Mrs. Winston's only child, and she couldn't make it to the wedding, either—"

"We'd come too, of course," Abby's mother broke in. Excitement heightened the color along her cheekbones. "Your dad and I've got a bit put by, and we always talked about taking a trip one day." She lowered her lashes. "Kind of like the honeymoon we never had. Anyway, that way John's mom would get to be at the christening, and we wouldn't miss it, either, and we'd have a trip. It'd be a real adventure," she ended in a rush.

Abby felt marooned, isolated and gradually slipping farther and farther from safe ground. While she smiled and heard her voice saying the right things, laughing, an intangible bubble walled her off. Michael wrapped his parents in a bear hug and talked of being the only one who could fly them to the East Coast. After all, he'd have to go, too. He'd also arrange for them to pay a fraction of the normal fare; dammit, he'd pay it himself. It was all a wonderful, wonderful idea.

An hour later Abby set out on the twenty-mile trip back from her parents' house in the north end of Seattle to the east side and the hateful job she must keep as long as possible. She despised herself for not telling her folks the truth about John and getting it over with.

When she crossed the Evergreen Point Bridge over Lake Washington, a setting wintry sun cast cool orange chips over the choppy waters. Abby glanced from the road, to the dense evergreen forest, to Mount Rainier, a giant gold-lit snow cone to the south and began to smile. She loved this place and loved her baby and her family, and she'd make her life come right. She didn't need a man to help her.

BY TEN, ABBY WAS counting off the minutes until the notice on the Laundromat wall could be flipped over to the side that read, No Attendant on Duty. In Case of Complaint Call: with her own telephone number added in black wax pencil.

Her art. Abby eyed the drunk snoring in a green plastic chair by the door. His ragged laundry had long since fallen to the bottom of the dryer, but she shied away from waking him. Her art seemed very distant. What would her parents say if they knew their daughter, their pride and joy, was managing a twenty-four-hour Laundromat? And Michael? What would he think, and Mrs. Winston? She felt sick again and sat with a thump at the end of the central row of chairs.

No one knew about this except Marie, and no one else would, if she could help it. Marie had badgered the truth out of her, and somehow being able to talk to someone made the discomfort easier to bear. The day would come when Abby could go back to her own profession, Marie insisted; this was temporary, and jobs were hard to come by when you were pregnant.

Abby pushed herself to her feet. Every move was becoming more difficult. She transferred two loads of wash to a dryer and inserted coins. The noise helped late at night, made her feel less alone. "Manager" was a laugh. She was the only employee. The man who'd given her the job came by every few days to empty the coin boxes. He said little, never looked directly at her but handed over her paycheck regularly every other Friday. The paycheck, Abby reminded herself when she was dejected, was all that mattered.

She wished someone else would come in. The drunk showed up regularly, always late, always reeling, and although she figured he only wanted a warm place to sleep, he frightened her. Her car had been acting up lately, and she worried it wouldn't start one night. The thought made her claustrophobic.

Some people left their laundry for her to do. They usually tipped. So did the customers who had her tend their dry cleaning in the large do-it-yourself machine at the rear of the store. Abby began folding a pile of towels and squelched her dislike for the work by telling herself for the hundredth time that in her condition she was lucky to have found something. Thanks to this job, her savings were still untouched.

"Good Lord!"

Abby froze. She'd know that voice anywhere. Still folding a towel, she turned slowly and looked into Nick Dorset's surprised amber eyes. She put the towel into a laundry basket and smoothed her dress. "Hi, Nick. Off your beaten track, aren't you?" *Oh, please, please, don't let him tell Michael.*

"You too." He dropped a bulging pillowcase and tugged off his gloves. "Never struck me I might not be the only one with washer trouble. Yours is out too, huh?" He met her eyes directly, and she saw him swallow. She made him uncomfortable, and she hated that. But he hadn't cottoned to the reason for her being there. If she could just keep up the pretense...

"You're lucky." Her brain seemed to be scrambled. "Uh, lucky. You can get your stuff right in. All the washers were full when I got here, or I'd be long gone."

"Right." He nodded, unzipping the black leather jacket. "Yeah, I'm lucky. I'll just get this load going. I didn't realize this was the closest Laundromat to our place." While he spoke, he shoved clothes into a machine, then shut the lid.

Several miles from Lake Vista; Abby hadn't realized it was the closest, either. The possibility of someone she knew coming in had never crossed her mind. Nick was looking around vaguely.

"If you didn't bring soap, you can get it from the dispenser," Abby said before she could stop herself. She mustn't risk any kind of conversation with this man for more reasons than one. He stirred feelings in her she shouldn't have, feelings that would horrify him if he as much as suspected them. And he represented a threat to her hope of finding an acceptable way out of her predicament.

He bought a box of detergent and started his machine. Abby finished folding and cast about for something else to do without giving herself away. She glanced at the wall clock. Fifteen more minutes, and she'd find an unobtrusive way to flip the sign. Then she'd breathe more freely, certain no one would ask for assistance and give her secret away.

"Abby, could we talk?" Nick had sat and pulled a book from his pocket, but it lay unopened in his lap. "About the day we had lunch?"

She lifted her chin with a sense of having to clear an air passage to her lungs. He was going to say he'd guessed everything about her and John.

"Please?" His smile made those long shadows beneath his cheekbones. "I feel bad about it."

She sank down beside him, clenching her hands together. "I'm the one who should feel bad. The food wasn't very appetizing, and I was lousy company." The dryer behind them stopped, and she glanced quickly over her shoulder. What would he think when she didn't take the clothes she'd folded with her? Nervously she added, "I was a bit down that day, I'm afraid."

"Because your husband's gone again so soon?"

Her scalp prickled. "He, er—" Overreaction would be death. The comment had no hidden meaning. "Yes."

"When will he—"

She leaped up. "Oops. Dryer's stopped. Don't want wrinkles."

"Abby." He walked beside her. "Is there something you'd like to share with me, something that wouldn't hurt so much if you had someone to talk to?"

Her pulse thundered. She'd been right to fear this man's intuition. "No," she replied with a forced laugh. "Of course not. Whatever makes you think that?" Her eyes went to the clock. Eleven. Instead of locking the customer's laundry in the supply room, she'd take it with her and make sure she was back before the woman came for it in the morning. That way Nick couldn't guess she worked here.

He didn't move away. "Let me help." Without making a fuss, she couldn't stop him from taking the other end of the sheet she held. He snapped the fabric efficiently, folding and passing in a manner that spelled practice. "Like old times," he chuckled. "This was always one of my jobs at home." With the last fold he approached her to take the sheet and covered her hands with his.

Abby parted her lips. Why couldn't she get enough air anymore? His fingers were warm and hard, strong. She closed her eyes and let him take the sheet from her. He must think she was strange. He was probably laughing at her behind those deep, deep eyes.

"I guess you're on your way now," he said quietly, and when she glanced up, she saw no hint of laughter. "It's icy out there now, Abby, and foggy. Be careful. You shouldn't be driving in conditions like these."

And in a condition like mine, she thought self-derisively. "Thanks," she murmured. "I'll be fine." The truth was she was terrified of slippery roads and the long deserted stretches where she feared her increasingly temperamental car would break down. She said, "No one needs to worry about me."

John Winston no longer mattered to her. She was glad they'd soon be divorced. But although she wanted her baby, she resented the way John had effectively spoiled her for another romantic involvement. How could she expect Nick, or any man, to show a woman alone with a child anything but decent concern? She piled one of the store's baskets high and gathered her coat and purse.

A rumbling grunt snapped Abby's attention to the man by the door. He snuffled and rubbed his bleary eyes. She dropped her coat and redistributed the load in the basket.

She kept her head down. Nick picked up her coat and leaned close beside her against a washer. "I'll carry that load out for you. It's too heavy."

Shuffling footsteps approached, but she didn't turn around. "I can manage." The old coot might be half pickled, but he could decide to notice any change in routine.

"You got a problem, missy?"

Abby gripped the rim of the basket in both hands. "No," she said too sharply and glanced sideways at the man. He swayed slightly. "Everything's fine, thank you."

He hiccupped and rubbed the back of one hand over his mouth. "Mister." His eyes didn't quite focus, but he aimed a glare at Nick. "If you don't want trouble, you better not mess with the help around here."

Chapter Four

For seconds Nick's face was blank.

Abby waited, her fists clenched on top of a washer. The too-familiar numbing sensation edged into her head.

"You got anything to say, mister? Or you ready to move on?" The drunk took a stumbling pace forward and clutched Nick's arm.

Nick carefully unwound the grimy fingers from his sleeve. He made no attempt to answer the man. Instead, he looked at Abby, and she read the expression in his eyes all too clearly: smoldering anger. "Abby," he said quietly, "do you work in this place?"

"Yes," she said. What else could she say? "But it's only temporary until..." Why had Nick, of all people, shown up and found her out?

He shook his head. "You don't belong here at all. Come on, you're leaving."

"The lady don't need your help." The man swayed. His stale breath constricted Abby's throat. "You want a fight, boy, you got it." He bared nicotine-stained teeth while he made a wavering jab at Nick's chest. The blow glanced off. Nick grasped the thin wrist as it passed and shoved the man into a chair.

"Sit still and shut up, buddy." He glared menacingly at the slumped form. "Better yet, go find somewhere else to make a nuisance of yourself."

She was going to die right here and now. "Please, Nick. He's okay. Everything's fine. I can't—I mean—I work here, okay? And I need the job." The game was up, all over: Nick would tell Michael, and then her parents would know. She made an effort to rally. "I can handle things. Really. I'm used to it."

"Is that supposed to make me feel better?"

He wasn't *supposed* to care one way or the other. Abby walked past Nick and stared unseeingly out the windows. Nick Dorset was a decent man with decent instincts. He must be wondering why John would allow her to do a job like this now.

Warm hands on her shoulders startled her. She glanced up into Nick's face. A wonderful face, lean, unforgettable. This was madness.

"Sit down, Abby—please. You look bushed." He steered her to a chair. "My stuff will be finished in a few minutes, and I'll drive you home."

Abby watched him silently. She'd have to think fast. He didn't know about John's desertion, but now he did know where she was working, and the set of his jaw showed his disapproval. He'd tell Michael for sure. The worst possible way for any part of her secret to come out would be secondhand. Her family would never forgive her if someone else told them the news. Somehow she had to appeal to Nick, to make him understand she needed the money she made here and persuade him not to say anything to Michael.

When the washer stopped, Nick piled his laundry, still wet, back into the pillowcase and met her eyes. "Is that yours?'' He inclined his head to the basket of linen he'd helped her fold.

"No," she said quietly and felt heat rush up her neck. "If you'd like to leave your things, I'll dry them and drop them off later." By then she'd have come up with a plausible explanation.

"There's nothing wrong with my dryer. You're coming with me now."

Abby bit the inside of her lip. "I'm not finished. And I have my own car. But thank you." She might like a strong man around, but not here, and not now.

"I'll wait." He slung his load over one shoulder and leaned tensely against the doorjamb.

"I said I've got my car," Abby said faintly. She didn't have the energy to keep up a battle of wits. "There are things I have to do."

"Do them." This was the flip side of Nick Dorset: totally intractable. "The heap you call a car will be okay in the parking lot overnight. From the noise the thing makes, I'm surprised it starts at all. You shouldn't be driving it."

A rumbling snore sounded. Her "protector" was once more drowsing and snuffling.

Abby picked up the book Nick had forgotten and said as she handed it to him, "I do have to drive myself. How would I get back tomorrow otherwise?" She was so tired.

"Something tells me you won't be coming back tomorrow. Michael doesn't know about this, does he?"

"Oh, please..." The right words, she must find the right thing to say. "Look, Nick," she stated resolutely, "I'm going to ask you a favor, but I need a little time to explain. Could you wait before you say anything to Michael?"

He studied her until she glanced away. "All right. I don't know what's going on with you, but something is. Maybe it's none of my business, but . . ." His sharply expelled breath was audible. He sat beside her. "Michael's my friend, and he feels about you the way I feel about my sister. If he'd found Janet working in—in a dump, I'd slug him for not clueing me in. But I won't say anything if that's the way you want it. Only, Abby, I'm not leaving you here tonight. You need the car tomorrow? Fine. I'll bring you back, and it'll already be here."

Abby started to protest, then changed her mind. "Whatever you say." He held all the cards. A few more weeks at this job were all she asked. They wouldn't make her rich, but they'd help.

Nick said, "Good," and leaned back in the chair. He smiled at Abby when she got up and willed all emotion from his eyes at her slight awkwardness. He'd like to get his hands on that son of a bitch Winston. Thank God the damned washer had chosen tonight to go on the fritz. He glanced at the creep snorting through flapping lips at the opposite end of the line of seats. No way would he leave her here with that.

Within minutes, she'd locked several baskets of laundry in the storage room, flipped over a sign on the wall and pulled on her coat.

They didn't speak until Nick had closed Abby into his car and climbed behind the wheel. She leaned against the door. Her uplifted profile, her neck, showed pale against the darkness outside.

He started the engine. "You leave the place unlocked at night?"

"The shop itself, yes. Anything portable is shut in the back room. A watchman checks the front from time to time."

"Is anyone really likely to wash clothes at one or two in the morning?"

He felt her look at him. "I guess, or they wouldn't keep it open."

Now what? Would she volunteer information, or should he ask direct questions? He waited, and the silence only lengthened.

Fog swirled in shifting tunnels before the headlights of his BMW. He'd tried to put her out of his mind. How he'd tried. In the past two weeks he'd worked up to seven miles a day on the track whenever he was in town, and Abby Winston ran every step of the way with him.

"I feel ridiculous," she said suddenly.

"Why?" He knew the answer. She was proud, and he'd made her feel as though she were a burden.

Abby rested her elbow on the window rim. "The lady-in-distress role is foreign to me. I'm a manager, Nick, a survivor. And I was fine back there—" she turned sharply toward him "—honestly I was. I know how it looked. But who's going to bother a— I'm fine there."

Who would bother a pregnant woman? she'd almost said. He pursed his lips. Her self-esteem was zero. She might be pregnant, she was also extremely, hauntingly lovely, more so to him because she was pregnant. He closed his eyes for an instant. There was definitely something wrong with his psyche.

He parked near the entrance to the condo, reached behind the seat for his laundry and leapt out to open her door. "We could both use something hot. Have soup or hot chocolate with me."

"You've done enough already." She held the railing beside the steps tightly, moving without her usual light step. "Let me make you something."

Still trying to save face, he thought. He was glad darkness hid the evil expression he knew he couldn't control well enough. "I bought this new drink mix I'm dying to try," he lied, praying he could keep her out of the kitchen while he found the old can of chocolate he knew he'd put somewhere in a cupboard. "This is just the night for it. Humor me."

She glanced back into his face, and for the first time in weeks he saw that marvelous, impish smile. "Okay," she said. "Lead on." He knew she was twenty-seven. When she smiled like that, she could have passed for seventeen, except for the fine lines of fatigue around her eyes and mouth.

A swift glance around Nick's condo unsettled Abby, made her feel like an intruder into his comfortable world. He wasn't a tidy man. As she stood awkwardly in the entrance to his living room, he toured the area, sweeping discarded clothes from couches and chairs, shoving newspapers and magazines into piles on tables, pausing for an instant to grab two pairs of shoes from a corner.

He grinned as he passed her, arms laden. "Sit. I'll do my famous hide-all trick, then make us that drink." He paused in the hall, looking back, laughing. "Sometimes I have nightmares my mother will show up and open the wrong closet. In my mind I see her lying in the rubble that falls out, calling me 'Nicholas Stuart.' That always meant big trouble."

Abby laughed, too, and walked farther into the room. The layout of this condo closely resembled her own. Nick's kitchen, open to the living and dining room, had a common wall with her kitchen. At the far end of the hall he would also have a master bedroom with its own bathroom. She could see the second bathroom door and the small bedroom beside it. In her own place, that would become her baby's nursery.

Nick breezed back and went straight into the kitchen. "Sit down, sit down," he called. "Oh, wait. Let's have a fire."

She'd already noted he did everything quickly. On his knees before the fireplace, he crumpled newspapers between the andirons and heaped logs rapidly on top. His shoulders moved powerfully beneath a dark turtleneck sweater. "There. Let there be flames." He set fire to the paper and rested on his heels an instant before checking over his shoulder. "Let me have your coat, Abby."

"I'm not—" Yes, she *was* warm enough for once. And she couldn't go on trying to hide her stomach from him. He already knew how pregnant she was. She shrugged out of the threadbare coat, annoyed at her own self-consciousness.

"Great." Nick took it and laid it over a chair, his housekeeping efforts evidently already forgotten. "Now, sit." He pointed imperiously to a smoky-blue couch. "I'll be a jiffy in the kitchen."

She crossed her arms and sank into the plump corduroy cushions. The blues and magentas were strong and appealing. Clearly he'd spared no expense on the decor.

"This is lovely, Nick," she said.

He stuck his head around a partition. "What did you say?" His hair stood on end in front, and he was in the act of pushing it more awry.

"This." She made herself look away. "Your home is lovely." He had that rare and irresistible mixture of masculine magic and total lack of self-awareness.

"Thanks. Coming from you, I'm flattered. Michael says you're very artistic." He went back to clattering with things she couldn't see.

Abby pushed herself upright. Her back ached. That was a new development she'd have to mention to the doctor. Wasn't it too early for backaches? She shook her head impatiently. Everything was fine.

"Let me help you." The kitchen was small, with counters lining two sides and a third Formica-topped space forming a central island.

Nick's muffled voice came from the recesses of a narrow corner pantry. "No need." He stood on tiptoe, reaching to the back of the top shelf.

Abby craned to see what he was doing. Two mugs were already arranged on a teak tray, and hissing milk climbed steadily up the sides of a pan on the stove. "There's a need!" She snatched the pan from the heat and held it over the sink.

"What's the matter?" He stepped back, holding a rusty tin in one hand.

"Well, one more second, Nicholas Stuart, and..." She laughed and it felt good. "Cleaning baked milk from stoves is pretty low on my list of fun activities."

"Mine, too. Thanks." Nick laughed, too, and took the pan from her. Then he caught her staring at the tin he held. "Ah, I can manage now," he said, the laugh fading to a sheepish grin.

"Your new drink mix?"

"Oh, what the hell. I was always a lousy liar." With a flourish, he inserted a spoon beneath the lid and pried it off. "There wasn't a new mix. I just didn't want to come in here alone, and I needed an excuse to lure you. Forgive me?"

When he looked like that, what woman could *not* forgive him? "I forgive you," she said softly, meeting his fine eyes. "And I love plain old chocolate of any kind." She started to turn away. "And I also didn't feel like going into an empty apartment any sooner than I had to.'' She'd said too much, but it didn't seem to matter.

They sat side by side, drinking silently, watching the fire, for several minutes before Nick spoke. "How do you feel?"

Tension shot back into her body. "Great," she said. "There's nothing like a fire and a hot drink to bring you back to life." Let him leave it at that.

"Mmm." He looked into his mug. "That wasn't exactly what I was asking."

Abby didn't answer. She couldn't answer.

"When—when— I'm not very practiced at this, Abby. When will the baby be born?"

A shaky feeling started in her arms and legs. "About the beginning of January, I think." As if the baby knew its mother was anxious, what felt like a tiny foot jabbed at Abby's side. She shifted involuntarily.

Nick watched her closely. "So, there's only a couple of months to go. You're seven months pregnant?"

"As far as I know." She'd never had this kind of conversation with a man other than her doctor. Even Michael was—well, he was Michael, and he glossed over any subject he considered outside his range.

"Is everything going smoothly? Does the doctor think you're as well as you should be?"

The baby kicked again, and this time Abby saw Nick's eyes catch the movement. She blushed violently. "I'm fine."

"What does that feel like?" He nodded at her abdomen. "You must feel very close to the baby when it's inside you."

The man was disarmingly natural. Abby took a deep breath. "At first I felt like a cage full of fluttering birds.

Now I think an elephant house might be more appropriate."

He didn't smile or move his gaze. Tentatively, he placed a hand on her belly and waited. The baby performed on cue, and Nick looked up, smiling broadly. "That's something," he said. "Marvelous." He smoothed her dress, pressing harder.

Abby blinked, her eyes stinging. John had never shown any interest in his child's development. He'd certainly never wanted to feel movement. From the instant he'd discovered she was pregnant, he hadn't touched Abby at all. She closed her eyes. For a crazy instant she was tempted to lean against Nick's chest, to ask him to hold her.

"Oh, good Lord. I'm sorry, Abby." Nick withdrew his hand as if it burned. Color stained his high cheekbones. "I'm sorry if I embarrassed you, Abby. I didn't think."

She cleared her throat. "It's okay. Nick, can we talk about my job?" *Keep on track,* she ordered herself.

He stood and set down his mug before putting more wood on the fire. "I thought Michael said you designed those display things in stores." His back was toward her.

"I did. I—" She swallowed. "I had a fall from a ladder and—"

Nick stood forcefully. "When? When did you fall? Did you see the doctor?"

His concern shouldn't make her feel so good, so warm. "It wasn't serious. I just decided to do something else until after the baby's born."

"You intend to go back to work then?"

She didn't meet his eyes. "I'll have to." She set aside her mug. "Nick, things will get better. But for a little while I'm not—" This was impossible. She'd never cried poor mouth to anyone, and she wouldn't now.

"You need money," Nick supplied bluntly. "I understand. We've all been there. But do you need it so badly you have to work in a Laundromat? I shouldn't have thought John would go for that. Or doesn't he know?"

This had to be over quickly. "He's at sea. He doesn't know I quit my job." At least she hadn't lied.

"I see. But Michael, and your folks—"

She cut him off quickly. "No! No, Nick. I can't go into it, but they're the real reason I'm asking, no, begging you not to mention any of this. I promise you I can work it out on my own. If I find I can't, I will go to Michael, and I know he'll help me."

Nick returned to the couch and sat sideways, facing her. "Do you know what you're asking?"

"Yes," she said evenly. "I'm asking you to pretend you know no more about me now than you did before you walked into that Laundromat tonight."

Abby thought she saw a hint of anger darken Nick's eyes. She was imagining things. "Can you do that, Nick?" she pressed, "Forget you saw me there?"

"Let's just say I'll forget it around Michael. Is that a deal?"

She hesitated. "A deal, I guess." He'd stick to it; she knew he would.

Nick made up his mind. He would ask now and her reaction would give him the confirmation he needed. "Abby." He waited until she looked at him. Her eyes were huge, the gray softer and more veiled than ever, if possible. "Abby, when's John due back? He's been gone a lot recently."

Her lips parted. Damn, he shouldn't have done that. She was going through enough already. But he had his answer.

"John?" The last traces of color drained from her cheeks. Nick made fists to stop himself touching her. "John is ... he's at sea."

"So you said. I wondered when he was coming back."

She stood and picked up her coat, bowing her head while she slid an arm into one sleeve. Silently cursing himself, Nick got up and stood behind her to help.

"This could be another long trip." Her voice was level but reedy. She gave a high little laugh. "I've learned to expect John when—when I see him."

"Sure." Nick wished he could haul back everything he'd said in the past two minutes. Abby headed for the door. "What time do you have to be at work tomorrow?" he asked.

"Oh, I don't know." She dug in her pockets, and he heard keys rattle. "I have to check my schedule."

He let her out and smelled the faint scent of some sort of wild flower as she passed him. "Will you call me when you're ready to leave? My number's on the tenant list. I'm on layover for ten days, so I can take you anywhere you need to go." He was sticking his heart firmly on his sleeve, and he'd sworn not to do that.

"Thank you," Abby said, without meeting his gaze.

He made sure she got into her condo and returned slowly to his own. Standing at his favorite place by the window, he stared into the street. Streetlights cast an eerie glitter on frost-covered shrubs.

The cold was in Nick's soul. He was no longer safely fantasizing about another man's off-limits wife. He was falling hard and hopelessly for a pregnant woman who still loved the husband who'd deserted her.

Chapter Five

Abby moved quietly around the condo. She'd finish getting ready and catch a bus to work before Nick had any idea she'd gone. Today she had the early shift, and he'd have no way of knowing that. When she failed to call, he was likely to contact her and discover she'd already been to the Laundromat and returned home. Soon he'd get over his natural protective urge and forget her. She was still worried he might make a chance remark to Michael, but all she could do was pray he wouldn't.

With exaggerated caution, she tiptoed to the door, with a brown sack containing a thermos of coffee and a cheese sandwich scrunched beneath one arm. She would find a way to thank Nick for his kindness of last night, but not now. The bus stop was a block away, out of sight of their building. All she had to do was get there.

Grimacing, she eased off the deadbolt, turned the handle and slipped onto the landing. With equal care, she slid the locks into place and turned toward the stairs.

"Morning. Thought I heard you up and about. Early shift?"

Nick. He sat sideways on the top step, his feet crossed at the ankles, his back braced against the wall.

"You couldn't have heard . . . I mean . . . I didn't make any noise." She bent her head and smothered a laugh. "What are you doing, Nick? Sentry duty?"

"Am I so awful you have to sneak away?"

"You know better than that. I just hate being a nuisance, that's all." She was glad to see him, even thrilled, and the feeling disquieted her. Abby sobered. "How long have you been out here? It's only eight o'clock. You were waiting for me, weren't you?"

"Yup. I figured you might try something like this. I was going to camp here all day if necessary."

Abby approached him, unsure what to say next. Nick swung his legs aside and offered her a hand. After a second's hesitation she gripped his fingers and sank awkwardly beside him on the step.

"What's in the bag?"

"Coffee and a sandwich. Want some coffee?" She only had one cup, but she could wash it out at the store.

"Thanks. Not now. I'll have some in the car." He smoothed a curl from the corner of her eye, and she flinched. "Abby, what's wrong—really wrong? You aren't doing so well, are you?"

She met his gaze defiantly. This was one guy who didn't give up on a cause easily. "I'm doing just fine, Nick. Terrific. Why shouldn't I be? Pregnancy's no big deal—happens every day."

"You're too alone with it."

Abby fashioned a brilliant smile. "Every woman's alone with pregnancy. No one else can do it for you."

"You know what I mean."

"Do I?" She set down the sack. Nick Dorset was a bright, bright man, and too perceptive. And she was beginning to like him too much.

"When are you going to give in and admit you aren't making it?"

Abby drove a hand into her hair. "I *am* making it, Nick. What makes you think I'm not? And why would you care?" She didn't want him to answer that. "For some reason you feel responsible for me—don't ask me why, unless it's because my brother's your friend. I'm perfectly in control, and if I weren't, it wouldn't be your problem. I had to take a little interim job, that's all. Why the big deal?"

He put an arm around her shoulder and shook her gently. "That's what I keep asking you." His strength acted to weaken her. She wanted to put her head on his shoulder.

"You're the one who's keeping secrets from her family," he continued. "If I wasn't pretty sure you were having a rough time, it would be one thing, but I am sure, and I'm going to have to play stand-in until you've got someone else around to help. I want to be here for you, because—for—for Michael's sake." His brown eyes reflected specks of light from the window over the stairs. He touched her chin lightly. "Would you be offended if I offered to lend you some money?"

"No! I don't need anything." Abby stood, immediately became dizzy and grabbed the banister.

Nick didn't notice. "Only till John gets back?" He picked up the bag and held his left hand toward her.

Abby looked straight ahead. "Thanks, but I've got enough money. I have to leave. All I need to ruin my day is to miss the bus."

"Okay, forget I mentioned a loan. Come on. The guy what brings you, takes you back. That's something else my mother taught me." He grasped her unresisting hand and tucked it through his arm.

"Your mother sounds like a nice lady. You and your family are close, aren't you?"

"She is and we are, thank God." He turned a sharp gaze on her. "But you think a lot of yours, too. I know that from Michael and from your overprotective instincts toward them."

She nodded. Confiding in him might feel good, it could also be very dangerous. Abby walked downstairs beside Nick. At five foot ten, she looked up to few men. Her eyes only reached his chin. She looked at him now, at his clear-cut profile, the sensitiveness of his slightly parted lips, his strong teeth. If only— She flexed the muscles in her jaw. If only Nick were part of her life? She was truly an idiotic dreamer. And a very pregnant, not-quite-divorced dreamer. What else did that kind of thinking make her?

Further argument about accepting a lift was pointless. Nick ushered her firmly to his car, and within fifteen minutes they sat outside the Laundromat. A fragile sun failed to stroke away the frost on the parking lot. Abby made ready to get out.

"Wait." Nick reached across and took her hand. "When do you get off work?"

She rested her head back and closed her eyes. He was like the proverbial dog with a bone. "I'm not sure. Look." She turned toward him. "Don't worry about me, okay? You've already gone far beyond the call of duty. I give you full marks for chivalry, recommend you for white knighthood, even."

He didn't laugh. "You sound flip."

"I'm not." She became uncomfortably warm. She had sounded flip and rude and ungrateful. "Thank you for everything, Nick. But forget me and get on with your life, huh? I'm not your concern."

He looked at her mouth while she spoke. She brought her lips together, but several seconds passed before his eyes returned to hers. She saw him swallow. The instinctive sensation inside her, long buried but not forgotten, spread fast and powerfully. Not now, maybe never again, should she allow this reaction, and never with a man she had no right to.

"Have dinner with me," Nick said quietly.

Abby received the invitation like an unexpected blow. She couldn't form a reply.

"Will you, Abby?"

"I've got to get into the store."

"Abby?"

What did he want from her? He couldn't be attracted to a woman seven months pregnant whom he thought happily married. Even without the pregnancy, he wasn't the kind of man to interfere in the marriage of a friend's sister.

"Can't you answer me?"

She started. "I . . . yes, yes, I guess so. Yes, I'll have dinner with you." *Fool. Poor, lonely fool.*

"What time shall I pick you up?"

Panic gripped her. "I don't know. Maybe we should do this another time. I'm not sure when I'll get off."

"I'll just stay and wait for you, then."

"Wait?" she croaked disbelievingly. "I've got a full day's work to do."

"How long is a full day's work?"

He had her. "Eight hours," she muttered. "Please don't stay or come back. I must drive my car home today."

He seemed to consider for a while. "Okay. But give me your keys for a minute. I'll bring them in to you."

Abby dithered, then found the keys in her purse. Nick took them and came to help her from the car. He smiled, bouncing the keys in his palm. "See you in a jiffy."

She still didn't move.

"Get in out of the cold." He waved, and she took a few steps backward. "Go on," he insisted. "I won't make off with your chariot, honest."

"Yes. Right." Abby clutched her brown paper bag to her chest and turned away. She didn't look back until she was inside the empty store. The place was cold, great misty moons swelling on each windowpane. She rubbed a hole and peered out.

At first she didn't see him. Then the noise of an engine grinding pulled her attention to the windshield of the Pinto. Beyond its white-coated surface, she saw his silhouette. He was checking out her car. The heavy warmth trembled into her again.

Nick slid out of the car and lifted the hood. He got a rag from the trunk of his BMW and bent over her engine. Checking oil and water—all those things she'd sworn to learn about as soon as she felt stronger. Day by day she became more aware of the need to become totally self-sufficient. But at this moment she loved watching Nick's lean body bend and stretch, his muscular jean-clad legs stiffen against the side of the car. Abby's sigh drained her lungs. The feelings she was developing for Nick Dorset were pointless and could be disastrous if they made her careless in what she said to him.

The hood slammed. Nick came toward the shop, wiping his hands. His straight back, the slight swing of his wide shoulders, accentuated the loose-limbed confidence of his walk.

"Whew." He expelled a cloudy breath as he came in. "It's almost as cold in here as it is out there. Here." He handed over the keys. "Believe it or not, everything seems fine. How's seven for picking you up?"

Abby spread her hands. "I really don't think I should, Nick. And you must have better things to do. You're very kind, but—"

He waited patiently, not attempting to interrupt. When she stopped, her lips parted, and he took a single step and kissed her cheek. "Seven?" he asked, his fingers lightly circling her neck.

Abby nodded, keeping her hands at her sides with difficulty.

"And, lady, you can trust me—with anything. I'm not a fool. I can figure a few things out for myself, and they're safe with me. Okay?"

She nodded again.

"See you." Fleetingly he smoothed her hair and left.

Abby stood motionless, watching him stride to his silver car and swing his long legs inside. He rolled down the window and waved, his grin broad, before driving away.

What? Abby wondered. *What things have you figured out, Nick?*

HE HAD TO TALK to someone, and Janet was the obvious victim. Nick ran upstairs and let himself into his condo. He calculated the time difference between Seattle and Omaha. Janet probably would be getting Penny's lunch.

Jeez, he wished it was a respectable time of day for a drink. What was happening to him?

Janet's phone rang seven times. Nick started to hang up. Damn. Maybe she was driving Penny somewhere, or meeting Crete at that little café in the basement of the building where he worked.

"Hello."

The receiver glanced off the cradle as he pulled it back. "Janet? Is that you?"

She laughed. "Yes, Nick. I'm me."

"Smartie. You always were a smart mouth. I thought you weren't there."

"I'm here."

Nick shook his head and smiled. "Good. Now we both know where we are. How's Crete?"

"Wonderful."

"Penny?"

"Wonderful."

"Mom and Dad?"

"*Nick...*"

"Are they okay?" He sounded mentally incompetent.

A sigh gusted along the line. "Mom and Dad are wonderful, too. What's the deal, Nick?"

He pulled out a dining chair and slumped into it. "Just felt like talking to you." That much was true. He crossed his legs on top of the table and grimaced at the marks the heels of his boots made on the glass.

"I feel like talking to you, too, brother. But why do I get this feeling you're about to drop a bombshell?"

"Because you don't have enough to occupy that fertile imagination of yours." Nick scrunched down, rested his neck on the chair's back and stared at the ceiling. "I'm on a long layover. I get bored, that's all."

"Thanks a lot. So bored you're reduced to calling me."

He ignored the remark. "Janet, have you ever had the feeling there was something different about me?"

Janet didn't answer.

"Are you still there?"

"What do you mean, *different*?"

He rolled his eyes. "*Unusual.* Not the same as most guys."

Janet giggled.

Nick shifted to rest his elbows on the table. "Listen, you. Be serious. This is serious to me. I wonder about myself sometimes. I mean, I've gotten fairly serious with one or two women. There was Lisa; I almost thought she was it for a while. But I could never quite... I don't know. Maybe I'm... different."

A muffled choking sound suggested Janet was working at control. "Nick, is there something you haven't told me?"

He groaned. "Like what? I don't mean I'm into whips and chains, if that's what you mean. Or that I've got a thing for some male flight attendant. Although—" he paused for effect "—there was this one who—"

"Stop!" Janet snuffled the way she always had when she laughed hard. "If there's one guy I'm not worried about in that area, it's you. Remember, you were the kid who ran the longest kiss contest behind the girls' locker rooms, and won. And if I'm right, you were only twelve at the time. So quit being squirrely and spit out your problem."

"I can't."

The line pinged and popped while Janet digested his announcement. Then she said, "You're in love. I knew it. The last time we talked, you sounded funny, and I knew you'd fallen for someone. Who is she?"

Nick scrubbed a hand over his face. He was in a big mess. How did he explain that to his sister? "You're running ahead," he said at last. "Way ahead. I don't know what I feel for sure yet."

"But you feel something for *someone*, correct?"

"Yep."

"So, follow your heart and see where it leads you."

"Straight into hell," he muttered.

"What?" Janet's voice rose. "What did you say about hell?"

"I'm in a bind, Janet. I don't think she really knows I'm alive."

She gave a short derisive laugh. "That would be a new twist. Who is this gorgeous paragon?"

"I can't say."

"That's ridiculous."

"I can't. Not yet." He stood and walked slowly around the table. "Maybe never."

A hard breath sounded. "You're driving me nuts. What do you want me to say? First you ask a bunch of questions about your mental health—at least I think that's what you were asking. Then you tell me you've fallen for someone. And now you can't tell me who she is. Tell me how to react, and I'll do it."

"Janet." He squeezed his eyes shut. A pain started in his temples. "This isn't your average situation. I'm not sure how to...I'm not sure... Damn it, I don't know what's the best thing to do next, and after that, and after that. She's kind of, well, off-limits in a way."

"Oh, God, Nick. Don't tell me." Janet gave her famous tuneless whistle. "She's married."

"On the head, kid. She's married to a one-hundred-percent creep who doesn't—"

"Understand her?" Janet broke in. "Nick, every man or woman who wants out of a relationship is misunderstood."

He paced, placing heel and toe deliberately. "You didn't let me finish. He doesn't want her anymore, only I'm not supposed to know that. He's left her, and I'm not supposed to know that, either. She's protecting the bastard, sorry, protecting him. She's not telling anyone he's taken off, not even her folks. I think I'm the only one who knows, and she doesn't know I do."

"Whoa! How do you know? Did you turn clairvoyant?"

"I just know, okay?"

Loud music blasted his eardrum. He jerked the phone away. Janet covered the receiver, then came back, sounding breathless. "Sorry, Nick. Penny gets bored when I'm on the phone. She does things to make sure I know she's still around. Kids are a challenge sometimes."

His throat tightened. "You're lucky. Kids are neat."

The following silence went on and on.

"Janet, I know this woman's on her own. She's my neighbor, and I saw her husband move out. I can see it all in her eyes, too, do you understand?"

"Yes," Janet said slowly. "Does she have children?"

"Uh, no. Why do you ask?"

"No reason, no reason. Just a feeling. You don't normally extol the virtues of parenthood."

Nick felt bone tired. "I didn't know I had."

"Forget it. Maybe I'm reading too much into everything you say. Tell me more about this woman, Nick."

He dropped to the floor and sat cross-legged, an elbow on each knee. He wished Janet were here, flesh and blood, looking right at him. "She's gentle, Jan, very quiet and soft, the kind of woman a man—this man—dreams about meeting. And she's got guts. I've been kind of trying to draw her out, and she covers up. She's more worried about hurting her parents and brother than what happens to her."

"You *are* in love!"

"Come on, Jan, help me, don't clown around."

He heard her tap her fingernail against the mouthpiece. "I'm coming to visit. Mom will help Crete with Penny. She's wanted me to get out there and see what you're up to. She thinks you'll open up to me better than you would to her."

"You're overreacting. No one needs to come. I just wanted advice. You asked questions and I answered. Now you're rushing out here. And why are you and Mom talking about me?"

"She's always talking about you, Nick. You should know that. 'When's that boy going to settle down?' You've heard the line. But you asked why I think you need help, so I'll tell you. You never said a word about what your friend looks like, that's why. She's gentle, quiet, soft. This is the guy who used to measure female brains in inches, thirty-six and above."

Nick couldn't help laughing. "That was in my youth. Abby's tall, five-ten or so, and thin—too thin. Short black curls, big gray eyes. Janet, she's the loveliest woman I've ever seen."

"Abby? Nice name. And she's married to someone else."

He sighed. "And she's married to someone else—at the moment."

"You intend to change that."

"Maybe. Hell, that's the problem. I don't know what I intend to do. But I do know I can't get her out of my mind."

Janet cleared her throat. "You've tried?"

"I've been running seven miles a day."

"You tried."

"Yeah, and it didn't work. Well, Janet, you must have things to do. Give my love to everyone."

"Nick."

"Yes?"

"Would you have room to put me up if I came for a day or two in a couple of weeks?"

He drove his teeth into his bottom lip and calculated. Abby would be seven and a half months pregnant then. *Oh, God.* "Of course I'd have room. I'd love to see you. It's been a long time since just the two of us were together."

"I'll let you know the date. Hang in there. If Abby feels anything for you, she'll tell you the truth about her husband."

"You're right."

"I am, Nick. She has to be the one to mention it, remember that."

"I'll remember. Bye, Janet."

He heard the way she slid the phone into its receiver. She was thinking. Nick checked his watch. Nine hours before he could pick up Abby. He'd be thinking, too.

Chapter Six

An open fire made up for almost anything lacking in the home decorating department, Abby decided. She'd stopped at a supermarket and bought two bundles of logs. This was the first fire she'd ever lit, and she was pleased it had caught and drawn so well. All those years of watching her father and Michael at work must have taught her something.

She stood back to look at the room again. Moving the couch and chair closer to the fireplace had produced a more intimate look. A hideous gap glared behind the grouping, but with luck she could keep Nick's mind focused on eating, and he wouldn't notice the emptiness in the room.

John had taken the turntable, but she still had her cassette deck and speakers. For the first time in weeks, she slipped in a favorite jazz tape and jogged in time to its beat into the kitchen.

Nick had better like Japanese food, particularly sushi. She'd tried to reconstruct comments Michael had made about Nick and she was certain she remembered something about eating sushi in Honolulu. She'd even splurged on a bottle of good sake. Nick might argue that they should go out as he'd suggested, but she'd soon convince him this was better, and after all he'd done, she owed him a meal at home and a chance to relax.

The house and her efforts in the kitchen were as appealing as they were going to get; now she'd better see what she could do with herself.

JAZZ. NICK SMILED and fingered the knot in his tie. Abby was playing jazz again after God knew how long. He used to hear her doing that late some afternoons when she got home from work. That was in the days when she occasionally smiled her shy smile on the stairs and wasn't quite so thin.

She was looking forward to a night out on the town. His hand shook slightly, and he studied his fingers with disbelief. Old Dorset, Mr. Cool, shaking like a high school senior going to his prom.

He hoped she'd like the restaurant where he'd made reservations. Canlis was one of the best places in Seattle. Its location, overlooking Lake Washington, was spectacular. He wanted to give Abby wonderful things. And wonderful food, things to make her feel good and be healthy, seemed a good place to start. He'd bought flowers, too, long-stemmed pink roses. Later he'd find a way to give her the rest of what she should have. He'd find a way to be with her . . . all the time. . . .

Nick tried to ignore his other thoughts and reached for his suit jacket. How long was it after a woman gave birth before she could— *Hell.*

ABBY TRIED NOT TO watch the clock in her bedroom. She already knew she had less than ten minutes left, and nothing she'd tried on made her look less like a melon. She avoided the mirror. Looking at herself wouldn't change a thing.

The dress she chose was one she wore in summer when she wasn't pregnant, another of her favorite cotton peasant dresses. She liked its blue-gray color because it did nice things for her eyes. The loose shape floated free from her shoulders and at least her legs looked good in it. Too bad it was intended for seventy degrees rather than thirty.

That was it, the best she could do. If Nick Dorset had wanted a glamorous companion tonight, he wouldn't have chosen her. Abby considered lipstick and discarded the idea since it only heightened her pallor, then returned to the kitchen. Where they would eat was still the big question.

NICK STOOD IN FRONT of Abby's door and shifted the roses from one hand to the other. He could think of a lot of guys who would laugh at this exhibition. He ran a hand over his hair and felt it spring awry again. To button the jacket or not to button the jacket? He did it up, undid it and grinned, shaking his head, before jabbing the bell.

The door opened at once. "Hi. Come in." Abby fiddled with a satin tie at the neck of her dress. Color swept into her cheeks. Nick's thighs tautened. She was fantastic.

"Here." He shoved the roses at her, and she almost dropped them.

They laughed.

"Roses?" She smelled them deeply before looking up at him, clutching the crackly package to her breasts. "I love roses. Thank you. I can't remember the last time... Thank you, Nick."

He shrugged. "They aren't anything." From the corner of his eye he noticed the fire. The room was warmer, less Spartan somehow. "Are you ready?"

She opened her mouth and closed it again before pulling him inside and reaching to push the door shut. "Do you like Japanese food?"

Nick looked more closely at the room. It had been prepared for guests, or a guest. His heart made an unaccustomed rotation. "I love Japanese food. Why?"

"Because I thought . . . I mean . . . Well, Nick, you've been such a dear to me it's time I did something for you, and I make pretty mean sushi. No one would employ me in a sushi bar, mind you, but I'm pretty good just the same." Her hands grasped the rose stems tightly. Nick wanted to warn her about the thorns but kept quiet.

She rushed on, "I made some stops on the way home and got all the stuff. They pounded the octopus for me. Do you like octopus?"

"Love it." He didn't want to be paid back for a couple of car rides. He wanted to take her somewhere special.

"You'd enjoy eating here, then? I got sake. I couldn't find that green mustard, but they had some hot stuff. And I found ginger slivers." Her eyes were huge and anxious.

Nick swallowed a sigh. Being with her, anywhere, was all he wanted. But he hated the thought of her spending money she couldn't afford and working some more after a day at that dump of a Laundromat.

"I messed up, didn't I," she whispered. Her gaze swept over him. "You're dressed to go out. I expect you'd rather do that."

"No." Nick smiled, snapping to life. What Abby needed most was cheerful company and a chance to do whatever pleased her. "I'd much rather eat here." He took the flowers and wrapped an arm impulsively around her shoulders, pulling her close. "I'll cancel our restaurant reservation. But you have to let me help." Her face was inches from his, her mouth a whisper away.

Abby felt his breath on her forehead. He felt so good, smelled so good, clean. She slid an arm around his waist and squeezed quickly before letting him go. He continued to hold her, gazing down at her body.

She rested a palm on his chest. "What is it?"

He started, looking at her face again. "I never held a pregnant lady before, that's all."

"I guess it seems strange," she said, trying not to stiffen.

"Different, that's all." He spread his fingers on her back, stroked lightly. "I was thinking how special it is to watch a life grow, to feel it."

Hesitantly Abby smoothed his lapel. She didn't want to move. "You're a special man, Nick."

"I doubt it, but thanks." He smiled into her eyes. His mouth was irresistible, wide, naturally upturned at the corners. Abby caught the glimmer of his teeth. How would his mouth feel, taste?

"What are you thinking, Abby?"

Her attention shot to his eyes. The expression there was intent. Did he sense how attracted she was to him, share some of the sensations that tempted her to reach up and kiss him?

She was dreaming, and she hadn't answered his question. Abby took a deep breath. "I was thinking we should get my roses in water and do something about dinner."

He laughed softly, tilting back his head. "You're right." He released her. "Come on. Let's create our masterpiece."

Abby followed him slowly into the kitchen, where he set about proving he knew a lot more about preparing sushi than she did. While she arranged the roses in a vase and found chopsticks, he mixed and chopped, wrapped concoctions in kelp and arranged them on platters. Soon one counter was laden.

"I'll heat the sake in the microwave," Abby said, decanting the colorless liquid into a glass jug. She assembled small pottery cups on a tray with a pot of green tea.

Nick stood back, surveying their handywork. "All ready," he announced and glanced toward the living room.

He had to notice the absence of tables. Abby swept up plates and chopsticks and napkins. "I thought we'd eat buffet style. Take what you like and come back for more." She avoided his eyes. "I have to do something about getting a dining table one of these days."

"I like buffet style and knees," Nick assured her. He leaned close, pushed back a curl from her temple and waited until she met his gaze. "Everything looks terrific in here. You light a good fire."

Abby started to relax. "My dad and Michael are the experts. This is the first one I've made myself, but I remembered watching them and did the same."

"I can't wait any longer for this food," Nick said, piling sushi on a plate. He poured a glass of sake and looked inquiringly at Abby, who shook her head. "Of course. Tea for pregnant people, I guess." He held a steaming cup and his glass in one hand. "Load up, and we'll sit on the couch."

Was he really as enthusiastic as he sounded? She could choose to believe so, and she would. "Sounds great," she said and put several pieces of sushi on her own plate, and mustard and soyu.

In the living room Nick put his food and the drinks on an end table and shrugged out of his jacket. He draped it over the chair and waited until Abby was seated on the couch before sinking easily down beside her and balancing the plate on his knee. "Oh, I love this stuff," he commented, sinking his teeth into a piece of tender salmon. "Mike and I have this favorite place in Honolulu, but I guess he told you that."

"Mmm," Abby managed around a mouthful of yellow tuna. "Do you like Hawaii?"

"Love it. The climate's great—in small doses. I prefer the seasons we have here."

"You come from . . ."

"Omaha, Nebraska. Nice. Home. But too cold in winter, and I just happen to think Seattle's the only place on earth I want to spend the rest of my life."

Abby's stomach tightened. Being relieved this was where he wanted to be would do her no good, but she was relieved just the same. "I love it here, too. I've never lived anywhere else. I was born in the north end of Seattle, in the house where my parents still live. Michael was born there, too. We went to the same schools, knew the same people—although Michael's two years older than me, and back then he never missed a chance to rub it in." She held her bottom lip in her teeth, smiling, remembering.

"That makes you twenty-seven."

Abby inclined her head, watching him get up and put more sushi on his plate. "It's not supposed to be polite to ask a woman's age." She sipped tea and regarded him archly over the rim of her cup as he sat again.

"I didn't," he retorted and brushed a knuckle along her jaw. "But Michael's twenty-nine, the same as I am. I'm not Einstein, but I can figure it out from there. And

by the way—'' he took her in thoroughly from head to
toe ''—twenty-seven looks fantastic on you.''

"Hah!" Abby pursed her mouth in mock skepticism.
"I bet you tell every female you meet the same thing."

"Wrong," he retorted. "Only the fantastic ones."

She chuckled. "You know a lot about me from Michael. All I know about you is that you come from Omaha. Spill."

He finished his sake, set his plate on the rug and spread an arm along the back of the couch behind her. "I'm a very complicated man, so this may take time."

"We've got time." She elbowed his ribs, and he caught her hand and held it.

He let out a bored sigh. "Nick Dorset, 29, six-two, one-eighty. One narrow escape but never married. Father an architect, mother a grade-school teacher. One sister, Janet, 31, degree in early childhood education but busy being married and raising one two-year-old daughter—Penny-the-prodigy." He sighed and frowned. "What else?"

"Achievements? Hobbies?"

"Boy, maybe I should go see if I can find my pedigree. You really want to know the little stuff?"

"I've got a feeling it's not so little."

"Where were you when I needed a fan club?" He rested his head back and looked at the ceiling. "Lettered in track in high school. Got an athletic scholarship to the University of Nebraska. Didn't make the Olympics. Did make it through the school of engineering. Air force—pilot. Fell in love for the first time, and can't get planes out of my blood. Got out of the service and went straight into commercial flying. Now I'm dreaming of owning my own business. I'd like to operate a float plane service between the San Juan Islands. How am I doing?"

"Great. You sound marvelous. And you'll do it with the float planes, Nick. I know you will."

He'd turned his face toward her. The room's subdued lighting deepened the shadows beneath his cheekbones and made his eyes unfathomable. Abby cleared her throat. He still held her hand, and she concentrated on the warmth of his strong fingers on hers. "There isn't anything very earth-shattering to know about me. I was an art major and went into store design, which I'm crazy about. Obviously, I didn't escape attachment. I'm looking forward to the baby: it's what I always wanted, although maybe not..." She blinked rapidly. "Maybe I could have timed my first pregnancy better."

"What do you mean?"

She'd slipped, said something she hadn't intended to say. "Nothing, really, except it would have been nice to be better established and settled."

"You can't always get things exactly right."

He was so direct. "No," Abby agreed. "You can't." She searched for a way to change the subject and grabbed for the first inspiration. "Running. You like to run, don't you? I've seen you heading for the track."

"Running keeps me sane sometimes. I—" He stopped abruptly and turned away. "Shall I turn the tape over?"

"Yes, please." His reaction puzzled her. "I'm going to start jogging."

Nick faced her, instantly frowning. "Not now, you're not."

She stared at him, irritated. "No, not now. Of course not now." He seemed to think she was some kind of invalid. "I meant after the baby's born. Having a baby doesn't mean a woman has to languish on a couch for the rest of her life, you know."

He smiled faintly. "I know that. My sister says she's never been fitter than she is since she had Penny. You should see that little kid go. I was just afraid you'd decided to handle exercise the same way you're handling the rest of your life."

Abby made fists at her sides and had to grab for her sliding plate. "How am I handling the rest of my life?"

He gathered their dishes and carried them wordlessly into the kitchen.

One step behind him, Abby tapped his back. "How am I handling the rest of my life, Nick?"

"As if you're invincible. Superwoman. Abby can do anything, and she doesn't need anyone, right?" He turned the faucet sharply to run water into the sink.

"I don't need someone to wash dishes, if that's what you mean." Immediately she hated the words. "Forget I said that. It was snippy. But leave that, please; I'll do them later."

He did as she asked, wiping his hands on a dish towel. "Can we sit and talk for a while? Or am I being kicked out?"

She *had* offended him. "Stay, Nick. I'm sorry if I'm not very good company. It's just that . . . I seem to fly off the handle easily these days. I would like you to stay." But not to ask questions, she thought.

Nick put in another tape and added wood to the fire. He sat on the couch and kept his eyes on Abby's face while she joined him.

"Any trouble at the Laundromat today?"

"No. I wasn't even busy."

"How many days a week do you work?"

"Six."

He loosened his tie and undid the top button of his shirt. "Seems like a lot when you're pregnant."

"It won't hurt me."

"I hope you're right. Abby." He slid a hand behind her neck and swayed her toward him until her shoulder rested on his chest. "If I'm pushing in where I don't belong, forgive me. But I care what happens to you. You're one of the world's special people."

She closed her eyes, grateful he couldn't see her face. "Thank you. But I'm fine, really. I can manage." He felt so strong, so very masculine.

Nick ruffled her hair and removed his hand. "And John will be back, and everything will be fine again."

The joy died. "Yes," she said. How would she cope? "Would you like some coffee?"

"Sounds great," Nick replied, and watched her slide forward and stand before going to the kitchen. Every second made him want her more...want her and the baby. He passed a hand over his face. The woman was still in love with her husband. She must be, or she'd admit the guy had dropped out for good.

"You take it black, don't you?" Abby called from the kitchen.

"Please." He noticed two books on the floor beside the couch and picked up the top one. *Becoming Parents*. The front cover showed a pregnant woman in a leotard lying on her side. Behind her a man reclined, also on his side, a hand on her belly, his face resting against her hair. Nick swallowed and began turning the pages.

Dishes clattered in the kitchen, and he closed the book quickly, but Abby didn't appear. She was running water over the dirty dishes in the sink, and he heard the dishwasher open. He should help.

Quietly he flipped through the book again, stopping at a section with the heading, "Guidelines for the Labor Companion." Brief instructions followed for dealing with various stages of labor. "If she loses control, be firm, keep talking, help her resume proper breathing. Massage her back or abdomen if this is helpful." Nick ran a finger down the page, picking out sections on irritability, nausea or vomiting, the urge to push or bear down, what to do when the mother wanted to give up. "Encourage. She may say she can't do it, that she's losing control or can't go on." Sweat broke out on Nick's forehead. All this stuff was foreign, the way women coped with natural childbirth—women and their husbands. Who would Abby have?

A small sound broke his concentration. Abby hovered in front of him, a tray of coffee cups in her hands. She stared at the book in his lap.

"Let me take that." Nick reached for the tray and put it on the end table. "Sit down and tell me about all this." She didn't need to be made to feel awkward. He took a deep breath through his nose. "You're going to use this method of natural childbirth?"

Abby sat down and took the cup he offered. "Yes. It's best for the baby, and I want to know everything that's happening."

Nick swallowed some of his own coffee and made himself turn another page in the book. "Sharing a baby's birth is a unique privilege," he read. The sensation in the pit of his stomach was like nothing he'd felt before. He'd like to share the birth of Abby's baby. His skin turned cold. Now he knew he was becoming unhinged.

"Are you taking classes or something?"

"I've had one. I go to Seattle for them."

He knew what he was going to ask, and that he shouldn't. "Isn't John supposed to go with you?"

She averted her face. "His work makes it tough to plan like other people do."

Nick pressed on, hating himself, yet unable to stop. "So who will coach you? That's what it's called, right? Coaching?"

Her hands shook. She gripped the cup tightly, her fingers curled. "I have a friend, Marie Prince, she... Well, she'll help if I ask her. If she's got time." Her chin came up. "And if that doesn't come off, I won't be the first woman to make it through without a coach. I'll learn the techniques well, and I'll do just fine."

How had she missed those books when she was cleaning up? Abby thought. She didn't want to discuss this, not with Nick. She didn't want to dwell on how alone she was likely to be when the time came. When she'd asked Marie to stand by, she'd admitted simply that she'd probably pass out and be useless. The class leader had volunteered help, if she was available, but that was iffy. Abby made herself smile at Nick and relax against the couch. How like him to immediately assume every father would make sure he was present for his child's birth. Nick would have been. The subject was something she'd never even broached to John.

Nick was watching her thoughtfully. "My brother-in-law was with Janet when Penny was born. Afterward he carried on as if he'd given birth himself. He said it was the greatest thing that ever happened to him." He grinned and set down his cup. "Seems to me great experiences should be shared."

"You mean I'll be selfish if I go it alone?" She forced a laugh. "If the horror stories are true, I might be prepared to spread a little of the greatness around. I have nightmares that I'll yell something stupid and make an ass of myself." Warmth flew up her neck. No one had ever made her tongue as loose as Nick did. Single men didn't want to hear all this.

"Do you suppose—" he began, then pressed his lips shut. He colored slightly. "I wondered if I could come to some of the classes with you."

Goose bumps shot out on Abby's arms. "Come? To childbirth education classes? Nick, you'd hate it."

"No, I wouldn't." He took her cup and put it beside his, held both her hands in his. "I'd be really interested. And then, if you needed me, I could...I could be with you for the delivery." He blushed furiously now. "I mean, I could take you to the hospital and cheer from the sidelines or something."

She doubted she'd heard correctly. He chafed her hands almost painfully, and she concentrated on watching his fingers move.

"Would you let me do that, Abby?"

"I don't know," she said slowly. Why would a man want to be present for the birth of another man's child? She'd curl up from embarrassment with Nick there.

"Will you think about it? Let me come to the classes, anyway. While—just while John's away. He'd probably be glad to know you had someone with you. And I know Michael would."

John, Michael. Abby's mind clouded. John didn't give a damn, and if Michael found out he'd fire questions with both barrels. "Don't talk to Michael about the baby or the classes. He's not comfortable with the whole thing."

Nick felt an unaccustomed trembling in his limbs. He could hardly believe he was pressing for this. "Stop worrying about what I may say to Michael. I've got the message you want him kept out of your business." She hadn't asked him not to tell John, he noted with more satisfaction than he was proud of. And she hadn't totally refused to let him be part of what was happening to her.

She was quiet now. Far from relaxing her, he'd managed to heighten her anxiety. Tentatively he stroked the side of her face until she looked directly at him.

"Just like you say, Abby, everything's going to be okay," he said, pushing his fingers into her hair. He mustn't go too fast or risk confusing her.

Abby nodded and covered his hand. She blinked rapidly, and his throat tightened. The lady was determined not to cry, not to give herself away. He started to pull her head toward him and met no resistance. Leaning back, he settled her face against his shoulder and rested his chin on top of her head.

"You're a kind man, Nick, the best. I'm going to look forward to seeing you with a wife and children of your own."

Nick stared ahead and through the windows at a dark, moonless sky. Oh, he was sterling, honesty itself. How fast would she run if she knew what he really wanted?

"Rest, Abby. Close your eyes. You look beat."

Her body untensed slightly. He felt the baby kick against his hip and suppressed a smile. Maybe he was going to pull this off, although a psychiatrist might enjoy figuring out why he wanted to.

Abby's breathing had become regular. Nick was surprised. She wouldn't be comfortable with the idea of falling asleep in his arms.

Despite himself, he drowsed.

The sharp click of a key in the lock snapped him wide awake. John Winston! Nick glanced down at Abby's bent head. She must be exhausted to hear nothing. His thoughts were scrambled. He heard the door sweep open. If he tried to put distance between himself and Abby, she'd be disoriented, then frightened. God, they couldn't do anything but face the music and find a way to explain the truth—nothing was happening here.

Careful not to awaken Abby, Nick craned to look over his shoulder, with a pleasant smile arranged on his lips.

The door slammed, and a man coughed. Heels clicked down the hall. "Hey, sis. Where are you?" Michael Harris said and halted in the entrance to the living room.

Chapter Seven

Nick quelled the urge to laugh hysterically. Michael Harris, of all people. And Nick was alone, at night, with Michael's married pregnant sister and holding her while she slept. *Think quickly,* he commanded himself.

"What the hell—" Michael began.

Nick cut him off, "Shhh." He pressed a finger to his lips and raised his brows. "She's sleeping."

Michael, still in uniform, slowly removed his cap and walked to stand in front of the couch. He shoved back his overcoat and splayed his hands on narrow hips. "What's going on here, Nick?"

"Shhh," Nick whispered again, making exaggerated pointing motions at Abby, who began to stir. "She'll be uncomfortable enough when she realizes she did this."

Michael sucked in his cheeks and took in the room through narrowed eyes. "This place looks different."

Abby started and lifted her head. "Nick?" She flattened her palms against his chest, looking at his face, bemused. He saw her sense Michael's silent figure an instant before she pulled quickly away and turned to her brother.

She'd fallen asleep, Abby thought frantically, actually fallen asleep in Nick Dorset's arms. She put a distance of a few inches between them and braced her weight on both hands. "Hi, Mike," she said lamely. He looked like an enraged parent, tight-lipped, stiff-backed. Good Lord, what was he thinking? Sure, it must appear weird for her to be with Nick like this, but she was hardly a candidate for some clandestine affair.

"Michael dropped in," Nick said, and Abby glanced at him, horrified. He sounded... *guilty*.

"If I'd known you might be busy, Abby, I'd have called first. You did give me a key to use—remember?— whenever John's away. Which seems to be most of the time, lately."

"Of course I remember." She wished Nick would say something intelligent. He was giving off awkwardness in signal waves. "I didn't think you were coming today," she said to Michael.

He took his cap from beneath his arm. "I guess not."

"Mike, listen," Nick stood, "whatever you're think-ing, you're wrong. Abby and I are friends, we—"

"I'm not thinking anything," Michael interrupted. "Why would I?" His slitted glare, first at Nick, then Abby, suggested he was most certainly thinking some-thing. She began to feel sick.

"It's good to see you, Michael," Abby said and heard her tone hint otherwise.

Michael didn't reply.

"It really is," she persisted.

"I don't understand this," Michael said. "It's wild. I didn't even realize you two knew each other, and I walk in on a cozy little domestic scene while my brother-in-law's away. Or is it domestic? How long have you two been 'friends'?"

"Michael, don't." Abby's skin crawled.

Nick gripped her shoulder. "Abby doesn't need any extra grief now, Mike. She's got enough. She needs to be calm," he finished uncertainly.

"Thanks for the instruction." Michael threw his cap on the armchair. "I didn't realize you were such an authority on what pregnant women need—apart from a broad shoulder to lie on." Abby had never heard him sound this way.

Nick dropped his arm from her shoulders. "Don't say things you'll regret, Mike. Abby and I are friends who decided to share a meal. She fell asleep while we were talking. Big deal. Let it go."

Michael looked anything but convinced.

Abby's heart did ugly things. "Nick," she said, keeping her voice level, "I apologize for zonking out on you like that. Some hostess. And I apologize for putting you through this scene, but Michael and I are very close, and we look out for each other when we can. He's doing his protective routine." She gave Michael a smile she hoped wasn't too fixed. "You always could be a pain when you felt righteous about something. In case you've forgotten, Nick played messenger for you the time you got held over in Chicago. Remember that?"

"Yeah," Michael said, while his expression flashed the rest of his reaction. *So what?*

Abby sighed. "Well," she pressed on. "Well, that's when Nick found out John's away, and he's, well—" She glanced at Nick who smiled thinly. He'd probably never speak to her again after this. "Nick's been very kind and helped me with—with a couple of things I needed done. So I persuaded him to let me make him dinner tonight."

"I see." The skeptical light remained in Michael's eyes. "And then—because John's away—you helped each other out with a little TLC?"

"For God's sake, Michael," Abby snapped. "I'm hardly a femme fatale. I'm more than seven months pregnant."

He looked first at her, then at Nick, and sat down suddenly on top of his cap. He pulled it from beneath him and hung it loosely between his knees. "I'm sorry." He ran a hand through his mussed black curls and met Abby's eyes. "I'm really sorry, Abby. I was caught off guard, that's all. You can imagine how it looked when I walked in here."

"Sure, I can," she said dully. This was her fault. She'd caused a rift between Michael and Nick. And because of her, Nick had been put on the defensive. "I'm sorry I caused this—for all our sakes."

Nick stopped her from turning away. "We're all sorry," he said with a laugh. "Forget it. I'm going to get out of here and leave you and Michael to talk."

"No." Michael leapt up. "Stay, please. I only stopped to see how you are, Abby." He grimaced. "You were a whole lot better before I arrived. Forgive a protective old brother?" He leaned to kiss her cheek.

Abby wrapped her arms tightly around his neck and shook her head before kissing him soundly. "Of course I forgive you. Only idiots don't like being cared about. Nick's the one you may have to convince not to punch you out."

"I'll let you off this time, Mike," Nick said. Both men laughed, but tension still arched between them.

"Why don't we all have coffee?" Abby suggested. "Or you two could finish the sake." She smiled at Michael. "You told me once that you and Nick enjoyed sushi, so that's what we had tonight, and I got sake to go with it."

"Nothing for me, thanks," Michael responded. "I think I'll get home and crash." He buttoned his coat, scanning the room quickly. His gaze came to rest on the empty dining area, and he opened his mouth before catching Abby's eye and bringing his lips together again.

She wanted him to leave and hated herself for the thought. He was telegraphing silent questions, and she wouldn't be able to put him off much longer. "Will you be in town for a few days?" Abby said.

"Until Friday. How about lunch tomorrow? I could come to the store and pick you up, if you like."

"No, no." She avoided looking at Nick. "I mean, yes I can get off, but let's not meet downtown. Does Hiram's at the locks sound good? I'm in the mood for seafood."

"I could still pick you up."

"I'll meet you there—say, at one? There's no point in you fighting the jam."

Michael showed signs of arguing. Abby put an arm through his and urged him toward the door. "Would you mind calling the restaurant for a reservation? Sometimes they get busy on nice days."

"Nice days?" Michael raised one dark brow. "We'll be lucky if it doesn't snow."

"Do it anyway, Mike," Nick said, and she caught his knowing grin at Michael. "You never know. There could be a crowd to watch sea gulls ice-skating or something."

"Oh, right." Michael slid on his cap and tipped it over his eyes. "Hiram's at one."

"I'll be there," she said faintly and listened until the front door clicked shut.

She couldn't look at Nick. She'd never be able to look at him again without blushing.

"Pretty bad, huh?" He turned her toward him. "But I guess I can't blame him for the outraged act."

Abby bit her lip hard. "I'm so sorry, Nick. I don't know what made me fall asleep like that. I've never been one of those people who nap for no reason."

"You've never been pregnant before, have you? I should think that's a pretty good reason, particularly when you keep insisting on overdoing everything."

"I've never been pregnant before, no. Maybe I am doing too much. I don't know what to say about Michael, about the way he behaved."

"Forget it. We must have made quite a picture. Poor guy had a right to overreact. But, Abby—" Nick breathed into his fist, watching her thoughtfully "—I do think you'd better consider confiding in Michael. He's suspicious."

She moistened her lips. "How could he be? I mean, of what?"

Nick shrugged. "I'm not sure. I just have a feeling he's looking for something. Anyway, think about it before you see him tomorrow. I'm sure if you appealed to him he'd agree to keep quiet around your parents. After all, it won't be long before John gets back—will it?"

Abby felt blood drain from her face. She was in a mess, and the situation could only get worse. "I'm not sure," she said evasively. "It could be awhile. But I'll think about what you say." She wanted to be alone now, to think. In two days she'd be signing final divorce papers. John was almost completely out of her life.

"Should we get those dishes finished?" Nick asked, beginning to unbutton a cuff.

She stopped him. "I'm going to leave them, tonight. I'll get up early, and they won't take any time. You must be ready for bed. I know I am. Thanks for the roses, Nick, and the lovely evening. And again, forgive my nutty brother."

"I've already forgotten the whole thing." He picked up his jacket and slung it over one shoulder. "I'm only next door if you need me, Abby."

"Thank you."

"You would call me, wouldn't you?"

"Of course." She wasn't sure she would, but she liked him more than ever for offering.

"Good night, then."

"Night, Nick."

He walked slowly down the hall. Abby followed, her hands clasped in front of her. She stretched around Nick to open the door and bowed her head as he passed.

On the threshold, he paused and turned back. "Thanks for a great dinner."

"You're welcome."

"This is the best time I've had in years, Abby."

She searched his face and found no trace of humor. "Well, thanks again, but I find that hard to believe."

"Believe it. Can we do it again? Next time I cook?"

What could she say?

"Abby? Will you spend another evening with me...soon?"

"We'll see. Good night, Nick."

Nick jammed his free hand into his pocket, stepping backward and feeling like a man moving through deep water. One pace in the other direction, and he could have kissed her. He kept smiling until she closed her door.

Drained, he leaned against the wall and rested his head back. He hadn't heard the last from Michael Harris about this evening. Michael could become a big problem unless he could be won over. Nick found his key and went into his condo. Michael would come around in time; he'd have to.

In the bedroom Nick looked at his bed, deciding what to do next. He was exhausted, but sleep was likely to be an elusive commodity. The answer to the problem came easily. He shucked his clothes and pulled on running gear.

ABBY PUSHED AWAY her plate. "That was wonderful, Michael. Sinfully good."

"You need to eat more."

Not again. "I eat plenty. I don't want to be a blimp after this baby's born."

Michael made a grumping sound. "Not much danger of that. How about dessert?"

"No, thanks. I couldn't. Don't let me stop you, though."

The waitress refilled their coffee cups, and Michael waited until the woman left. "About last night, Abby."

Here it comes, she thought, and concentrated on the boats gathering in the locks outside. "It's interesting, isn't it," she said.

After a short silence Michael said, "What?"

"The locks," Abby replied. "The way the boats gather in this huge pen to go from salt water to fresh, forcing their way upriver like salmon."

"They're going into a lake," Michael remarked shortly. "Lake Washington isn't a river. And the boats don't have to force anything, they wait for the lock water to pump them up between Puget Sound and Salmon Bay, and off they go—upstream, no sweat."

Abby glowered at him. "Thanks for the lecture. You know what I meant."

"You meant to avoid the issue, and it's not going to work. What's going on with you?"

"Nothing, damn it." She pushed back her chair, collided with the diner behind, and cringed. In a lowered voice, she added, "There's nothing going on with me that I can't handle," and immediately regretted the last few words.

Michael leaned across the table. "And what does that mean, nothing you can't handle? If everything's peachy, why is there anything to handle at all?"

Abby let out an exasperated breath. "You're putting words in my mouth. Why are you so determined to find problems?"

"I'm not. But I'm not a fool, either. Abby, I really feel rotten about last night. I'll have to apologize to Nick. But something's going on. I knew it the last time I saw you at the folks'. Will you let me in on the big mystery?"

The temptation to confide in him almost broke her. Abby drank some water, trying to stay calm. "I've had some difficult weeks, that's all. That isn't unusual, I'm sure." If she told him even that she was short of money there'd be no turning back, and he'd dig out the rest of her sordid little story before she was ready.

"Okay, you aren't going to come clean without a fight, so I'll just have to push you, Abby." He covered her hand on top of the table. "Last night was the first time I've been in your condo in weeks. There are things missing, Abby. The dining set? The clock? I didn't take inventory, but there was a lot gone, and I don't understand it."

Her heart had started a heavy thudding. So much for her theory that Michael wasn't observant. "I'm making some changes." Changes came in many forms, she thought, divorce was just one of them.

"Changes?" Michael repeated. "Waiting until John's away and getting rid of half your furniture? What's he going to say about that?"

Abby stuffed her hands in her lap and made fists. She didn't want to hate John, but at this moment her feeling for him came close to that. "We did it before he left. He knows."

Michael regarded her for a long time. He rested back in his chair, never taking his eyes from her face. "Abby, you have to have some idea when John's due home. You always did before."

She started pulling on her coat. "I don't know this time. He has to take trips when he can get them." Getting out of here was all that mattered to her for the moment.

"Funny he's making back-to-back trips suddenly. I never got the impression John was that dedicated. At least not as long as good old Mom kept coming through with the bucks." He paused, clearly stricken by what he'd said. "Forgive me. I—I should never have said that."

"It's okay," Abby said. What Michael implied was absolutely true: John was an overindulged only child who needed to grow up. Not that his development was her problem anymore. She stood, reaching for her purse. "Lunch was great, but I've got to run. I'll call you, Michael, okay?"

"I don't leave until tomorrow." He paid the bill and hurriedly trailed her outside. "Could we get together tonight, go see Mom and Dad maybe?"

She faced him, smiling, praying her eyes wouldn't give her away. "I can't tonight, Michael. You see them and give them my love. I talked to Mom this morning. Remind them I'll be over for dinner on Sunday. Have a good trip, huh?" She pecked his cheek, holding back tears. "See you when you get back."

"Take care, Abby."

She turned and half ran to her car. Behind the wheel, she set her face in a grim mask. All the books said babies sensed if their mothers were unhappy, even before birth. She would *make* herself be happy. She'd concentrate on this little person of hers and nothing else.

AT LEAST THE DRUNK hadn't shown up tonight. Abby had already locked the storage room and put on her coat when the big hand on the wall clock clicked to the half hour. Ten-thirty. She flipped over the sign, made one last tour of the shop and walked out to the Pinto.

Isolated flakes of snow fell, and a thick film of ice covered the little car's windows. Snow in November, particularly before Thanksgiving, usually boded a hard winter in the Northwest. Abby searched for an ice-scraper and remembered breaking the one she'd had last winter. She took a credit card from her wallet and went to work, shaking her hands every few minutes to keep her circulation moving. Tomorrow night she'd put newspaper over the windshield to avoid this.

The engine didn't want to turn over, but on the fourth try it caught sluggishly and she set off, peering over the wheel at slick streets. The defroster wasn't enthusiastic about its task, either.

The bad weather had made hermits of all sensible people. By the time Abby turned onto Coal Creek Parkway and headed west, not another vehicle was in sight. Widely spaced streetlights served only to highlight a thickening snowfall. Dense evergreens crowded the sides of the road, and Abby drove slower and slower, knowing, without having to see, that a skid could land her in a deep brush-choked ditch.

She stopped for a red light, and the engine died.

Pumping the gas while she turned the ignition key, Abby noted a service station on one corner. Lights illuminated the pumps, but no attendant was in sight. She turned the key again and closed her eyes with relief when the car jolted forward.

Another six miles, and she'd be safely home. When the car quit again, Abby figured she still had five miles to go. This time repeated efforts produced only flat clicks that let her know the battery was dead.

Abby got out and lifted the hood. She waited fifteen minutes, flapping her arms and stamping her feet. One car sped by. Both she and the Pinto were probably next to invisible, Abby decided and started walking back to the intersection.

By the time she reached the service station, her feet felt nonexistent, and every muscle in her body ached. The place was closed, but at least there was a telephone booth. She tried Marie's number and hung up after fifteen rings.

Abby walked out of the booth and stared up, narrowing her eyes against the snow. Cold air seared her throat. Nick would come, but did she want to ask him? The answer troubled her deeply. More than anything else at this moment, she longed to see Nick's tall figure walking toward her. She had no right to want him.

Abby searched the phone book and found Nick's number. She inserted a coin in the slot and began punching buttons, pausing between each digit. She almost hung up when she heard his voice.

"Hello," he said, and then, when she didn't answer, added, "Who is this?"

"Nick," she replied quietly, "it's Abby."

He hesitated. "Abby, you sound funny. What's wrong?"

She gritted her teeth, screwing up her courage. "My car's broken down on Coal Creek Parkway. I'm near Sunset Highway, at a gas station. It's closed. Everything is because of the snow. I've tried to get hold of—"

"I'll be right there. Stay put."

"Nick, just a minute. I'll walk back to the car. It's on the right side of the road heading—"

"You'll stay where you are. Close the door of the phone booth and try to keep warm." He hung up.

The telephone booth had no door, but Abby huddled inside the glass sides, her arms tightly crossed. She shouldn't have called Nick. She was being unfair, preying on his goodness.

Within minutes she heard a powerful engine. A car swept to a partial stop at the intersection, then the silvery gray BMW roared into the station forecourt, screeching to a halt inches from where Abby stood. Nick got out and ran around. Abby was surprised to see him in his airline uniform, gold stripes glittering around his jacket cuffs. He wore no overcoat or hat, and speckles of snow clung to his hair by the time he caught her hand and pulled her into the car.

"Get in," he ordered. His features were strained. The muscles in Abby's jaw trembled. She wished he would hold her.

When he sat beside her, with the car still running, he turned up the heater and then stared through the snow-caked windshield, his arms crossed. "I've been watching for you," he said. "I needed to see you."

She drew up her shoulders. Something was happening between them—had happened—and it shouldn't have. "This is a pain, Nick. I guess you were right about my rotten old Pinto."

"That's not the point."

"What . . . what is the point?" Could she dare to hope they were held together by something more than his concern for a friend?

Nick slid his hands around the steering wheel. "It's about time you guessed the point, but you won't face up to the truth."

If he'd touched her, run his hands over her, he couldn't have produced a more electric reaction. She mustn't read too much into his words. "I'm not sure what you mean."

"Aren't you?" He reached behind his seat for a blanket before speaking. "I can't get further into it now. But we will. And in the meantime, this has got to stop," he said tightly. "This crazy job you insist on doing must go. I got called in. Another hour, and I'd have been gone. It's too dangerous for you to be driving around at night in a car that's only fit for the scrap heap."

"You're overreacting," Abby retorted and immediately turned her face away. "I shouldn't have called you. Why didn't you say you had to leave, Nick?"

He draped the blanket over her. "I'm just glad I hadn't left yet. Like I said, I'd been waiting for you to get back." His hands lingered at her sides, and his face was close. Abby could see the light from the dash reflected in his eyes, feel his soft breath, almost believe his lips had pressed hers. "I always seem to be waiting for you, Abby. Even when I don't realize it." He passed a palm slowly over her cheek, ran his fingers into her hair, and he did kiss her fleetingly on the temple before he turned back to grasp the steering wheel.

Abby looked at him. His face was inscrutable in the muted green light. "Why were you waiting for me?" The ache in her thighs, the swelling heat from her breasts, was an almost forgotten sensation. It felt right and she wanted it.

He continued to stare ahead. "I—I needed to ask a favor."

"Ask. What is it?"

"Nothing. I'll tell you when I get you home."

She must concentrate, she thought. "Nick," she said barely audibly. "I think a dead battery's all that's wrong with my car. Could we jump it, do you think? I've got cables in the back."

His mouth turned down. "I don't want you driving that thing." He turned eyes that glinted toward her. "I realize I don't have the right to ask anything of you, but I'm going to, anyway. Please, Abby, give up this job. If money's the big problem, let me lend you what you need until you're on your feet. No one need ever know, not John, not Michael and your folks. If it would make you feel better, you can write out some sort of note and pay me back when you can."

Miserably, she shook her head. "I can't—"

He rested two fingers on her mouth. "You can. All I have to worry about is me, and I can afford to help you."

Getting Nick involved had been a terrible mistake. Abby gently removed his hand. "Thanks, Nick. But it's not as bad as you think. I really can manage very well. Just drive me home. I'll get a new battery and put it into the car tomorrow and get it checked over. Now, let's go, or you're going to be late."

Unthinking, she pressed her fingers into the hard muscle of his thigh. She heard breath escape Nick's lungs and started to withdraw her hand. He covered her hand quickly, holding it in a vise. His leg was rock hard, and his fingers twined through hers, pulling hers fractionally higher. He was aroused, unbearably aroused. *Oh, God.* She bowed her head and willed her clamoring responses to stop.

"Nick, this is no good. I don't understand it, but I know it's no good."

"Abby," he blurted out. "If only... oh hell, not now. This isn't the right time to get into anything that means so much. But, Abby, I wish you'd give up working at—"

"No," she interrupted, "stop worrying." She laughed and withdrew her hand while a cold place formed around her heart. Her body pulsed. "You're a frustrated mother hen, and I love you for it." The breath lodged in her throat. What a dumb thing to say. She prayed he hadn't noticed.

Nick was quiet for seconds, his head bowed, then he silently let in the clutch and drove back to Lake Vista.

Outside her door, Abby stopped and faced him. "Thanks a million, Nick. You saved my life. I'll try not to bother you again." She put a hand against the wall behind her for support. "Have a good trip."

"I'll be back on Monday." His smile didn't reach his eyes. "Can you stay out of trouble till then?"

He felt responsible for her, Abby thought and looked away quickly. "Just concentrate of taking care of yourself, Nick."

"Wait," he said. "I almost forgot. Get your door unlocked while I fetch something."

Abby watched him go into his condo. By the time she'd switched on the light in her own hall, he was back, with a large cardboard box in his arms.

"This is why I was waiting for you to get back." His smile was almost a boyish, caught in a half truth smile. "One of the reasons, anyway. I didn't want to leave it on the step because it's heavy." He carted his burden past her into the kitchen and set it on a counter.

"What is it?" Abby asked, but he held her arm and walked her back to the doorway. "Leftovers," he said. "I'm famous for going out of town with partly used stuff in the refrigerator and then coming home to a bunch of ruined food. Do me a favor and use it up for me. Throw out anything you don't want. The meat's been frozen once, so I didn't want to freeze it again, and it was too much for dinner. I always overestimate." He was hurrying now.

"Anything else I can do?" Abby asked to his back. He strode inside his condo and emerged with a flight bag, his raincoat and cap. He settled the cap on his head and dug in his pants' pocket.

"I've got one plant still trying to live." He worked a key off his ring. "The one by the living room window. Don't ask me what it is." His golden eyes met hers, then lowered fractionally to her mouth. "If you think of it, would you water the thing?"

There wasn't enough air. "Yes," she said softly. "Can I do anything else?"

He hesitated. "You could... Abby, don't take any chances, please." They key clinked against her ring as he dropped it into her palm.

"Have a safe trip, Nick."

He took a step toward the stairs, then turned back and shot his free arm around her shoulders. Tipping his head sideways to keep his cap visor cleared, he kissed her mouth briefly. "For luck," he said and pulled away an inch to study her. "Luck for both of us." He kissed her again, harder, his lips parting hers, his tongue passing her teeth to reach far into her mouth.

Abby moaned deep in her throat and clung to him, weak as she never remembered being weak. Nick pulled back, his eyes somber and penetrating. "We'll have luck,

Abby. We'll see to that.'' He left in a rustle of water-proof fabric.

Abby stood still, listening until the downstairs door banged, closing out the sound of his running footsteps.

Chapter Eight

"Go away," Abby mumbled and pulled the quilt over her head.

The intercom rang again, more insistently this time. Someone was leaning on the button.

She rolled onto her back. Monday, her one day off, and some clown had to bug her first thing in the morning. *Monday!* Nick was due back today, and she had his key. Abby scrambled from bed and tottered down the hall to the intercom speaker. "Hello," she said, cleared her throat and repeated, "hello."

"Finally," a woman's voice said. "Let me in, will you? It's freezing out here."

Marie Prince. Abby looked heavenward and released the latch on the outer door. Just what she needed, Marie's pseudobored don't-give-a-damn act on the very day Abby was due to sign away the marriage she'd thought was forever.

She opened her front door, left it standing wide and scuffed back to the bedroom. There would be no more sleeping now.

Seconds later she heard the door slam. Abby tossed aside her nightgown and pulled on underwear. She took a sleeveless dress from the closet and rummaged in a drawer for a turtleneck to wear underneath.

"You're all belly." Marie entered the room and flopped on the end of Abby's bed. She laughed. "And boobs. The rest of you is as thin as ever, thinner maybe."

Abby kept her mouth firmly closed and struggled into the sweater.

"Why don't you buy some proper maternity clothes? They've got some cute stuff."

"Why bother," Abby said from inside her dress. "Seven weeks, and this will all be over. And—" she wiggled her head clear "—as you just got through pointing out, I haven't gained much weight, so my regular things will fit as soon as I get back in shape."

Marie, propped on her elbows, swung her feet while she assessed Abby minutely. "You're a good-looking woman, beautiful in a way. The sooner you start making a new life, the better."

Abby found a pair of panty hose without runs and sat to put them on. "You're talking about finding another man, aren't you, Marie?"

"Mmm. What else is there?"

Not for the first time, Abby felt deeply sorry for Marie. She really wasn't whole without a male in tow. "Marie," she said patiently. "A woman with a newborn baby is hardly every man's idea of desirable. And, believe it or not, there are even women—me, for one—who don't spend every minute dreaming of Mr. Wonderful. I'm a bit soured on romance these days." Perversely, Nick's face, his tawny eyes smiling, passed through her mind. And his touch. They'd passed to a new level, and there'd be no going back. She slipped on flat shoes and began making her bed around Marie.

"You said you'd keep in touch," Marie said, standing and helping with the covers. "I haven't heard a word from you in ages."

Abby glanced up, contrite. "I'm sorry. Things have really been a bit crazy. Today..." She faltered, deciding how much to say. Then Marie's eyes settled on hers, and the old understanding was there. Abby warmed to this little woman all over again. "It's been almost three months since John filed for divorce. Everything's ready. This afternoon I sign the papers, Marie. It only took ninety days and a date in court, and that was that—over. I knew what was coming, and I'm glad in a way, but I still feel a bit upset about it." She made much of smoothing the pillow shams.

In an instant, Marie was at her side, standing on tip-toe to hug her. "I thought it must be about that time. Call it second sight. Something made me decide to come over here today. I'll come with you to the lawyer's office, if you like. It's rough to do those things on your own."

Abby smiled. She pushed Marie's long hair behind her shoulder. "You've got a good heart, Marie. Too good for your own comfort sometimes. Thanks for the offer, but I'd rather do this alone. The lawyer said John's signing *in absentia*, which I suppose means he won't be there, so at least I don't have to face him. He's probably sunning himself on some beach in the West Indies." She sounded bitchy, and she detested that. "How about some coffee?"

"I thought you'd never ask," Marie said, leading the way to the kitchen. Abby noticed she didn't push her offer of company at the lawyer's office. Poor Marie, she tried so hard, but she wasn't heroine material.

Abby started coffee while Marie toured the living room, picking up magazines, dropping them, always on the move. "Where did the roses come from?" she called.

Abby stopped, holding the filter suspended over the percolator. "My neighbor gave them to me," she said.

"The guy who works for the same airline as Michael?"

"That's the one." Let it drop, Abby thought uncomfortably.

"The one who looks like a male model?"

Abby closed her eyes and suppressed a smile. "Nick's a good-looking man. He's also very nice."

"He didn't find these beside the road. These are strictly hot-house variety."

Trust Marie to pick up on every little thing. "You don't take anything in your coffee, do you, Marie?"

"No. Let's talk some more about this neighbor of yours."

"There's nothing to discuss." Abby carried two mugs into the living room and handed one to Marie. "Sit down somewhere."

Marie remained standing over the vase of roses. They'd been buds when Nick brought them, now they were wide open and fragrant. "He just rang your doorbell one day and said 'I brought you these. Not for any reason, just because I'm nice.' Right, Abby?"

"Don't be silly." She was remembering the box of "leftovers" he'd dropped off. The meat he'd "overestimated." Everything was fresh and untouched, and carefully selected for her, she knew. To back up his meat story, he'd thought to take off the original wrapper and use fresh plastic. She wondered how he intended to explain the chicken he'd included, and the box of chocolates.

Marie had sat on the edge of the armchair. Abby became aware of being studied closely. "Are you going to say any more about this man, or do I have to dig it out of you?"

"There isn't any more to say. You have a vivid imagination. I made him dinner one night, that's all, and he brought flowers. No big deal."

"No big deal!" Marie came half out of the chair. "Of course it's a big deal. Here you are having a relationship with a perfectly marvelous male, and you don't even bother to keep me posted."

Why had she told Marie anything? Abby wondered. She could have said she bought the flowers herself, if she weren't so honest.

"Have you been out anywhere?"

Abby shook her head. "Stop dreaming, Marie. For my sake, turn off the fairy-tale syndrome. Look at me, will you? Really look. What man in his right mind would want to take me anywhere? Nick is just a good neighbor. He's the kind of man who likes to do nice things for people. Can we leave it at that?"

Marie gave a short laugh. "Good neighbor Nick, sure, if that's the way you want it. But I'm not fooled, and neither are you. Pregnant or not pregnant, the guy's got a thing for you. I've heard some men get turned on by pregnant—"

"Marie," Abby broke in threateningly. "End of subject, understand?"

Marie buried her nose in her mug. She slid back in the chair and crossed her ankles.

They drank in silence, and Abby got up to refill their coffee. Another hour, and she'd have to leave for the lawyer's office. She checked her watch and remembered

Nick. She should have made sure what time he was due in just in case he didn't have a spare key.

"Abby, have you thought about what you'll do after the baby comes?"

Abby set down her mug. "I've thought about it." And she didn't want to talk about those thoughts to anyone.

"I've been thinking about it, too, a lot." Marie glanced at Abby, faint pink spreading over her milky skin. "You're still keeping everything to yourself, I suppose? Not telling your family?"

"Yes," Abby said. "I have to. I told you I wanted to make it through on my own as much as possible."

"Bringing up a child alone can't be so easy."

Deep inside Abby, something twisted tightly. "A lot of people do it. I won't be a pioneer."

"A lot of people do it, and a lot of little kids suffer because they do."

Abby stared at Marie. "Are you saying my baby's going to suffer because—"

"Because it won't have a father around? I guess that's what I'm saying. Who'll look after it? Are you going to stay home?"

"You know I can't do that." Cold slipped over her skin.

"Your mother, then? I suppose she could babysit."

"No!" A panicky feeling gripped Abby. "My mother's too old for that, now. She didn't have Michael and me until late. I couldn't let her try to bring up another child."

Marie got up and knelt on the floor beside the tape deck, reading cassette titles. "But someone does have to bring up a kid, right? Is it right to let some stranger do that while you run a taxi service, picking up and dropping off, and always too tired to enjoy any of it?"

"I don't know what you're getting at, Marie. I'll just have to do the best I can with what I've got. At least my baby will be loved. A lot of single mothers, and fathers, manage very well."

"So you already said. I just wondered if you'd considered the alternatives, that's all."

Abby massaged her temples as if she could stop the ache there. "There aren't any alternatives." She wanted to add that she needed encouragement, not more doubts to worry about.

"Yes, there are." Marie scooted around to face her. "One, anyway. Children do best with two parents. A real home. Abby, there are dozens of couples who'd give their eye teeth for this baby you're expecting. There's someone out there—a couple—who would take it and give it everything you can't: security, the best food and clothes, an education when the time comes—"

"Stop it." Abby's jaws hurt from gritting her teeth. "This is *my* baby, *mine*. And no one else can give it the kind of love I can give. I can't believe you would say this to me. You're supposed to be my friend."

"I am." Marie scooted across the rug to sit at Abby's feet. She held her knees. "I'm sorry if I always come on too fast and too strong. But I am thinking of you."

Abby's mind retreated. What Marie suggested was unnatural; it was madness. "Don't talk about it again."

"Are you really worried about how you'd feel if you gave up the baby, or is it your family's reaction you're thinking about?"

"I don't want to discuss this."

"Then there's John's mother, I suppose. I wonder if John's told her about the divorce."

"Marie. I can't take any more of this. These are things I have to face, and I can't, not yet. I don't think Mrs.

Winston knows about the divorce. In fact, I'm sure she's still waiting to see her grandchild for the first time." Abby choked and covered her mouth. "I didn't want to do this to any of these people. And I didn't want it to happen to the baby or me. I'm no martyr, Marie: I do care what happens to me, and in the end I'll come out okay. Will you leave it at that?"

Marie crossed her ankles and stood effortlessly. "For now, Abby. But someone has to make sure you do keep looking out for yourself. I've got to get to some office in Bellevue, so I'd better go."

"Yes," Abby said faintly. "Thanks for stopping by."

"I'll be back," Marie commented, winding a blue angora scarf around her slim neck. "I won't push. But I know you'll think about what I've said."

MICHAEL OPENED THE DOOR to his apartment before Nick had time to ring the bell. "Hi, there, Mike," he said, a prickling sensation climbing his spine. "Do you see through doors these days?"

The other man wasn't smiling. "You got my message. Good. Shut the door behind you. I'm having Scotch. Is that okay for you?"

Nick followed him into the living room with its vaulted ceiling and glass wall overlooking Lake Washington. The apartment complex was ten miles from the condos but still in Seattle's east side suburbs. "Scotch is great. Ice, no water." He pretended not to notice Michael's grim mood and went directly to the window. "You've got a hell of a view here, Mike. I never could figure out why they called my place Lake Vista. When the leaves come off the trees, we could probably see a corner of the lake if we climbed on the roof, but that's about it."

"*We?*"

Nick glanced quickly at Michael, who shoved a glass into his hand. "Just a figure of speech. What's up?" Something was eating Michael Harris. His blue eyes had that opaque quality they sometimes took on when he was trying to control his anger. Nick's stomach contracted. The guy was angry about something.

"I wanted to talk."

"No kidding." Nick felt the unfamiliar stirrings of anger himself. "The message I got when I landed made it sound like I was slated to be the star witness at an inquisition." He fished a crumpled sheet of paper from his pocket and read aloud "'I need to ask you a few things. I'll be at my place for as long as it takes.'"

Michael gulped his drink. "That says it."

"You could have started with a 'Dear Nick,' or even 'Hey, you.' What's eating you, Mike?"

"My sister," Michael announced without preamble.

Nick took a slow sip of his own Scotch, leveling his gaze on Michael over the rim of the glass. He clinked the ice cubes together. "Are you still trying to make something out of the night you found us at Abby's place? I thought we'd covered that."

"Not well enough. I need answers, Nick, facts. And I can't get at Abby. She's closed herself off from me—something that's never happened before—and I'm worried to death, damn it."

The going could get rocky, Nick recognized. He'd have to tread carefully. "Aren't you making too much out of things? Her condition could account for her changed attitude toward you. She's kind of drawing in with her baby, maybe gathering strength. She'll come out of it."

"There you go again," Michael said tightly. "Spouting like a professor of obstetrics, or female psychology or something. And when did *you* get so all fired close to

Abby? You're very comfortable interpreting her moods, aren't you?''

"This won't get us anywhere, Mike. Why not spit out exactly what's on your mind, so we can face it.''

"Okay.'' Michael slammed down his glass on the teak dining table. "Okay, if that's how you want it.''

"I don't *want* it at all,'' Nick retorted, exasperated. "*You* do. I'm just an unwilling participant.''

"Are you saying you aren't involved with my sister at all?''

Nick's scalp tightened. He passed a hand over his face. "We aren't . . . haven't been romantically involved, if that's what you mean.''

"Nick, my folks are asking questions. Where's John? they want to know. Why doesn't Abby talk about him? She had dinner with them on Sunday—yesterday. I got back late last night, and my mother was on the phone almost before I got through the door here. Evidently Abby hardly said two words all evening, and when my mother tried to talk about the baby's christening—there's been talk of going to John's mother's home in New York for that—Abby clammed up. Mom said she thought Abby was going to cry. I tried to get her at work this afternoon and couldn't.'' Michael stepped close to Nick. "She's left the store. She doesn't work there anymore. Hasn't for over a month. If the folks knew that, they'd have said so. Something's going on with her that she's not talking about. I'm afraid to push her in case she moves even farther away. But you know, don't you, Nick?''

Nick repressed an urge to flinch.

"I may be way out of line,'' Michael continued, "but a man doesn't take an interest in a woman who's carrying another man's child. He doesn't find ways to be with her and spend time snuggling up to her—''

Nick's fist connected with Michael's jaw almost before he knew he'd moved. "Oh, God," he muttered and grabbed to stop Michael from tripping backward over a chair.

Michael wrenched away, touching his fingertips to the corner of his mouth where a thin trickle of blood showed.

"Mike," Nick began, reaching for Michael's shoulder.

"Forget it. I didn't realize defending a maiden's honor was big with you."

When Nick swung again, Michael dodged and caught his wrist. He gripped Nick's tie, backing him up a step before he held his ground. "I ought to kill you," Michael muttered hoarsely. "Do you think I'm mad? You messed around with Abby, and John took off. That's what happened, isn't it? You've ruined her life, and when you get sick of your little games, you'll take off, too, you son of a bitch."

Something snapped in Nick. He straight-armed Michael, smacking the heels of his hands repeatedly into his chest, pushing him away, step by step, until his calves met the edge of a couch and he sat with a thump.

Nick stood over him. "Shut your filthy mouth, Michael. Shut it. What Abby told you about our friendship is true. I wouldn't be living by her in the first place if you hadn't told me the condo was for sale. Abby and I were only nodding acquaintances for months. We didn't meet properly until a few weeks ago when you asked me to let her know you weren't getting in on time from Chicago.

"When I found out she'd left her old job, I asked her to tell you, but she was afraid of worrying you. The same as she's afraid of worrying your folks with her problems."

Michael found a handkerchief and wiped the blood from the corner of his mouth. His hand shook. "What's happened between Abby and John? Not that I like the bastard." He colored and looked away.

Nick sat beside him. "Mike, we're being asinine. Neither of us has the right to tell Abby what to do with her life. She hasn't told me what's happened between her and John Winston." That much at least was true. "And it's not my business, any more than it's yours. She has said she wants to get on her feet—on her own—and prove she can cope without help."

"She's not in a condition to cope alone. Is she working somewhere else? I've got to know what's happening."

"If you interfere, she'll close you out. I'm an outsider, and I can see things more clearly than you. If you love her as much as you say you do, don't push, and don't tip her hand about the job or your suspicions about John to your parents. Let her tell you everything when she's ready."

Michael rallied. "Why would she confide in you if you hardly know each other?"

"Probably because we've been messing around, don't you think?" Nick was irritated. "I moved in next door about the same time as she must have become pregnant, but, being the swift mover I am, I'm the father of her child. How do I know for sure why she's confided in me? Maybe she needed someone nonthreatening who wouldn't tell her what to do, and I was the only available candidate."

"Oh, hell." Michael buried his head in his hands. "I'm sorry, Nick. What else can I say? I love Abby. She's always been so gentle, and I hate feeling helpless. I can't stand by and do nothing."

"Mike," Nick said and fetched their glasses, "drink this and listen for once."

Michael looked up questioningly at him.

"Abby's a big girl, and she's letting all the people in her life know she wants to go it alone now. Stay out of her business until she invites you in."

Michael drained the liquor. "Do you think John's left her? Be honest with me, Nick."

He considered how much to say. "I think it's possible."

"So do I." Michael leaned back and closed his eyes. "And maybe it's for the best. I'll do what you ask, if you'll do something for me." He lifted his lids to gaze unblinkingly at Nick.

"Name it."

"After what I've said, this is going to sound off-the-wall, but I do trust you, Nick. Keep an eye on Abby. Let me know if you think she's in real trouble, or if she seems ready to open up. And in the meantime, look after her for me."

Nick bowed his head over his glass. "Sure, Mike, I'll do that for you."

Chapter Nine

Nick drove too fast, Abby decided. But now that she thought of it, so did Michael. Flyers had to have quick reflexes, and they were probably naturally attracted to speed and challenge. She winced as Nick cut between two cars in the fast lane. They were crossing the floating bridge between Mercer Island and Seattle itself. A steady drizzle fell, and lights on tall standards cast wavery reflections across the wet surface of the span. Blackened rims of crusty slush were all that remained of the previous week's snowfall.

Abby glanced at Nick. She'd been repeatedly glancing at him ever since they'd left the east side shortly before seven. "Are you sure you want to go through with this?" she asked, willing him to say he'd rather not go with her to a childbirth education class, after all. "If you've changed your mind, I don't have to go tonight." So far, she'd attended only one class, read the course books and halfheartedly practiced the conditioning exercises they outlined. If Nick hadn't pressured her, she probably wouldn't be going now. "I could make up this class later."

Nick kept his eyes on the road as they entered a tunnel. "You don't have a whole lot of time left to squeeze these classes in, my girl. And, no, I don't want to change my mind. You did put those pillows and books in the car?''

"In the back seat," she confirmed, her heart sinking lower. Since he'd returned from his last trip, all her efforts to dissuade Nick from taking her to this class had failed. On Monday, he'd shown up on her doorstep and persuaded her to share pizza. The following evening he'd "made too much" Chinese food and "needed her help." Last night she'd worked, but when she got home, Nick sat on the top step outside her condo, waiting, with his irresistible smile and a request for her to watch a movie with him, because he "hated watching movies alone." And each time they'd been together, he'd found a way to raise the subject of childbirth preparation. Finally he'd lulled her into revealing the class schedule and accepting his offer to take her tonight. Abby pulled her shirt farther down over the one pair of maternity jeans she owned. The prospect of his being there while she went through the ungainly exercises mortified her.

"You're supposed to go to eight sessions?" Nick asked, startling her. He took the exit to Rainier Avenue. He didn't wait for her response. "You waited too long to finish the course. You'd better figure out a way to graduate early." He laughed as he changed down gears.

Abby laced her fingers tightly together. She couldn't echo his laughter. When the time came for her to deliver her baby, she'd be alone, anyway—wouldn't she? Going to the classes without a partner had seemed pointless. Nick was...Nick was a special person, but even if he offered, could she suffer the embarrassment of having him present during her labor? She couldn't. She flexed her hands and wound her fingers together again. Whatever she learned would be useful. Everyone said proper breathing alone could make all the difference in coping with contractions.

"You're quiet," Nick said. "What are you thinking about?"

"Not much."

He smiled at her. "Can't you tell me? No? Okay, I'll tell you what I'd probably be thinking." Ahead a light turned amber, and he braked. "I'd be thinking I had six weeks before the most scary event in my life. I take that back—at the risk of quoting clichés—I wouldn't go through this at all. I'll never understand where women get the guts."

Now Abby laughed. He was wonderful to be with, natural and warm. "I'm not afraid, Nick. It's a thrill to look forward to meeting someone who's been invisibly with you for months. I know this person of mine. He likes music—jazz, of course. He's happy when I'm happy, and when I'm miserable, he gets real quiet, just like I do." She stopped and stared unseeingly at shop windows.

At the firm pressure of Nick's hand on hers, Abby looked down at his long fingers. His palm was wide, and the thumb that he ran briefly up and down hers was strong. The light changed to green, and he shifted gears again.

"You keep calling the baby *him*. You really think she's going to be a boy?"

"No," Abby said, aware he was trying to keep her mind occupied. "I think *he's* going to be a boy."

"Uh-uh," Nick said. "Wrong. This baby's a girl. I've seen her hip action, and no boy could manage that." They arrived at a square red-brick building, and Nick parked beside the curb. "This is the place, and we're two minutes late."

Abby watched him get out and pull her pillows and the books from the car. She joined him on the sidewalk. "Hip action? What's with the hip action?"

"Come on." He put an arm loosely around her shoulders and started for the glass double doors. "Just believe me. That kid sashays in there. Definitely feminine."

Abby smiled, concentrating on what he said with a small part of her brain. She walked automatically, then nodded when he checked a board for the room location. Distantly, she heard him continue to joke. Their footsteps echoed along a deserted corridor that smelled of wax. They turned a corner, and he said "this is us" while he looked at a number over a door.

The room felt crammed and airless. Abby registered other couples, smiling, sitting on pillows on the floor, then started at the sound of her own name.

"Abby, that's you," Nick had bowed close to her ear. "Yes," he said loudly and continued to look at her, frowning. "This is Abby Winston."

A petite middle-aged woman smiled and indicated a vacant area. Abby walked there with Nick, let him take her coat and held the hand he offered tightly while she sat on a pillow he dropped. He sat beside her, holding the other pillow on his lap. "Nick" she heard him say and glanced at the blond woman again. She must have asked his name. He'd only given his first one. Abby took a deep breath through her mouth. This was the instructor, and she'd think Nick was Abby's husband. Stinging heat rushed to her face.

"Six weeks," Nick was saying. "We're taking the crash course."

The ripple of laughter that circled the room brought Abby's mind into focus. She was sitting like a zombie, allowing Nick to pinch-hit in a situation he wasn't qualified to deal with or responsible for. Movement all around her followed the instructor's request to get comfortable. Some women remained seated, others curled up on their side. Each man faced his partner.

"Abby and Nick." The instructor bent over Abby. "I'm Louise. Ask questions whenever you need to. You won't have a problem catching up with the rest of the class if you put in some extra time between sessions."

Abby avoided Nick's eyes. "Yes," she said firmly. "What should I do now?"

"Lie down," Louise said, "or sit. Most women are more comfortable lying. We're going to get into partner awareness of tension. Have you spent any time with the course books?"

"We both have," Nick put in, taking Abby's hands. "It looks as if the side position with the pillow under the knee would work best to begin with."

Louise patted Abby's shoulder and grinned. "They say some men get the same physical sensations as their wives during pregnancy. Nick's obviously worked out how that heavy tummy feels. Use the side position for a start."

The woman went to the next couple, but Abby didn't move. She closed her eyes.

Nick made circles with his thumbs on the backs of her hands. "Lie down," he whispered. "Everything's okay. Open your eyes and look at me. Concentrate on my face and forget where you are and all the other stuff that's bothering you."

Abby opened her eyes but couldn't seem to move. "I can't do this, Nick," she said. "We shouldn't be here, *you* shouldn't be here." But she couldn't look away from his eyes. They smiled, touched her soul.

He put the second pillow on the floor and laid a palm on her cheek. "We're both exactly where we should be.

Unwind, sweetheart. Lie down. This is going to help you."

Under his hand her skin turned to fire. The rest of the room, the people, went away. Mesmerized, she let him guide her down. He lifted her upper leg and positioned the pillow she'd been sitting on between her knees.

Nick sat cross-legged and leaned close. "You did read the books, didn't you?"

Abby passed a hand over her brow. "Yes. But how do you know all this stuff?"

"I got my own copies. Remember, I said I was interested and I wanted to come?"

"You got you own copies?" She couldn't believe he would go out and buy books he didn't need and read them. "Why did you do that?"

He touched her face again, and this time he kept his hand across her cheek, his fingers ruffling the hair at her temple. "I did it because I care what happens to you, Abby. I want to be here, with you. Now concentrate. What are we going to do next?"

She only felt his hand. His voice lulled her. She looked directly back into his eyes. He meant what he said. Nick really wanted to be here for her.

"Abby, are you listening? What comes next?"

"I don't remember."

"Yes, you do. Tense and relax. Tense and relax. Let me see how you look when you tense—scratch that." He laughed softly. "Show me relaxed. I know tense; I can see it right now. We've got to learn what it takes to touch-relax you. The gate theory makes sense to me—cutting down the perception of pain by blocking its path with a gate of skin stimulation. But I have to be able to tell which areas you tighten up and what kind of touch works to reverse the process."

Abby grimaced. "The directions are coming back to me now. Are you sure you want to go on with this, Nick? I won't mind—"

"Relax," he ordered. "I'm going to lift your left arm. I'll move it around. You let it go limp and heavy."

He supported the arm, bending and flexing her elbow, rotating the shoulder, flapping her hand back and forth. "Okay, Abby. Now go limp."

"I *am* limp." She wasn't limp; she was tight, and trembling inside and responding to him in the last way she should be responding now.

"Abby, you are *not* limp. I could stake a tree with this arm. Are you ticklish?"

She narrowed her eyes. "Why?"

"Because of something I read in that book. You know the piece I mean?"

"If you tickle me, Nick Dorset, I'll never forgive you." She pulled her bottom lip between her teeth, and Nick watched, somber for an instant, before bowing to press his mouth to her ear. He kissed it gently, and the little hollow behind the point of her jaw. Abby's spine felt formless. Instinctively she turned her cheek to brush his. The slight roughness of his beard area electrified her.

His fingers tightened on her arm, and he hesitated before lifting his face away a fraction. She couldn't see his face, and she wanted to, to read his eyes. "You are ticklish," he breathed. "And I want to feel the weight of this arm now, or I'll find your sensitive spot and do my worst. The relief when I stop will make you relax."

"Sadist." She closed her eyes and tried to do as he asked. Her muscles softened slightly, and warmth crept steadily into her cold hands and feet.

Nick set down her arm and supported her bent knee. With his other hand he massaged her thigh. For an instant Abby tautened. She looked at his face, his freshly anxious eyes. He smiled. "Let go again, Abby. But keep your eyes open this time. We'll have to figure out a method of keeping you focused—a piece of music, or something visual to concentrate on. The book says you aren't supposed to drift too much, or you won't be ready for each contraction."

"I . . . Nick, why are you doing this?" As soon as she asked, she knew what she longed to hear.

Nick stroked her calf with long, sweeping motions. "Because I want to."

She grappled with his words. They were simple, beautiful to her . . . too simple. Her mind darted back to the night he'd rescued her in the snow. Then he'd let her know how aware he was of her as a woman. But he'd never mentioned that encounter again. She returned her attention to his face. "Thank you for helping me, Nick. I wish I could do something for you."

"You are." He rested both hands lightly on her side. "This feels tight. Think about the muscle over your rib cage and imagine the tension flowing from there, through my hands and into me."

"What am I doing for you?" she persisted, every nerve in her body fluttering.

Nick regarded her solemnly. "You're giving me the pleasure of getting to know a beautiful woman and appreciating that she's also very bright and talented. No woman ever affected me the way you do, Abby."

He spoke as if he meant what he said, as if he cared. Abby opened her mouth, and Nick immediately pressed a thumb against her lips.

"And now," he said, unsmiling, "could you please give me some encouragement here by cooperating? I want to lead you through the relaxation series in the book and make sure the instructor thinks we're doing it right so we can practice at home. It's also past time to start getting the breathing patterns and contraction timing down."

She tried. Each gentle order he gave, Abby attempted to follow, constantly pulling her mind back from the stray trails it followed. "Take another long sigh and concentrate on your shoulders," he said. She shrugged them loose. He'd spoken of their practicing at home, as if he were her husband. "While I rub the back of your neck, see warmth coming in there and the stiffness going into my fingers." She felt his fingers. She remembered how they'd looked holding hers in the car. Whatever was happening to her with Nick, she'd lost the will to fight it, didn't want to anymore.

"Do you feel more peaceful?"

"What?" Abby lifted her head. "Oh, yes, yes I do. Thank you." She didn't feel peaceful. Even the skin on her face and scalp responded to him with an intensity she'd never known, she realized with surprise.

"You two are good at this." Louise, making her constant tour of the room, paused and knelt beside Nick. She placed his hand on Abby's belly. "She'll be getting more Braxton-Hicks contractions from now on. You'll be able to feel them too, a kind of pulling up."

Nick frowned, passing his hand higher, then lower. "Are they the start of labor?"

Louise smiled. "No, just the uterus's way of getting ready for the real thing. They increase uterine circulation and help the cervix thin and soften. You'll both know the difference when true labor begins."

At nine, Abby and Nick collected their belongings and headed back to the car. Once more Nick put an arm around Abby, this time holding her more firmly to his side. She glanced up into his face, and he smiled at her.

"Feel less threatened?"

"About the classes? Yes, I guess."

"Good. But I really meant do you feel better about having me with you. It embarrassed you at first."

"No—"

"Yes, Abby, it did. And that's understandable. But you won't feel so badly next week, will you?"

"I...no. Not if you want to come. But I do feel guilty. It isn't your job."

"It's someone's job, and I don't see anyone else around."

"So your conscience makes you feel you have to fill in. I could cope on my own, Nick. I'm a very capable woman."

He opened the car door and helped her in. He rested an elbow on the door and stared down into her face. "I already know how capable you are. But you *do* need a partner for these classes. And wanting to be that partner has nothing to do with my conscience. When are you going to figure that out?"

Before she could reply, he slammed the door and stood in front of the hood, waiting for a break in the traffic before he got behind the wheel.

Abby kept the pillows on her lap, clutching them. Okay, he was one of the world's gentle, responsible people, and he wanted to help her for a time. So be it. She'd leave the subject alone. She could certainly use someone to rely on. She trusted Nick. If there was one person she'd like to have with her now, he was it. Her mouth dried out. What if he were around only for a while? Just long enough for her to—love him? Yes, she was afraid she'd fall in love with Nick, and then lose him.

He started the engine but didn't immediately pull away. "Are you tired?"

She turned questioningly toward him. "No. Why?"

"Did you eat dinner before we left?"

"No—yes, yes I did." Good Lord, if he found out she hadn't, he'd be plying her with food again.

Nick met her eyes briefly before he maneuvered from the parking place to cross two lanes of traffic. "You're a lousy liar. You haven't eaten. Neither have I. Let's go out on the town."

Abby held the pillows closer. He couldn't mean that in the traditional sense, but she should be the one to make sure he at least had a meal after all he'd done this evening. "My treat this time," she said lightly. "What kind of food do you feel like?"

"When I invite a lady out, *I* pay. And I choose the place, too—no arguments entertained. It's my masterful side sneaking out, the one I keep hidden most of the time."

"A closet chauvinist," Abby said and gave a short laugh while she visualized how she looked in her baggy blue flannel shirt worn with jeans and tennis shoes. Her coat was the favorite black wool, voluminous and comfortable, but rapidly taking on the greenish tinge of age. Nick also wore jeans, she remembered. A good sign. He wasn't likely to pick a restaurant where they'd both feel out of place.

Nick took a left turn from Denny Way onto Fifth Avenue and headed for the gulches between the towering glass and concrete buildings of Seattle's business district.

"Do you like the kind of music George Winston plays?" He leaned forward over the wheel, checking in each direction, and took a sharp right onto Pike Street. "I know I usually hear nothing but strains of Dixieland coming from your place."

Apprehension sickened Abby. She wanted to go home but couldn't hurt him. "I like George Winston very much," she said. "His stuff is different, melodic, not typical modern jazz. Why do you ask?"

"Because he's playing at a place off Pioneer Square. We could eat and catch his second set. Would you like that?"

Why now? Abby thought. Why did a man who liked the things she liked and seemed on her wavelength in almost everything have to come along when there seemed no way their relationship could go anywhere?

"Abby? Will you let me take you there? The fare's strictly American-bar: beer and nachos. If you want something else, we can go to another restaurant first."

"No," she said hurriedly. "I enjoy that kind of thing." She'd agreed to go. Abby ran her eyes glumly over a group of bums slouching beneath the pergola in Pioneer Square. With luck, the dress where they were going was strictly Army and Navy store, and she'd fit right in.

The dim interior of the club they entered was a blessed equalizer for all patrons. Nick found a corner table, and Abby took a chair facing the stage. A back-up group played soft synthesized music, and a few couples danced slow and close on a minute floor. Conversation hummed loudly enough to dull the music, and blue cigarette smoke hung beneath the thin beams of spotlights directed at the ceiling.

Abby ordered orange juice and tonic water and laughed when Nick said "Make that two" as if he drank the concoction all the time.

"You don't have to be on the wagon just because I am," she said when the waitress had left.

"I have to get in shape for the big event, too." Nick pushed a candle to one side of the table and leaned closer.

"Do you think all this smoke could be bad for the baby? I didn't think about it."

A helpless urge to cry almost undid Abby. She glanced away, feeling the tears well up. "You're wonderful. I hadn't even thought of that. But I don't think one trip into a smoky room will do any harm."

He stretched his hands, palms up, across the table.

Abby stared at them and slowly put her two clenched fists on top. Something was happening between them, and it wasn't born of Nick's sense of decency. Pregnant or not, the tingling in her thighs was purely sexual, and the glimmer in his eyes was anything but that of a concerned friend.

Nick bent his elbows, closing her hands inside his and lifting them. He kissed each of her knuckles slowly, as if lost in thought before he said, "I'm afraid to say what I want to."

Her body ached. Simply looking at him, the sensation of his fingers, his lips on her skin, aroused Abby as she'd never been aroused. "You can say anything to me." Her voice was husky, hardly more than a whisper that he strained to hear. She cleared her throat. "What is it, Nick?" Wanting him to be completely open, afraid what that could mean, Abby smiled and felt her insides draw together. Every silent message he sent told her he was falling in love with her. If he said as much, what would she say, what could she say now?

He was quiet for a long time, then a deep breath lifted his broad shoulders. "It's not such a big deal, really. I shouldn't have made it sound so dramatic." He smiled and pressed her hands before releasing them. "My sister, Janet, is coming in a couple of days. She's one of those people who clean corners with a toothbrush and cook gourmet meals three times a day. I wondered if you'd mind using a critical eye on my condo before she gets here and helping me figure out some good places to take her."

Abby's stomach felt as if a large hand had squeezed it. Disappointment sent goose bumps crawling over her skin. She rallied, tapping her fingernails on the checkered tablecloth. "I'd like to do that, Nick. Give me a few hours to think about it. She might like to see this area of town. When I think of Seattle, I always think of Pioneer Square and the waterfront. And Snoqualmie Pass. I bet she'd fall in love with the mountains. There's a pretty good snow pack already, and there could even be skiers. If we have a clear day, you could take her up one of the lifts."

"Great idea," Nick said, but his eyes held an intense light. Sad? Why would he be sad? "Would you meet her, Abby? Come over to my place and visit? She'll only be here three days."

Abby crushed a desperate longing to hear Nick say she mattered more to him than his sister, than anyone. She wanted too much. His friendship should be enough. "I'd be pleased to," she replied mechanically, wondering what his sister was likely to make of Nick's interest in her.

George Winston played his set. His music, poignant modern interpretations of beautiful old pieces, brought joy and longing. Nick's hands, covering hers once more, gripped tighter.

"You loved that, didn't you?" he asked when it was over.

Abby turned her head away.

"Didn't you?" Nick pulled her wrists toward him. "Look at me."

She kept her face averted. "His music twists my heart, if that isn't trite." He mustn't know that listening to beautiful music with him was almost more magic than she could bear.

"You twist my heart," Nick said softly. "I don't want this night to end, Abby. I...oh, Abby, I wish I could take you home and know I'd never have to let you go."

Blood throbbed in every part of her body. Some emotion he hadn't analyzed must be carrying him along. He couldn't know what he was saying.

"You'd soon get sick of that, Nick. I'm a bit much to hold these days. But it's a nice idea." And her heart said, *I wish I could hold you forever.*

He released her hands. "One day you'll understand. When you stop believing whatever mind tapes you've been taught to play. You're beautiful, my... you're beautiful."

She could hardly breathe. "We'd better hit the road. Some of us need more beauty sleep than others—not that it helps a whole lot."

Nick sighed, then smiled brightly and presented his profile. "I resent that. Many women have said this is an irresistible face. And the body, well..."

"You know perfectly well I meant *I* needed beauty sleep." Abby smiled wryly. "We both know how gorgeous you are. I'm sure you're as bad as Michael. He leaves trails of broken hearts wherever he goes. At least, he does if you believe what he says."

Nick held her hand as they wove a path to the door. On the sidewalk they both stood beneath a streetlight, fastening their coats against an arctic wind that slapped discarded newspapers against buildings.

"Abby," Nick said and cupped her jaw, "I'd like to kiss you again, and not for luck this time."

Her throat closed. She stared up at him.

"Do you understand?"

She shook her head, afraid he'd somehow see the uprush of emotion she felt.

"What is it—loyalty to John? Is it so wrong to kiss someone who cares about you? I think you want to."

Abby rested her weight against him. His fingers splayed wide in the small of her back, then slid up between her shoulder blades. She lifted her head, and he lowered his mouth slowly over hers, opened her lips languorously and slipped his tongue inside. A quiet place formed inside her, but only for a moment before the clamoring came, and she returned the kiss with an ardor that rocked them both. Nick pressed his mouth hard from side to side and drove his fingers into her hair. He brought his teeth together on her lower lip, and she moaned. Abruptly Nick raised his head and guided her face beneath his jaw. She felt the rapid beat of the pulse in his neck.

Seconds later she roused herself, hugged his broad body quickly and pulled away. She trusted him, knew he'd be there for her if she needed him, but she couldn't allow the sexuality between them to escalate, not until she knew what the future held.

"You are so lovely, Abby. I thank God I know you," Nick said, shielding her from the wind with his body.

"The light's changing," she said shakily.

"A lot of things are changing," he responded.

"Let's cross."

Holding each other close, they hurried to the other side of the street where the BMW was parked. Nick helped Abby get settled and climbed in beside her.

He locked the driver's door and faced her, hooking his knee over the console. "About what you said back there, just before we left the bar—" he pulled her chin up "—about me and other women. I've been pretty much a loner the past few years, Abby. I'm not into breaking hearts. And what I hate most is to watch the heart of someone who means a lot to me being mangled and not being able to do much about it.''

His face mesmerized her; the serious glint in his eyes, the hint of white where his teeth showed between slightly parted lips. He knew something was very wrong in her life and was obliquely asking her to let him help.

Abby fixed her attention on the signal. ''You're a good man, Nick. Maybe too good. We should get home.''

"YOU'RE QUIET, JANET."

"So are you. You haven't said a word in ten minutes.''

Nick spread his fingers on his thighs. ''I didn't realize. Sorry.''

"You're nervous.''

He laughed and stood. ''You noticed. Observant girl.''

"I'm known for my sensitivity.''

"Oh, Janet, it's good to have you here, even for a little while.'' Nick faced her, looking down into her upturned face. Scrubbed. Janet always looked scrubbed and healthy…and dearly familiar. ''Did you sleep well? Is the bed okay for you?''

"It's great. But you didn't have to give up your room for me. I could have slept in the spare one, or on the couch.''

"No way. Nothing's too good for my sister. How's everyone back home?''

Janet crossed her arms. ''We did that number last night, remember? Everyone's just terrific. Nick, for God's sake, settle down. You're as nervous as a cat. I already know your Abby is married…I'm not shocked.

Worried about how things are going to work out, but not shocked. So stop chewing your fingernails.''

Hell, Nick thought, Janet *didn't* know Abby was pregnant, but she soon would. "She's not *my* Abby, unfortunately. And I never chew my fingernails." He should tell the whole story, just spit it out.

"I was speaking metaphorically."

"Look, Janet—" he had to tread carefully "—don't say anything. I mean, be careful what you say to Abby. We understand each other, you and I. Our brand of humor and so on, but—"

"What do you think I'm likely to say to the woman? I won't make cracks about penalties for bigamy or anything. Quit panicking."

Skirting an issue was always hazardous, Nick thought. What if Janet drew the same conclusions Michael Harris had at first? He turned his back and leaned against a wall. "She doesn't know how I feel about her," he said in a rush. "Not for sure."

Rustling behind him was all he heard.

"Janet, do you understand what I'm saying?"

"I understand," she said softly. "You idiot, Nick. You never did know how to let your feelings out."

He pressed his temple to the cool plaster. "I guess I didn't."

"And you haven't let her know she means a lot to you?"

"No. Not really. And, Janet—" he swung around "—she mustn't find out yet. You said I had to wait for her to come clean about her marriage, and she hasn't. She's too vulnerable now. If she thought she'd hurt me, if she couldn't . . . feel something special for me, she might insist she did, anyway. I don't want that."

The doorbell rang, paralyzing him. Abby. He shouldn't have suggested she come. It was a rotten idea with things the way they were.

"Nick," Janet whispered. "Trust me."

He nodded.

"Well?" The doorbell rang again.

Nick couldn't concentrate. "Well what?"

"Let her in, Nick." Janet stood and faced the door.

"Right, right." His brain felt like mush. He rushed to the door and swept it wide, grabbing Abby's elbow and hauling her inside. "Abby, this is my sister, Janet. Janet Ross. Janet—Abby Winston."

When he sought Janet's eyes, she looked not at him but at Abby. He saw a swift downward glance, and then Janet was striding forward, smiling, to shake Abby's hand.

"So you're Abby," Janet said loudly. "Nick's been telling me all about you."

Nick's blood drained to his feet. Great going, Janet, he thought. *Great going, Nick. It's your fault.* "Come on in, Abby," he said and shook his head slightly at Janet. "We're plotting Janet's itinerary. She thinks Seattle's dreary, so I've got to reprogram her opinion."

Abby looked into eyes the same tawny brown as Nick's, with the same warm, humorous quality. Brother and sister strongly resembled each other. The woman was also tall, a feminine version of Nick with her curly brown hair grown to shoulder length. She was going to like Janet Ross, Abby decided, even though there'd been a flash of surprise not quickly enough hidden when the woman realized Abby was pregnant. Evidently Nick hadn't told his sister quite everything about her.

"Hello, Janet. I'd have known you even without Nick being here." Her hands felt too big, and there was nowhere to put them. She soldiered on, "Are you sure you two aren't twins?"

"I'm the baby," Nick said and immediately reddened.

"He's fourteen months younger, and I never stop hearing about it." Janet laughed, looking at him hard before she indicated a coffeepot and cups on the dining table. "How about some coffee, Abby?"

Abby longed to touch Nick, to tell him to loosen up. Clearly her pregnancy was an embarrassment to him. She didn't want to be here.

Janet had started pouring coffee. "I'm sorry, Janet," Abby said, her smile wavering. "I can't stay. But thanks for the offer."

She felt Nick looking at her but kept her attention on Janet, who set down the pot. "Are you sure? Nick said you'd be able to spend the day with us."

Abby retreated, taking slow steps backward. "My work schedule changed. I'd really like to come, but you know how it is." He'd be glad of her sudden change of mind—they both would.

"I don't think I do know how it is," Nick said quietly.

A shiver climbed up Abby's spine. His mouth had settled into a hard line. She wiped her right palm on her skirt. "Just one of those things." Her tone wasn't light enough. "I'm sorry if I've upset your plans."

He eyed her squarely. "Are you? Thanks. Maybe you should have thought about my plans before."

Abby swallowed, aware that Janet stood motionless by the table. What must the woman be thinking? "I never intended to complicate your life." She turned her face away. Every word they spoke sounded damning.

"Isn't it time you quit that dump you insist on working in? You know it worries me. Doesn't that count for something?"

"Nick," Janet broke in, "isn't this a conversation you'd rather have without me?"

Nick didn't appear to hear. He'd come so close to Abby that she had to lift her head to meet his eyes. His face was pale now, even his lips. "Michael knows something's wrong with you. After that...after he was here with us, he took a few more potshots at me, and he's figured out..." He stopped, with one hand raised, as anguish slowly darkened his eyes. He looked over his shoulder at Janet, then back to Abby. "Oh, my God. I'm sorry." He pulled her into his arms. "Forgive me. Please forgive me. I don't have any right to speak to you like that."

Abby's body became rigid. "It's okay." She touched his sides, but he didn't release her. What did Michael know? That she was working in the Laundromat? Had he told their parents? "Let me go, Nick," she whispered. Nick, she thought, had presented Janet with a picture she'd find as hard to decipher as Michael had the night he'd found her with Nick. Because of her, this visit would probably be strained, ruined. "Please, Nick." She closed her eyes. He smelled clean, fresh from the shower. His hair was still damp.

"Do you really have to go to work?" He lessened his grip, then slowly moved away until he held her at arm's length. His eyes pleaded with her.

"Nick," Janet interrupted. "If Abby has to work, she has to work." She gave Abby a pained smile. "Pray your baby's a girl. Boys never stop wanting their own way from the day they're born."

Abby returned the smile gratefully. "I think you're right, but I also have a feeling this is a boy. Nick insists otherwise, something to do with the baby's hip action, whatever he means by—" She stopped. Sweat broke out on her back and the palms of her hands. Every word she spoke twisted the situation more. She must get away.

"We've got a girl," Janet said, coming to stand beside Nick. "Penny. I expect Nick's told you how I go on about her all the time." She grinned broadly, and the atmosphere softened. "I won't bore you with pictures now because I know you're in a hurry. But I'd like to show her off. Could we get together before I go back? I've got tomorrow, if I can get rid of Nick for an hour. There's nothing I like better than a chance to share war stories about early childhood survival—for the parent."

Abby wanted to hug the woman. "I'd like that. Yes, let's do it. Lunch at my place."

Nick wasn't listening. "It's slick out there again, Abby," he said. "Drive carefully, please."

Shut up, Abby wanted to say, *before you make your sister draw totally wrong conclusions.* "I'll be fine." She turned back to Janet. "Your brother is a frustrated father. He thinks he has to look out— He worries about me," she finished lamely.

"He's always been a bit like that," Janet agreed.

"Did you get a new battery?" Nick continued as if no one else had spoken.

"Yes," Abby said, exasperated, and opened the front door. "My car runs like a Rolls-Royce these days."

As she entered the hall, she called to Janet, "See you tomorrow, Janet. Come whenever you like. Thanks for being so understanding about today." And to Nick, she added, "Make sure Janet sees the good stuff around town. The Seattle Center. Take her on a ferry across Elliott Bay. And, Nick, is there something I should get in touch with Michael about quickly?''

He shook his head sheepishly. "No. I was lashing out, I guess. He is worried about you because he found out you aren't at the store anymore. But I put him off. There's nothing to worry about."

Nick's next action left her weak. Janet had returned to his condo, leaving them alone. He moved swiftly, held her face in both hands and kissed her mouth possessively. She responded instinctively until they drew away, breathless.

"We're going to talk, Abby. If you insist on keeping up that job, make sure you're free on Monday morning. I'm taking you out—somewhere away from here—and we're going to get a few things straight."

"I don't know—"

"Monday, Abby. Promise me."

She pushed open her unlocked door, a million confused thoughts tumbling through her mind.

"Abby Winston, will you answer me?"

"Yes, Nick," she said quietly. "I'll see you on Monday morning."

She closed the door behind her, shutting him out, and dropped to sit on the floor. Pressure was going to come from all sides and blow apart her carefully made plans; she could feel it. Her head throbbed. What she needed was sleep, but for Janet and Nick's benefit, she'd have to go out, even though she wasn't really working.

Her back ached. Tightening in her belly made her wince, and she leaned back on her arms. The Braxton-Hicks contractions the childbirth education instructor mentioned had been coming more frequently in the past twenty-four hours. She lay flat on the carpet, and her uterus pulled in sharply. The baby rolled. Abby closed her eyes and tried to relax. A few more weeks, and her baby would be here.

Tears squeezed from her closed eyes and seeped, hot, across her temples. *Her baby.* She laughed and cried at the same time.

NICK HALF LISTENED to the Seattle Space Needle elevator guide spout facts. "The Needle is five hundred feet high. It was built as part of the 1960 World Fair Grounds and left as a permanent structure for the city residents and our visitors to enjoy." The girl spoke fast with little inflection. Nick studied his shoes and wondered what Janet was thinking. She'd said little after Abby had left the condo or during the half hour drive into town. What was Abby doing now? He passed a hand over his hair.

"From the observation deck you may enjoy a 360-degree view of the city and the surrounding scenery," the guide droned on.

They shot steadily up the graceful structure toward its space saucer crown. Nick met Janet's eyes, and she returned his regard steadily, her thoughts unreadable.

At the top, they started a slow circle of the deck and Nick pointed out landmarks as they went. He dropped a coin into a telescope and made Janet look at the Olympic Mountains and Elliott Bay with its jumble of commercial and pleasure craft and the smattering of container ships and grain vessels.

When they'd walked the perimeter of the circular structure twice, Janet planted herself in a deserted area and confronted Nick. "Are you going to tell me?"

He swallowed. He'd known the questions would come, more questions, and that they might be stickier than the others. "What do you want to know, Janet?"

She brushed back her shiny curls. Janet only seemed to get lovelier, Nick thought abstractedly. "Well, brother," she said, "if you're going to be difficult, I guess I'll have to help you out. You love Abby. I'd have to be blind or mentally incompetent not to gather that."

He looked past her toward Puget Sound. "I do love her."

"You were pretty rough on her at your condo."

"I know. But I wanted her to come."

Janet turned to rest her elbows on the window ledge. "Didn't it strike you she might be embarrassed?"

He shoved his hands into his pockets. "To be with us?"

"Stop hedging. You omitted one little thing when you told me about her. That was dumb, Nick. Was I likely *not* to notice she's pregnant?"

For an instant he didn't know what to say. He cleared his throat. "I wasn't sure how to explain."

Without looking at him, Janet reached out a hand and waited for Nick to hold it. She urged him beside her at the window. "Is it your baby?"

Nick exhaled, bowing his head. "No, damn it. I wish it were, but it's not. Do you believe that?"

"I believe it. You've really let yourself in for something, haven't you?" She looked up at him. "Are you sure her husband is out of the picture?"

"I'm sure he's left her. Her brother is, too, although Abby doesn't know that yet. The only thing I'm not sure about is whether she still cares for John Winston."

"But you want her...to marry her."

He sighed. "It's all I want. And I want that baby, too. I know it sounds crazy, Janet, but I feel as if the kid were mine. Am I mad?"

"No." She patted his shoulder. "Just a very unusual man. And from what I've seen of Abby, she's just as unusual. And, Nick, I think she loves you, too."

His stomach dropped. "How could you know that?"

"I saw it in her eyes. In the way she looked at you."

"What am I going to do, Janet?" Helplessness shaded the new hope she'd given him.

"Keep on loving her until she's ready to admit she loves you, too."

Chapter Ten

"Hold my hand," Nick said. "This probably isn't such a hot idea."

Abby took another step and slipped.

Nick cursed under his breath, shooting an arm around her waist. "I told you to hold on to me, Abby. Those boots of yours weren't made for packed snow. I don't know why you suggested coming to—"

"I didn't."

"—a ski area in your condition." He stood still, waiting for her to look at him. "You did suggest it. You said—"

"No, I didn't. I did suggest Snoqualmie Pass would be a nice place for you to bring Janet while she was visiting," she interrupted evenly. "I agreed to talk to you today, that's all. Coming here was your idea. So can we have this discussion you insisted on and be civil to each other and maybe enjoy the scenery now that we're here?"

Nick turned her toward him. "I've been rotten this morning, haven't I?"

"Absolutely rotten, Nick Dorset. Horrible."

He touched her cheek hesitantly and tucked a stray curl inside her woolly cap. "What should I do about it?"

She caught his hand and held it in both of hers. "Tell me what's eating you, Nicholas Stuart."

"Oh, oh, Nicholas Stuart—that bad, huh?"

"That bad." She studied his face, his hair whipping this way and that, the way his tan intensified against the snowy backdrop below a glaring blue sky. He should be dressed in brilliant gear like the few skiers who passed, skis and poles over their shoulders, on their way to the lifts. She imagined him rocketing downhill, sleek, powerful . . . laughing . . . white teeth . . . crinkling eyes . . .

"What is it, Abby?"

She inhaled sharply, focusing on his eyes. "I was just thinking. I guess I was miles away."

"Thinking about what?"

She shook her head, laughing. "Sometimes a vivid imagination is a curse. I could see you skiing, and you looked—" She released his hand. "You looked marvelous. Do you ski?"

"Yes, you?" His regard didn't waver.

"Yes. Michael and I both learned when we were little, and we kept it up. Our folks couldn't afford it, really, but they always managed to give us the things they were sure we had to have."

"They sound like special people. I'd like to meet them one day."

Abby turned clammy inside her old parka. "I'm sure they'd like that, too," she mumbled.

Nick tucked her hand firmly through his elbow. They picked their way toward an alpine-style lodge, its roof sharply sloped and edged with painted flowers.

"I'd like to ski with you," Nick said. "Can we do that next winter, do you think?"

Abby watched their breaths make white clouds and tried to decide how to answer. "That would be nice." Her

tone had the right noncommittal note. There was no de-
nying what she felt for Nick, and he'd given enough signals that he could see himself as more than simply her
champion while she was alone. But he didn't know she
would always be alone. When he did find out, he could
decide to run. Heading off deep involvement now could
save them both.

"It's bound to be pretty quiet in the main lodge," Nick
said. "Not too many people come up on a weekday this
early in the season. We could hole up in there and talk.
At least it'll be warm, and we'll have a good view of the
slopes."

"I don't want to do that." Abby pulled him to a halt.
"We can ride the chair to the top of the Thunderbird run
and sit in the little lodge up there. They always have a
fire, and you can see forever."

"No," Nick said, turning incredulous eyes on her.
"You're not riding a ski lift in your—"

"Condition! Why not? They stop the chair for non-
skiers to get on and off. I'll be fine and I want to go."

"You sound like a spoiled kid," he said grimly. "'I
want to go.' You aren't warmly enough dressed, and I
don't want you falling."

She pulled her hat firmly over her ears. "Are you
coming with me, Nick, or am I going alone?"

He grumbled under his breath, the word "women"
sounding clearly from time to time while he guided her
with exaggerated care to the lift station. When the operator had stopped the rotating cables, Abby slid quickly
into a chair and fastened the safety bar under her belly.
The fit was snug, but she made no comment. When Nick
was beside her, the machinery ground again, and they
swept slowly upward, swinging gently, the distance beneath their feet and the slopes widening.

"Isn't this something?" Abby shouted, lifting her face to the stinging wind. The sun turned the snowpack to an undulating carpet of glitter. Isolated skiers sped downhill, knees flexing to absorb each turn, poles flashing as they nicked the snow's surface. Abby laughed. "I can hardly wait to be down there again."

"You will be," Nick called back. "I've seen some fairly small kids up here, too. The baby should be able to start before too long."

Abby tipped back her head, laughing delightedly. "He's not even born, and you've got him on skis. You're wonderful."

"Am I?"

She glanced at him and quickly away again. "The old male ego never quits, does it? Sure, you're wonderful, Nick." The top station was in sight. She unhooked the seat bar. "We're almost there."

A strong arm immediately pressed across her stomach. "Stay put. Don't move a muscle until they stop the chair."

Heat crept beneath the cold skin on Abby's cheeks. "I didn't intend to jump off in midair." How could he be so aware of her pregnancy yet so unconscious of her swollen shape. He always touched her naturally with no sign of the distaste John had shown from the beginning.

Slipping and sliding, leaning on each other, they made their way from the chair dismount and up an incline to the circular lodge. Warmth rushed to meet them as they opened the door, as did the smell of burning cedar from a central fireplace.

At ten in the morning most skiers had already started their day on the slopes. Apart from Abby and Nick, only two other men and a counter hand were in the lodge. Abby chose a table with a clear view across the Cascade

Mountains and peeled off her parka and cap. She stuffed the cap and her mittens into a sleeve and laid the coat over an empty chair. Nick shed his outer clothes and went to the counter. He returned with two mugs of hot chocolate, pulled the chair from the opposite side of the table and sat beside her.

"Janet said you two had a nice lunch on Saturday," he said. "A 'good talk,' she said. Whatever that means."

Abby blew holes in the cream on top of her chocolate. "It means what she said: that we got along well. We found a lot in common. I really like her. It's too bad she couldn't stay longer." She glanced at Nick. "From her pictures, Penny's a doll. She looks a lot like you and Janet."

Nick gave her a sidelong look. "I've been called a lot of things, but never a doll."

She elbowed him, grinning. "You know I didn't mean that. Although, according to Janet, you are certainly God's gift to the world."

"What's that supposed to mean?" The mountains seemed to hold his attention now.

"Only that your sister thinks you're wonderful. I know all about what a good student you were, the star you were on the college track team and your sparkling service record—crack flyer and so on. And, more important, you're a nice guy."

"According to Janet."

Abby met his eyes and didn't hesitate. "According to Janet and me. You're the nicest man I've ever met." She hadn't meant to add that.

But Nick's face showed only the faintest flicker as he wrapped his hands around his cup. "Thanks," he said. "Every man needs a fan club."

The tiredness she'd come to dread edged into her muscles, her bones. Nick made no attempt to start a serious discussion. A sudden brittle silence yawned between them, and Abby sensed that whatever was said to break it could change things for good.

"Do you trust me, Abby?"

"Yes."

"You came right back with that. Are you sure?"

"I'm very sure. But why did you ask?"

Nick rested an elbow on the table and supported his chin. "Because I'd like us to be...I'd like to feel we were very good friends, the best."

His tone, the rigid attitude of his body, puzzled her. "I don't think I've ever had a better friend than you, Nick."

"But you aren't comfortable enough to be honest with me about everything."

She didn't like the direction he was taking. "I am honest with you."

"I don't think so. Or perhaps 'honest' isn't the right word. 'Open' might be better. I don't think you're open with me about the important things in your life. Maybe I don't have the right to expect you to be, but—"

"You have the right. I gave you the right by making you a part of my life. It's me who doesn't have the right to ask so much of you."

He turned to look at her. "You can ask anything. Could you tell me what's really going on with you right now?"

She covered her mouth, expelling a slow breath.

"Try, Abby. Start anywhere." He rubbed her shoulders and rested his hand on the back of her neck.

"I don't know where to start," she replied, so low that he brought his face closer. She added, "I don't know what I should say and what I shouldn't say."

Gently he brushed a kiss across her temple. "It's okay. Just be quiet if you want to. I didn't mean to push you."

Instinctively Abby leaned toward him. The force of her need for him terrified her. "Thanks for understanding." She'd made what could only be a terrible mistake. She'd fallen in love with Nick Dorset.

It was there in her eyes, Nick thought exultantly. The shy surprise of early love. He was winning. If he could keep himself from rushing in and frightening her off, she'd come to him whole, without John Winston's ghost.

She gazed at him for a long time, her lips barely parted, before she straightened deliberately. "I have been doing a lot of heavy thinking lately," she said. "Do you remember seeing a woman coming to my place? Small, with blond hair?"

"Not really."

"Marie Prince. I've known her since grade school. She comes over quite often. You must have seen her."

She was anxious. Nick scooped her hand from her lap and squeezed it. "Maybe I have. I just don't recall," he said.

"Anyway, Marie said something a couple of weeks ago that made me think. Sooner or later you have to face up to things, don't you?" The great gray eyes pleaded for a response, a specific reaction he couldn't give without knowing what Abby was thinking.

"Marie was talking about what children need," she went on. She tugged at the neck of her green sweater. "Not just material things, although everything seems to come from that in the end."

A coldness climbed Nick's spine. Abby was close to some sort of panic. "Kids need love most of all, Abby," he said as calmly as he could. "Like the rest of us. It doesn't sound as if your friend told you anything you didn't already know."

"No, no, Nick. That's not it. I mean, that's not what I'm trying to say."

"Okay," he responded carefully, "go on. But take it easy, Abby. You're uptight suddenly."

"Do you think it's a terrible thing for a mother to give up her baby?"

Nick realized his mouth was open and brought his lips together. Abby snatched her hand from his and began pulling on her cap and gloves.

"Abby," he whispered urgently. The lodge was fuller now. "What are you saying?"

"Nothing." She dragged on her parka.

Nick stood and reached for his own jacket.

"You don't have to come," Abby insisted. "Stay and enjoy the scenery. You have to leave tomorrow. You should enjoy your last day off."

His brain felt numb around the edges. "Where are you going?"

"Home. I'm tired."

"Home?" A blast of icy air hit his face as she opened the door and walked onto the broad deck surrounding the lodge. "How can you go home if I don't? You came with me." He caught her arm and swung her around. "Why are you running away from me? And what...Abby, why did you ask about mothers giving up their babies?"

Wind snatched at the curls not covered by her cap. He saw the start of tears in her eyes.

"I don't want to talk about it." She hurried across the deck, her boots slithering on glassy ice. "I shouldn't have said anything."

Nausea hit Nick with weakening force. He closed his eyes for an instant. "Stand still, Abby. Now." The deadly apprehension he felt flattened his voice.

"Let me go, Nick. Just let me go. Stop feeling responsible for me."

He grasped her elbow and pulled her under the eaves of the building. "Don't tell me what I can or can't feel," he said. She was crying now, her head bowed. He held her against the wall, and she clutched the front of her jacket. "Abby, look at me. Finish what you started to tell me."

"I need a tissue." She sniffed and raised her brimming eyes to his. When she blinked, tears made their way down her cheeks.

Nick searched his pockets, finding nothing but his keys and wallet. Abby wiped her face with the backs of her fingers and sniffed again.

He remembered the kerchief he wore around his neck, took it off and handed it to Abby. "Blow your nose with this. Then start talking." Whoever coined the phrase "slowly dying inside" must have felt what he was feeling now. Watching her cry tore him apart, but he couldn't comfort her without softening too much to be able to keep pressing for answers.

"Marie called me last night." The blue scarf, held to her lips, moved with her breath. "She asked if I'd thought any more about what we talked about before."

"About what babies need, what children need?"

"Yes. Marie mentioned how many people can't have children and want them desperately. She...she was saying how hard it is to work and look after a baby. And how expensive things like day care are."

Heaviness pressed into Nick's chest. Her tears flowed again, and the scarf muffled her voice. He folded his arms, gripping the fabric of his parka at his sides.

Abby made a choking noise and blew her nose again. "When you spend all your time getting a child ready to go to a day-care place and then picking him up and working in between, you've got to be too tired to enjoy him. A child knows when you don't have what it takes to be a real parent, when everything he does—the things children *should* do—makes you mad. That isn't fair, Nick. I don't want my baby to be unhappy."

Anger began to eat at Nick. "And this Marie what's-her-name says you're going to be the kind of mother who makes her child's life a misery?"

"No! Well...she just wanted me to think about the future, and whether or not I'd be doing a better thing if...if...oh, Nick." Her shoulders came up, and she seemed to shrink.

"If?" He was being merciless, but backing away now could only harm them both. "If what?"

She lifted her head and wiped her eyes once more. "I don't know why I'm blubbering about this. I'm just trying to decide if it would be kinder to give the baby up for adoption." Struggle contorted her features. "Some couple could give him everything a child needs. A nice home and clothes and toys and good schools. I—"

"Don't!" His head was exploding. "Don't say any more. Damn it, don't say it again." He put a hand on each side of her face and rested his forehead on hers. "I can't believe you let this...this *friend* make you even consider this. Abby, you told me how you know your little person. You said he liked your kind of music and was happy when you're happy. You said you were excited and just looking forward to meeting him. And you meant it,

Abby, you really meant it. God, how can you think of giving him up? How many children has Marie Prince had?''

"None."

"So what makes her someone you'd listen to? *Nice* clothes, *nice* toys? What about love, Abby, what about the most important gift you can give any human being?''

"Adoptive parents love their children. I have to be sensible, realistic.''

"You have to live with yourself. If you don't keep this baby, you'll be destroyed. And your family, what about your family?'' He squeezed his eyes shut, willing her to mention John. She had to know he ought to be asking how John would react to the idea of losing his child to strangers. Her face, when he touched it, was icy. He tipped up her chin, smoothed her cheeks. "What is it you're not telling me?''

"Nick." Her voice came faintly, high and thin. "Hold me, please.''

He hesitated, vaguely conscious that he was also close to tears. "Sweetheart . . . Abby, I—'' *I love you,* he thought vehemently. But he mustn't say it. She wasn't ready to deal with another possible commitment. "It's okay, love. It's all right.'' And he did hold her, wrap her tightly in his arms, rock her gently until the choking noises faded.

"It's not, Nick. There's only me to decide what to do and to cope.''

The air seemed abruptly thinner. He stopped breathing altogether. "Why do you feel that?''

Her sigh fanned his neck. Her nose was a cold spot against his chin. "I'm divorced. John and I are divorced now. He filed in September, and it's all over.''

Nick gritted his teeth against a whoop. She'd finally told him what he'd longed to hear, and it was more, far more than he'd dared hope for. John Winston wasn't her husband anymore.

"John never wanted a baby. Things hadn't been very smooth for us for a long time, and the pregnancy was the end for him." She looked up at him. "John isn't all bad, Nick. I don't want you to think I'm blaming him for all that's happened. But he's out of my life now, and it's going to take a while for me to get completely stable again—financially, I mean. I can do it. I'm good at what I do, but I had to quit until the baby's born because I couldn't work on ladders or climb around like I have to."

"I understand," Nick heard himself say. At this moment he felt he understood the world's most obscure mysteries, that he could take on any challenge. *Abby, marry me,* his heart told her, *be my wife and let the baby be mine, as well as yours.* He had to hold back. The timing must be perfect, and she must have a chance to recover from the hurt and disappointment of one failed relationship before he could expect her to risk trying marriage again.

A rolling movement against his belly surprised him. He stepped away, still holding Abby's shoulders, and glanced down.

"Oh, dear." She gave a jerky laugh. "Another county heard from. The baby's been listening to all this discussion, and he's probably...cold." Her mouth came together in a straight line, and she turned her head away. "I can't give him up, Nick. I'm too selfish."

"You're not selfish, my love. You're just a mother with a normal mother's instincts. Let's get down to the car and back home. We both need to warm up." He chuckled. "I guess I should say we all need to warm up, although I think you do a pretty good job of keeping the little tyke snug."

My love. Abby nestled into the arm Nick put around her. He'd called her his love, and sweetheart. His behavior all morning had been that of a man in love.

"When we get back," he was saying, "you should rest. You've had quite a workout for a lady as pregnant as you are. Have you seen your doctor lately?"

"Last Friday. He said I'm in great shape," Abby responded. Nick sounded like a concerned…husband. Her need was creating the illusions her starved soul yearned to be true.

Driving back to Bellevue, Nick kept up a stream of chatter and laughter. He touched her hands frequently, lifted the backs of his fingers to rub her cheek or jaw, reassured her constantly that everything would be fine, that *they'd* work out her problems.

The BMW wound downward between snow-laden banks and evergreen forests, droopy branches sagging beneath the white coats they'd wear until spring. Abby tried to use the relaxation methods from her childbirth books, concentrating on first one tight muscle, then another, clenching harder before deliberately letting go. Her efforts failed. What kind of a woman fell in love with a man while she was carrying someone else's child—when she'd been separated only months and divorced a few days? Was she depraved, without moral standards?

"Speak to me, Abby. Let me know you're still here."

She breathed in sharply and glanced at Nick. "I'm here. A bit tired, that's all. Thanks for taking me into the mountains. It's so lovely. Clean and new."

"That's the way your life's going to be, Abby," he said softly. "With the baby. You'll see, it'll all come straight."

"I hope so." Unthinking, she laid a hand on his thigh, then drew in a sharp breath at the instant jolt in the hard muscles and tried to withdraw it.

Nick stopped her. "I like your hand where it is." He pressed it closer. "Don't hold back from me any longer, Abby."

"I—" She turned hot and cold by turns. "I don't want to. But we both have a lot of thinking to do."

Nick fell silent. He was digesting what she'd said. Surely he couldn't fool himself into thinking their future—if they had a future together—wouldn't be tough. Abby pulled her hand from beneath his and played with the zipper on her parka. They still had so much to figure out about each other. Or maybe they had nothing, nothing at all, and this little dream she'd slowly allowed to form would drift away like their breath on the cold mountain air. Abby closed out the idea. Whatever happened, this man had made a place in her heart that would always be his.

"I'll be out and back in a day on this trip," Nick said.

Abby turned sideways. "I see." He behaved as if he owed her an accounting of his schedule.

"I leave again Thanksgiving Day, but I'll be in town for the class on Wednesday night."

"I'm glad you made me carry on with the course," she said.

He kept his attention on the winding roads. "We'll both be glad I did when you deliver."

Shyness paralyzed her tongue. His being there while she gave birth would be more humiliation than she could take.

Abby clenched her fists. "Nick, you're a dear, but you probably won't even be in town when the baby's born. The chances are he'll decide to arrive while you're on the beach in Waikiki.'' *Leave it,* she longed to say. *Please let it go.*

He laughed easily. ''I'll arrange my schedule to let me be around when your due date gets close, and I can keep switching if it takes a bit longer than expected. The book says first babies are often late.''

''No, Nick,'' she insisted, keeping the desperation she felt out of her voice. ''Don't make any special arrangements on my account. I'm going to use a birthing room and midwife for delivery. Midwives are great at helping out these days. The daughter of one of my mother's friends had a baby last year, and her husband couldn't cope, so the midwife took over. It went perfectly.''

The sudden pull of the brakes jolted her forward. Nick slowed rapidly and drove into a turnout. He switched off the engine and swung his long body to face her, drawing up one knee. ''Let's get a few things straight, Abby.''

She concentrated on a point outside the window and said nothing.

''Okay, clam up if you like, but listen, anyway. Some things shouldn't be done alone. You didn't get pregnant alone, and you shouldn't have to deliver the baby alone.''

She felt her face turn scarlet and bowed her head.

''Sorry if that's blunt, but it's true. John's out of the picture. No one else has shown up to hold your hand through this, and you haven't even told your family what's happening. That leaves me, and I'm going to be as hurt as hell if you shut me out.''

''I'm not shutting you out,'' she said. Her cheeks were throbbing now. He *couldn't* be there, he simply *couldn't.*

''So you'll tell me when the baby comes?''

''I'll tell you.'' God forgive her, she was telling Nick what he wanted to hear. And she hadn't exactly lied. She'd tell him—afterward.

She heard leather squeak as Nick moved, felt him bend over her. "You're all very organized and logical, Abby." He stroked her hair, pushing it back from her ear. Softly he kissed the side of her neck, the hollow beneath her cheekbone. "But I'm going to have to make sure one person isn't left out of the calculations."

"Who?" she whispered.

A finger and thumb, strong but gentle, tipped up her chin. "You, Abby. I'm going to make sure you come out of this happy."

"I—"

His firm lips covered hers, cutting off what she'd been about to say. What was she going to say? Nick's mouth moved slowly, opened slowly. His teeth were smooth against her tongue. Carefully he slid his arms around her shoulders. For a second he pulled back, looked down into her eyes, glanced at her mouth and gradually, so gradually, lowered his lips to hers once more.

MARIE HELD OPEN the door to Jake's and shivered, hopping from foot to foot until Abby passed her and they were both inside the warm bar.

"Boy, Bellevue's come a long way from the dead burg it used to be," Marie said, pulling off her gloves and eyeing the customer-crammed sea of dark marble tables. "Remember when this town was just a place for extra Seattleites to sleep? Over there," she announced triumphantly. "In the corner. Quick, before someone gets it." She took off, arriving at the empty table neck and neck with a man built like Mr. Universe. Marie put a hand on the bicep bulging under his left sleeve, smiled coyly and slipped into a seat. Abby saw her friend's shake of the head and knew Marie was turning down an offer of company.

Abby waited for the man to leave before she joined Marie. "How could you do that poor little guy out of a place to sit, *and* your delightful company?" she asked through her teeth.

Marie's eyes became widely innocent. She flapped a hand. "Sometimes you just have to make sacrifices. Beneath those muscles I could feel a tender heart, and you know my record for breaking hearts. I decided to spare him."

Abby laughed and unbuttoned her coat. She and Marie had spent the afternoon trudging around the Bellevue Square shopping mall while Marie bought clothes and Abby attempted to keep her mind off her aching feet. Marie lived in Seattle but insisted that the fifteen-mile drive to the east side was a small sacrifice to get at "all those yummy shops." Abby could make it from the condo, south of Bellevue, to the downtown area in ten minutes. Today she'd rather have spent her spare time on the couch.

"How many kinds of rum are you going to try, Abby?" Marie asked when a waitress arrived. "I'll have a sampler of beers, please—ah—Ballard Bitter, Anchor Steam and Whatney's."

"Perrier for me, please," Abby said, and to Marie, when the waitress had walked away, she added, "Do they really have the world's largest selection of rums, do you suppose?"

Marie shrugged. "Who knows? But it sounds good and makes a great gimmick." She slid into the corner of her bench and stretched out her legs. "Let's get back to you and your Nick."

"He's not *my* Nick," Abby responded testily. Her straight chair did nothing for her throbbing back. The pain had been there all day and no position seemed to relieve the discomfort. But at least she could breathe more easily this afternoon, and for some reason she'd begun to feel she had a waist again. "I don't want to discuss Nick."

"But you have fallen for the guy. You said so."

"I say too much to you. And I didn't say I'd fallen for him."

"You said you felt something different for him, and that he was different from any other man you've known. That sounds like more than casual interest."

Abby's Perrier and Marie's three miniglasses of beer arrived. Abby took a swallow and arched her back. Her belly tightened almost painfully, and she shifted, taking a deep breath.

"Are you okay?" Marie swung her feet to the floor and leaned across the table. "You look a bit green."

"I'm in pain," Abby said grimly. "It's called a sick-of-being-pregnant pain. Everything aches."

Marie looked startled. "Pain? It's too soon, isn't it? Do you have to go to the hospital or something?"

"Good Lord, no." Abby shook her head wearily. "I've got three or four more long weeks of this to go, so loosen up and drink your beer."

"If you say so," Marie muttered skeptically. "Nick went to the class with you again on Wednesday, you said. He must really be something."

"He is," Abby said and snapped her mouth shut. Marie was fishing, and catching too much. "Did you spend yesterday with your folks?"

"Yesterday? Oh, Thanksgiving, yes." Marie rolled her eyes. "Always go home to good old Mom and Pop for turkey day. How about you?"

"I did, too." Abby instantly relived the previous day's joyless celebration, her parents' puzzled faces, Michael's failed attempts to get her alone.

"Did Nick go with you?"

"Mmm? Oh, no, of course not, Marie. What are you saying?"

"You still didn't let on about the divorce—to John's mother, either?"

The baby made a sluggish revolution in Abby's belly and settled in a position that put pressure on her bladder. "Drop the subject, please, Marie. It's nice of you to be interested, but you can help me most by leaving that part of my life alone."

"Sorry." Marie buried her nose in a glass.

"I don't mean to be snippy," Abby apologized. "I'm not sure of my own feelings on anything anymore. You must see how it would feel to be pregnant by one man and in love—"

"With another?" Marie's brilliant green eyes stared unflinchingly into Abby's face.

"I...yes, damn it. And he feels something for me, too. He's wonderful. For the first time I feel—loved, I guess, is the only word. He loves me, but I don't think it's the same kind of love I have for him. He wants to be there for me." Abby ran a finger down the outside of her cold glass. "I won't need him so much soon, and then he'll go on his way. He's got too much to offer to get tied down by a woman with a child. Nick will marry someone gorgeous and have kids of his own."

"You're gorgeous."

Abby looked away. "This isn't his baby."

"That doesn't seem to be putting him off. Abby, the guy's got to be crazy about you, or he wouldn't be around now. He's got a case on you despite the baby, and he's waiting until the two of you can get together—really together.''

"Marie, don't." Abby blushed. Whoever had suggested that pregnant women couldn't be turned on sexually was either male or had never been pregnant.

"You want him, too, Abby. Admit it."

"No...yes, yes I do. But I can't see how he could feel that way about me like this.'' She splayed a hand on her belly.

"Abby.'' Marie lowered her voice. "Like you said, you won't be pregnant much longer. Don't give up a chance at a fresh start. Sure, you're probably right that a baby could put a man off. Do something about it. I'm not a hard old bag, just dead cold sensible when it comes to looking at what's out there for each of us. If I was in your place and a Nick came riding out of the dust to carry me off, I wouldn't think twice about going.''

Abby swallowed more Perrier and carefully set down the glass. "And if he is just hanging by a thread waiting for me to come to him—do I allow him to take on the dead weight of a woman with an infant? I don't think so, Marie. He's been one terrific friend, and I couldn't do that to him.''

"You're not getting my message, Abby. I know how mad you get every time I suggest this, but you keep leading into the obvious. Come to Nick fresh. You can be the one to have his children—if that's what you're aching to do—later.''

"Give up my baby. That's what you're telling me to do again, isn't it?" Abby stood and buttoned her coat. "I'm going home.''

Marie moved swiftly, cutting off Abby's exit. "Think about it, will you? Everyone would be better off. You, Nick and the baby.''

"Excuse me, Marie."

"I'm coming with you."

"It would be better if you didn't. Give me time to get over what you've just made me feel."

"What have I made you feel, Abby—uncertain? That would be a start."

"I've never been more certain in my life. Whatever happens between Nick and me, this baby will be part of it because he's part of me. I'll see you later, Marie."

Abby's heart thudded. She held her back straight and walked the length of the bar, past a counter banked with crushed ice and studded with fresh fish, then the restaurant beyond. Her hand was on the plate-glass door to the street when the heavy rolling sensation hit her belly once more. Three times in the past two hours she'd had to empty her bladder, but she'd never make it home if she didn't stop again.

The ladies' room was to her left. In the bathroom, she locked the door and hung her purse on a hook. Uneasiness made her hands shake.

Minutes later she slowly took down her purse. She hadn't really had a bloody show, but there was some pinkness.

At the sink, she ran cold water and splashed her face. What had the book said about membranes breaking? It could happen early, she knew, but that didn't mean the baby was ready to be born.

A sharp line of pain burned down one groin and into her thigh. She'd done too much walking today. For once she'd be sensible and ask the Laundromat owner to find a replacement for her tomorrow. A day in bed, and she'd be fine again.

Chapter Eleven

Abby pulled up her knees and waited for the pain to pass. This one hadn't been bad, not as bad as some of the others. Breathing deeply through her mouth, she checked the bedside clock. Almost an hour since the last contraction. All afternoon there had been regular twenty-minute intervals between each wave of discomfort.

Thirty-seven weeks, or thirty-eight, she wondered? The sweat on her body turned cold as the pain dulled. No, thirty-six weeks. She was thirty-six weeks pregnant. Healthy babies were often born a month early. But this was probably only something the book had called false labor. Were false labor pains longer or shorter than true ones? She couldn't remember. Her longest contraction had lasted less than a minute, thank God.

Sweat burned the corner of her eye. She was tired. If this was the real thing, she didn't have the energy to go through with it, anyway.

After returning from Bellevue the previous afternoon, she'd gone to bed and slept until the first pain had awakened her at two in the morning. The day had passed, long and gray. After the early morning pangs there had been lengthy periods of physical relief. But she'd struggled with bursts of panic. And thirst; she'd drunk glass after glass of water and trudged back and forth from the bathroom too many times to remember.

Abby pushed the covers down and shoved awkwardly to sit on the edge of the bed. She needed to urinate again, and walk. The temptation to lie on her side had been overwhelming, and she'd given in, but the position did nothing to lessen either the pains when they came, or her anxiety.

Another surge of agitation welled up in her, like the others, and indecision. Earlier she'd lifted the phone several times to contact the doctor, then changed her mind. She turned her head to see the clock again. Four. Her doctor's office hours were over. Too late to call for advice now—except to the hospital.

The patch of sky visible between the bedroom drapes was already dark again. Another night would start, endless and empty, except for the pains and this frantic tightening in her muscles.

She ought to eat something, Abby thought, or at least get another glass of water. In the bathroom, she drank more water and washed her face. Without knowing why, she combed her hair and put on some lipstick. She began to feel more human and sat on the toilet seat gathering energy to go into the kitchen for food.

Nick had returned in the early hours of the morning. His familiar step had sounded on the stairs, hesitated outside her door and continued into his condo. He must think she'd gone to work today. Her car was in an end slot. He wouldn't have seen it when he'd left to go running. Abby always knew when Nick went running by the softer thud of his shoes. He'd be expecting her to return from the Laundromat soon. The wretched tears welled up again. She wanted to see him. She was frightened.

Abby folded her arms on the side of the sink and rested her forehead. On the other side of the wall, Nick was doing... what? Lying on the floor, as she'd seen him do often now, and listening to music? Reading one of his ever-increasing pile of magazines about aircraft and flying? If she asked, he'd come to keep her company. She smiled against her arms. He'd want to practice breathing, or making her relax. No, she couldn't ask him to come, not when she might be in labor. If she was, he'd insist on coming with her to the hospital, and that was out of the question.

Don't underestimate the power of water. Somewhere in the book she'd read how a warm bath could relieve backache.

While the water ran into the tub, Abby collected clean clothes. She wanted to be dressed, in case... This *was* labor, she admitted to herself. Early, but real, and she would have to organize her thoughts enough to get ready.

The bath felt wonderful. Even the pain that came, pulling her instinctively to a sitting position, seemed easier to take with the warm water lapping over her skin.

Abby climbed out reluctantly, fresh determination shooting a sense of urgency into her. She walked about the condo, gathering the supplies she'd need for the hospital. At one side of her small suitcase she packed a little pile of clothing for the baby. Her contractions became regular again and more frequent, still more localized in her back than her belly. There was time, but she should call the hospital.

Before she could dial the number, the urge to use the bathroom came once more, and a stronger pain, much stronger. Abby concentrated on her hands, flexed the fingers, while she took a deep breath and then let it out slowly. She felt sick. Think, she ordered her straying brain, think. Her next breath, through her nose, was hard to hold, but she kept the air in her lungs, drawing it down to her stomach, then letting it escape through her mouth.

This spasm left her drained. The trip to the bathroom was punctuated by two stops for contractions. "It hurts," she said aloud, then covered her mouth. If she allowed herself to go to pieces, she'd be lost, and maybe the baby would suffer.

When the next contraction had peaked, she returned from the bathroom to the bedroom and called the hospital. The midwife's calm voice reassured Abby. She answered "Five minutes apart. About a minute and a half" to the woman's question about the frequency and length of the pains. "I don't know," she said when she was asked if her membranes had ruptured. The instructions were short "You should come in now, Mrs. Winston. We'll be expecting you."

Abby hung up and snapped the suitcase shut. She walked slowly to the living room, taking her coat from the closet as she passed. Her car keys were on the kitchen counter.

In the dining area she hesitated, looking at the wall phone. What if the pains were so bad that she'd have an accident while she was driving? She arched her back, clamping her hands on her hips. She *could* do it. She *would* do it.

"Oh, no," she groaned and leaned against the wall. A contraction hit, a blow that pierced her back and bore downward. Her fingers, instinctively splayed over her stomach, felt the bulge strain outward, then sink slowly back. "Fool, fool," she muttered. No, she *couldn't* do it, not all of it, not completely alone. She mustn't drive.

Her breathing came in bursts now. She was out of control. Gasping, she wrenched the phone from its cradle and dialed Nick's number.

"Where have you been?" he almost shouted when he heard her voice. "I've been watching for your car for hours. I've got my coat on. I was going to the Laundromat. How did you get in without me seeing you?"

Shut up, Abby thought, closing her eyes.

"Abby? Abby?"

I need you. Organize the breathing. That was what she should do. The book said . . . damn the book.

"Abby! For God's sake, answer me."

"Nick," she whispered. "Could you drive me to the hospital. It's all I need . . . the drive . . ."

"Oh, hell. You're in labor. Get to the door. Unlock the door." His phone crashed down.

The pounding on her door seemed to come before she'd taken a step. She worked her way along the walls, hanging on. She heard her name. Nick was shouting her name and hammering on the door. She had to stop. For an instant she was afraid she would vomit, but the nausea passed, and she shuffled on.

The chain on the door had never felt heavy before, or stiff. It came loose, clanked down, and the deadbolt clicked in slow motion. Abby swung back against the wall, sinking into darkness with yet another contraction. She couldn't do this anymore.

"Good God, Abby. How long have you been like this?"

She didn't answer. Nick put his arms under hers and eased her to the floor. He knelt beside her and held her chin, tilting it up. "Look at me and stop panicking," he said loudly. "Keep your eyes open. Use my face as a focal point."

"Yes," she said and began to cry. Useless, she thought, she was useless, and she couldn't go through with this. "I can't do it," she told him. "I don't want to."

"I know," Nick said. Beneath his tan he'd paled. "But we'll make it, my love. Did you pack a bag?" When she nodded, he stroked her hair back. "Where is it?"

"In the bedroom."

He was back in seconds and kneeling again. "How close together are the contractions?"

"I don't know. Close. All the time." She opened her mouth and closed her eyes.

"How long have you been here on your own?"

She grimaced. "Since yesterday. I thought I was just tired."

"I should have called to see if you were home, damn it. I didn't think." Nick kissed her closed lids and carefully pulled her up.

She laid her face against his neck, pushed her fingers into his vibrant hair. His familiar scent and the feel of his skin on her cheek calmed her. She loved him. Abby lifted her lids and looked into his face, deep into his dear, beautiful eyes. "I love you, Nick. I'm sorry. I love you so much, my darling. I shouldn't say it, but I do." She must be delirious, but if she didn't tell him now, she might never have the guts. He could forget her afterward and go on, but he was with her when she needed him most, and she wanted him to hear the words.

His lips on hers brought her eyes wide open. His own eyes were closed while he kissed her lightly, sweetly. "You're my life, Abby," he said when he lifted his head. "I love you, my sweet lady. I have since I first saw you. Everything's going to be okay."

He half carried her downstairs, pausing when she couldn't make it through a contraction without stopping to breathe over the wave of pain.

"No," she complained weakly when he fastened the seat belt loosely under her belly, but he held her hands until she stopped trying to push it away, and she felt a warm sleepiness for several seconds before the next contraction.

Nick joked, held her hand, shook her gently each time she began to sink away from consciousness. "Concentrate," he said again and again. "Count the streetlights. Out loud. Let me hear how many."

Abby counted. And Nick counted each time another contraction swept in. She did as he instructed, organizing her breathing, changing the pattern sometimes if he told her to, making it somehow. They'd make it, just like he'd said. On the bridge between Mercer Island and Seattle, her legs began to shake uncontrollably. "Nick," she said, bracing her hands on the dashboard.

"Everything's great," he said. "Start contraction. Breathe, one—"

"Nick," she interrupted urgently. "The pain's changing. I feel strange. I'm going to throw up."

"No, you're not. What do you feel, shaky?"

She nodded.

"Transition," he commented. "You're really moving, kid. Good girl. You may be so good at this you'll want to do it every year."

She couldn't smile. "How much farther?"

He steered the car up a steep hill between tall old buildings. "We're there. I'm going to get a wheelchair." He drove to the hospital entrance, flipped off the ignition and ran around to open her door. He put his face close to hers. "Do as I say. Take several shallow breaths."

"I can't."

"Do it. Count in your head. Then blow. Do it!"

She used the tops of her lungs, keeping her eyes on Nick's face. In her mind she thought *one, two, three*, and then she blew.

"Good," Nick said. "Do it again while I get a wheelchair."

He ran through the doors, and for an instant the panic rushed back into Abby. She clutched her coat. Her body trembled. Then Nick was back, easing her forward into the chair. He slammed the car door and pushed her into the brightly lit foyer.

"I have to sign papers," Abby said through gritted teeth. "They told me that."

"Later," Nick replied, punching an elevator button. "Which floor for obstetrics?" he called to a passing nurse.

"Three." She smiled broadly and patted Abby's hand.

She'd be looked after here. The tension drained out of her once more. Another contraction broke the moment of relief, and Abby breathed deliberately.

When the elevator doors opened on the third floor, a woman in surgical greens turned from a desk to face them. She looked critically at Abby and took the wheelchair from Nick.

Questions came fast but calmly. Abby answered as best she could, with Nick filling in what he knew. No one challenged his presence. Twice he was called "Mr. Winston," and both times he answered unflinchingly.

The birthing room, all pastels, mauve and pink and blue-gray, was warm without a sign of the equipment Abby had expected.

"Help your wife put this on," the midwife instructed Nick, handing him a gown before she drew a curtain across the open door and left.

Abby took the gown from Nick. She was too tired, too desperate, to blush. "Thanks for everything," she said. "I'll always be grateful, Nick."

He didn't move.

"Stop worrying," she said and paused, gripped by another pain.

"Keep your eyes open," Nick said. He held her shoulders, massaging. "Give it to me, sweetheart, give up the pain. Come on, one, two, three, four—blow. Let's get you into that fashion piece and finish this thing. I'm ready to meet your little person."

She shook her head. "You can't go through this, Nick. I can't—" She had to bear down. She stared at him, stricken, and he smiled, stroking her cheeks, then her belly with broad motions. "The baby's going to be born," she said faintly. "I can feel it. I want to push."

Nick frowned. "Don't push until they examine you. Hold your breath. The cervix has to be fully dilated, or you'll tear."

Abby managed a smile. "Dr. Dorset. Oh, Nick, you really read that damned book. Thank God you did. I think I refused to concentrate on the words for some—" The pushing sensation came again.

"Up," Nick commanded, taking her weight with one arm around her waist. He unbuttoned her coat, tossed it over a chair, then leaned her against him to unzip her dress.

She should feel horribly embarrassed, but she didn't. She let him undress her to her slip.

"Okay, love. I'll hold the gown. You get out of the rest of your things."

He made a screen with the shapeless striped garment and they managed to maneuver her into it. Nick sat her on a chair and gathered her clothes into a heap before calling the midwife.

Abby found she didn't want to lie down. She sat on the jointed birthing bed with her knees drawn up. Nick stood at her shoulder, holding her against his chest.

"Your cervix is dilated to eight centimeters, Abby," the midwife pronounced. "Doing a beautiful job. But we need two more centimeters before you do any more real pushing. We could use warm compresses on the perineum to help soften things up and avoid tearing. Would that be okay?"

Abby agreed, and the wet, warm cloths were applied between her legs.

"The baby's early," she said, holding the hand Nick offered. "Is it all right?"

The midwife, Rosa, as indicated by her name tag, rubbed Abby's legs. "Everything seems perfectly fine, Abby," she commented, moving the compress to check the cervix once more. "According to your records, you're coming up to thirty-seven weeks, which isn't unusually early. When did your membranes break?"

Abby pulled her thoughts together. "I'm not sure, but it could have been in the middle of yesterday afternoon. I'd been shopping. There wasn't much fluid."

The pressure began again, and Abby dug her fingernails into Nick's hand.

"Okay," he said, "okay. You're doing beautifully. We're almost there, right nurse?" He pressed the heel of one hand into the base of Abby's spine, freed his other hand and began a rhythmic massage of her belly.

Rosa studied her watch. "Almost there," she agreed. "It'll be soon, Abby. It's ten o'clock now, so your membranes ruptured about thirty hours ago. Next time, dear, remember to call when it happens.''

Abby felt disoriented. Another desperate desire to push came, and she held her breath until it passed. ''I wasn't sure it had happened.'' She sighed, then yawned, and the tension seeped away slightly.

''Mr. Winston.'' The midwife looked at Nick. ''It might be a good idea if your wife bore down gently each time the urge passes. Do you have a preference for position?''

Abby raised her chin, and Nick kissed her mouth before looking back at the smiling midwife. ''Maybe we could move back to a chair? She doesn't seem to like lying down.''

The midwife agreed and left them alone again as soon as Abby was settled on the edge of a chair.

''We don't have long to go, Abby.'' Nick knelt between her knees. He surrounded her with his arms, and she pressed her face to his neck, clinging to his shoulders. ''Lean forward, sweetheart. Put your weight on me. Tell me the minute you feel something different...so I can yell for help.'' He chuckled. ''I'm still working on that medical degree. I'm only up to almost-delivery in my studies.''

A distant question made fleeting contact in Abby's head. How could Nick be so calm? Then she let him take her weight.

Another contraction came, then several minutes' respite. Leaning on Nick felt so good. Two more pains, almost without interval, swept in, rose and ebbed, and Abby breathed as Nick instructed. He stroked back her damp hair, and she turned her lips to find his palm.

"Did you discuss anaesthetic with them?" he asked. "I guess you'd have to have it pretty quickly if you were going to."

The response was hard to form. "I don't want it," she managed. "I'm going to make it through, and it'll be better for the baby."

"Brave kid," Nick said against her hair, and she felt him smile. "But it's okay if you feel you need it. The book—"

"Says so," she finished for him, trying to laugh, but ending with a sharp intake of air. "This is it, Nick. It's burning hot there. I can feel the baby's head."

"Nurse!"

His shout startled her. A second later, two nurses swished through the curtain, and Nick was already lifting her onto the birthing bed.

"I don't want to lie down," she said, desperately holding his shirt. "I want—" She couldn't say anymore.

Nick moved behind her, supporting her whole weight. "You don't have to, darling. Squat," he ordered, then said to the midwives, "That's okay, isn't it?"

"Whatever works," Rosa said. She held one of Abby's thighs while her companion supported the other. "The baby's crowning. Burning now, Abby?"

"Yes," Abby groaned. "Yes."

"Now," Rosa said, all business, "grunt and push, then let go and let the baby do some of the work."

Abby tightened her gut. The pain meant something, was achieving something. She laughed and choked and lost her focus. The contraction overwhelmed her, and she cried out.

"Concentrate, Abby," Nick said into her ear. "Force back against me, and think about your breathing."

Abby panted, waited for Rosa's command and pushed again. A popping sensation made her gasp. She glanced into a hanging mirror and saw the baby's head emerge. Excitement threatened to scramble her efforts again.

"The head!" Nick's voice came to her in an unnatural yell. "I can see it. God!"

The second midwife squeezed Abby's thigh. "A small push, Mrs. Winston, and we'll have the shoulder," and within seconds she said, "and now the other shoulder."

Abby squeezed her insides tightly, and the tension flowed out.

The baby was born.

Abby sobbed and turned her face up to Nick. "We did it."

"Yes. Oh, yes." His face was drenched. Sweat and tears. His hair clung to his temples. The effort must have drained him, too.

Abby slumped. "Is he all right?" she said, gasping, sliding more heavily into Nick's arms. "Is he?"

"Looks good, so far," Rosa said, working rapidly over the baby. She wiped the tiny face Abby could hardly see, and the body. "A boy, Abby. But it sounds as if you already knew that. And no tearing from you. Excellent."

The tiny body moved, arms and legs flexed and jerked, and the baby cried.

Emotion expanded Abby's lungs, filled her throat, and then was let go in another wash of tears. "I want to hold him." She laughed through the tears, looking up at Nick.

"That's something," he said in a voice she'd never heard him use. His lashes clung together. "That's really something." Fresh tears welled along his lids, let go, and he ignored them. He stroked Abby's hair absently and helped settle her back on the pillows.

"Now, Mr. Winston, I expect you'd like to cut the cord." Rosa had clamped the umbilical cord in two places and held surgical scissors toward Nick.

"Yes," he murmured, taking the instrument without hesitation. He snipped through the now-limp cord in the spot Rosa indicated, and Abby saw his throat move. He let the midwife take the scissors from him before he passed the back of a shaky hand over his eyes.

Abby swallowed her sobs, watching Nick, watching his face show the same emotions she felt. She loved this man so much, couldn't imagine having or wanting another here in his place. This child, in this moment, belonged to both of them.

"Here." Rosa lifted the baby and placed him in Nick's hands. "Why don't you introduce your son to his mother?"

The nurses busied themselves with Abby. She felt more pressure and knew the placenta was being expelled, but she only saw Nick and her son.

Nick stared at the little boy for several seconds. With one hand, he unbuttoned his own shirt and pulled it loose before lifting the baby to face level. His heart thumped painfully, and the blood in his veins; his body yearned toward this tiny creature an instant ago unborn, in this fragment of time thrust into the world—and, through Abby, become a part of himself. He cradled the infant against his naked chest, closed his eyes at the blind snuggling and reaching of the wobbly face and minuscule fingers. Blood and mucus streaked his skin. He held the baby closer, kissed his forehead, his downy cheek, bent over him, murmuring, not knowing what sounds he made, yet sure they were right.

Abby made a sound, and he looked into her bright eyes, returned their gentle smile. He leaned close. "You made a perfect child, Abby. Hold him."

The miniature body squirmed against Abby's breast, and she couldn't stem her sobs. "He's beautiful." Her throat burned. This little one was so soft, so helpless. Fierce protectiveness tightened her grip, and she smiled at Nick through her tears. His face blurred. "He's going to have a good life; you'll see."

His reply shocked her. "John Winston's a bastard," he said, his voice harsh and strangled. "I hate his guts, but I love the son of a bitch for giving me this day."

Chapter Twelve

"Wake up, buddy."

Nick stirred, opened his eyes a fraction and yawned.

"Nick, wake up."

Consciousness hit him in shock waves. "What? Abby, what's the matter?"

A hand, clamped over his mouth, silenced him, and he looked up into Michael Harris's serious blue eyes. "Keep it down," Michael whispered urgently. "She's asleep. Come into the hall where we can talk."

Nick scrambled from the couch, shoving at his disheveled hair, rubbing the stubble on his jaw. Early daylight from a gap in the blinds made a pale stripe on one wall. He went to Abby and pulled the sheet higher over her shoulders. Her face was smooth and untroubled, faintly shiny, her heavy lashes flickering occasionally. She sighed and threw a hand over her head in a childlike way. Thank God, Nick thought, at last her hard times were over.

"Come on. Before she wakes up," Michael insisted, gripping Nick's elbow to propel him through the door.

"When did you get here, Mike?"

In the dimmed light of the hospital corridor, Michael faced him. He was in uniform, and his tie was pulled loose. "I got in at five this morning and decided to risk calling Abby. I had the damnedest feeling I ought to, and when she didn't answer, I called here. Nick, is she okay? And the baby? He's early."

"They're both fine," Nick said. He was still groggy. "Did you see Justin? He looks like Abby."

Michael's expression cleared, and he smiled. "I haven't seen him yet. Justin, huh? I'll be damned. It's hard to think of him as here and real."

"Come on," Nick said. "I'll get the nursery nurse to bring him to the window where you can see."

Michael followed him down the hall. "Can't I hold him? Amend that. I've never held a baby, so I'll need time to get used to the idea, but I'd like to see him up close."

"Only mother and father get to hold the baby for the first couple of days," Nick said and immediately clamped his mouth shut. He scrubbed at his face. "Michael, they may call me 'Mr. Winston.' I brought Abby in last night, and they thought I was her husband. There wasn't time to set them straight. Don't say anything about who I really am, okay? Abby needs someone around, and..." Nick's stomach tightened. "It's the way we want it, do you understand, Mike? The baby may be John Winston's son because he fathered him, but last night—and today—I've got more right to call him mine."

"I see." Michael stared into Nick's eyes. "It is definitely over between John and Abby, isn't it?"

"Yes."

"And you two are in love."

"Yes. But we didn't say more than four words to each other until John was out of the picture. I want that absolutely clear, Michael."

Michael hesitated, pulling the knot of his tie farther awry. A low cry came from one of the birthing rooms, and he flinched. "I believe that, Nick. Thanks for being here for Abby. Were you with her when the baby..."

"Was I there when Justin was born?" The tentative light in Michael's eyes made Nick laugh. "Yes, I was. And boy, that was something, Mike. She was great. I couldn't handle that number, but she sailed through."

"It wasn't too hard on her?"

"Hard enough. I can't imagine it's ever too easy." He grinned. "In fact, there were a couple of times when she said she'd changed her mind, but I persuaded her to go through with it, anyway. Let's have a look at Justin."

Outside the nursery, Nick tapped on the glass, and a nurse in a rocking chair, holding a baby, glanced up and smiled. She got up and rolled a plastic infant bed in front of Michael and Nick.

"What do you think?" Nick asked, turning his head sideways to peer at Justin. "Good-looking guy, huh?"

Michael didn't answer.

Nick elbowed him. "How about all that hair?"

"Jeez," Michael said under his breath. "Five pounds, ten ounces. How does anything that small make it?"

"He's not so small," Nick said. "They've got one baby under four pounds. The one in the incubator at the back. Justin's about three and a half weeks early. The midwife said he probably wouldn't have been more than seven pounds if Abby had made it to term. And he's healthy as he is."

"He looks like a little gnome," Michael said, grinning. "All wrinkled. Like a prune."

Instantly indignant, Nick looked critically at Justin. "That's a hell of a thing to say, Mike. He's a good-looking kid." He pushed his fists into his pockets. "Abby's been to hell and back in the past few months. Trying to do everything alone. She's going to need help, and I don't just mean financial help."

Michael rested an elbow on the windowsill and continued to study the baby. "You don't think John will come through with support once he sees the boy? How could he resist someone this cute?"

"I thought you said Justin was a gnome." Nick spread an arm across Michael's shoulders. "I don't want John Winston's support. Abby won't, either. They're divorced and he's out of the picture."

"Divorced?"

Nick's arm slid off when Michael straightened. "They've been divorced several weeks. I don't think she's heard anything directly from him since he left."

"Do you want to marry Abby?" Michael asked quietly.

"Don't jump the gun," Nick replied. "We need time to know what we want for sure. But I do love her, Mike. Do you know how that feels?"

Michael's blue eyes fixed reflectively on a point above Nick's head. "I don't know. I guess not."

"It's weird," Nick said. "I know I never loved a woman before. It's like . . . nothing can get in the way of it, nothing else is as important as it used to be."

"Sounds dangerous to me. But you've got good taste, I'll give you that," Michael said. "Maybe if I met someone like my sister, I'd risk my reputation and get involved. I've got to call my folks. And I'll have to tell them the truth about Abby and John . . . and you." He set off purposefully toward Abby's room.

Nick caught up and stopped him. "Let Abby explain to her folks in her own way, when she's ready."

"It's time they knew. You see that, Nick—"

Nick interrupted quickly, "Of course. But Abby wants her mother and father to have a chance to enjoy Justin first. I know how they feel about divorce. Abby told me. She hopes once they're involved with the baby, they'll accept the other more easily. And I'd like it if they didn't view me as an undesirable intruder."

"When do you intend to spring it on them?"

"*I* don't intend to tell them at all," Nick said patiently. "You aren't listening to me. This is Abby's show. If you want to do something for her, then play it her way and let her know you're behind her whatever she decides. And Mike—" he took a deep breath and passed a hand over his eyes "—Abby and I haven't gotten past the stage of admitting we feel something for each other. She's got…we've got a way to go to know what we want in the future. So don't say too much about this conversation, okay?"

"Okay." Michael's smile spread slowly. He grasped Nick in a bear hug. "For what it's worth, I'm rooting for you if you're right for Abby. Can I see her now, please?"

Nick knew his own grin was sheepish. "I know I come on a bit strong sometimes. I've got a lot at stake here. We all do. Go see her. And if you say Justin's anything but wonderful, I'll flatten you—later."

Chuckling, Michael led the way back to Abby's room, passing a midwife in the doorway.

"Good morning, Mr. Winston," she said to Nick. "Dr. Morris would like to have a few words with you when he gets here."

Cold shot up Nick's back. "Who's Dr. Morris?"

"Consulting pediatrician on call," she replied. "Don't worry. Everything's going to be all right. Justin needs some intravenous antibiotics, that's all. He'll also need some pretty close monitoring for a couple of weeks, but then he'll be ready to go home.''

Nick looked from the nurse to Michael, who frowned. "Antibiotics for what?" Nick asked. "What's wrong with him?"

"Dr. Morris will explain in more detail. But Abby's membranes ruptured a day and a half before she delivered. That invites infection. We automatically suction gastric fluids on any baby in those circumstances, and Justin has a Group B strep. Not uncommon. The bath Abby took yesterday afternoon probably didn't help."

"You mean Abby and Justin are sick?" Nick shook his head, confused. "They're going to be here for two weeks?"

The midwife twisted the stethescope hanging from her neck. "Mrs. Winston is asymptomatic. No symptoms. She'll be transferred to a lying-in room shortly and go home in a day or two. The baby must finish the course of antibiotics the same as an adult. In this case the medication is administered intravenously and can only be done under medical supervision. There's nothing to worry about. You can spend as much time as you like with him. Please try to make sure Mrs. Winston understands all this, too. She's bound to be apprehensive, and she'll need your reassurance." A buzzer sounded. "Can you do that?" she asked, waiting for Nick's affirmative nod before leaving at a trot.

"Damn it all," Nick groaned. "What else? I might have known things were going too well."

"Save it," Michael said sharply. "You heard what the woman said. No big deal. Now, let's make sure Abby doesn't get uptight."

Abby strained to hear the masculine voices outside the curtain. One was Nick. Relief warmed her, and she deliberately unclenched her fists. Waking to find him gone had filled her with desperation. The other man spoke again, and the curtain was pushed a few inches aside.

"Michael!" she exclaimed, delighted. "Get in here. Nick called you." She saw his uniform. "You came straight from the airport? You must be exhausted."

He smiled, still poised half inside and half outside the curtain. "Not as exhausted as you, I bet."

Abby swallowed. Every few minutes she wanted to cry with happiness. "Will you come in here, Michael Harris?"

"You look great." He edged just inside, and Nick had to steer him farther into the room.

"I feel great." She looked at Nick, at the dark shadow of his beard, his dear, smiling eyes. "Thanks to Nick," she added. Michael might as well know how she felt.

"I didn't do anything," Nick said, crossing to slump on the edge of the couch.

"Sis—" Michael approached the bed, and she patted the edge. He sat gingerly. "Nick and I had a talk. I know about John and the divorce."

"This isn't the time, Mike," Nick said firmly. "Abby, I took Mike to see Justin. He's a handsome kid, isn't he, Mike?"

"Fantastic," Michael said, reaching for Abby's hand. "Exactly what I would expect from you. You're going to have to give me lessons in holding babies, though. He's such a little guy."

"Not too little," she replied and turned her face to Nick. "Did the nurse tell you about the infection?"

Nick shifted to the very edge of his seat and propped his elbows. "Yes. Abby, you were in labor on your own for a long time, weren't you?"

"It wasn't bad at first. I wasn't even sure it was the real thing."

"I was next door, and I didn't know. You should have called."

Michael cleared his throat. "Abby, I've got to get Mom and Dad here. They'll never forgive either of us if we keep them in the dark much longer."

She sighed. "I want to see them, too. But, Michael, I'm not ready to tell them the truth about John and me, okay? I've got John's mother to think of, too. He obviously hasn't told her, or she'd have contacted us."

Michael stood slowly and buttoned his collar. "Whatever you think is best. I'll pick up Mom and Dad now and tell them there wasn't time to alert them when you were brought in. And I'll explain how Nick came to your aid." He glanced at Nick and gave a wry grin. "I am grateful for that, Florence. And I honestly believe you two might make a great item." He worked his cap on and tilted it over his eyes before pushing up the knot in his tie. "It'll probably be about an hour before I get back. Anything else I can do for you?"

"Yes, please." She rummaged in her purse on the bedside table and produced a scrap of paper. "Give Marie Prince a call for me. She'll want to know about the baby."

Michael grimaced. "Do I have to?"

"Michael," Abby said admonishingly, "Marie's okay. Just give her a call and tell her not to come to the hospital. I'll see her when I get home." She ignored the grumbling noise Nick made. "I know you two never hit it off, but she's had a rough time ever since she was a kid. You never saw her rotten home life. Underneath the tough act she's soft, and she's always been a friend to me—as best as she knows how."

"Okay, okay," Michael muttered as he slipped past the curtain. "I'll call her."

Nick immediately took the place Michael had vacated on her bed. He placed a hand each side of her and leaned close. "I've probably got morning breath, but could I please kiss you?"

She smoothed his hair, watching his eyes, and kissed him slowly. "You must want to go home, Nick. You've been so wonderful."

"You mean I do have morning breath, and you're telling me to go home and clean my teeth."

Abby laughed and immediately winced at the pulling in her womb. "There's an extra toothbrush in the drawer—especially for fathers. You almost qualify, and I don't want you to leave—ever." Heat burst into her cheeks. "Nick, what I said at my place before we left. You know, about love?"

He sat back and held her hands. "I remember."

"Well—" she bowed her head "—I don't want you to think you owe me anything, or that I'm going to be a nuisance." She couldn't go on.

"You could never be a nuisance to me, unless—" Nick put a finger beneath her chin and tilted up her head. "Did you mean what you said?"

All the air had gone out of the room. "Yes," she whispered. "So much it hurts. I do love you, Nick. But—"

"Shhh. I love you, too, Abby. Sometimes it feels as if I've loved you forever. I don't want to remember the time before."

Tears again, Abby thought, and felt them slide down her cheeks. "I don't know how you could have fallen in love with me, the way I've been."

"You don't know much. I couldn't not fall in love with you. You were one sexy pregnant lady, and now, well…" They laughed. "Do you understand all this stuff about Justin?"

Abby sobered instantly. "It's my fault, Nick. I should have realized the membranes had ruptured. Then I took a bath, which was totally stupid. But the nurse said he's absolutely normal and very strong, and the medication will set him right."

"It's going to be tough driving back and forth for two weeks. You probably should find a place to stay close by."

Impossible, Abby thought. She couldn't afford a second apartment, even for two weeks. "As long as I can spend a couple of hours a day with him, it'll be okay," she said.

"But how will you make it here from the east side every three hours for feedings?"

Abby pulled her hands away. "I'll give him a bottle when I am here. Otherwise a nurse will do it. They'll hold him—"

"Bottle?" Nick interrupted. "I don't understand."

"I'm not nursing Justin," Abby said evenly. "That's why I had the shot after delivery."

Nick screwed up his eyes. "I don't remember any shot."

"I had a shot," she explained patiently. "Some stuff called Trace to suppress lactation."

"Isn't mother's milk best, particularly for a baby who's premature?"

"Yes. But not essential. And this is a decision I had to make because—" She hesitated as a nurse entered the room.

"Good morning, I'm Linda Acres. I'll be with you until this afternoon." The woman's broad smile took in Nick and Abby. She settled her rimless glasses more securely on her snub nose. "Justin's already getting his medication. We'd like to move you to another room, Mrs. Winston. But we wondered if you and Mr. Winston would like to stop by the nursery and give Justin his bottle. He can be held quite easily even with the drip, and I'm sure you'd enjoy it."

Abby looked at Nick, met his eyes and saw a softening there. "We'd like that, wouldn't we?" she asked him.

"I'll get a wheelchair." Linda Acres turned away.

"No." Abby swung her legs over the edge of the bed. "The sooner I'm on my feet, the better. I can make it."

Nick helped her into her bathrobe, and they walked, their arms around each other, to the nursery.

Justin had been moved to a separate room, and a long tube ran from one tiny leg to a drip bag suspended from a hook. Abby gripped Nick's arm convulsively, but he shook her gently and smiled.

"Your boy's waiting for you," the nursery nurse said brightly as they pushed open the door and went inside. "Dr. Morris was already here and left. He had an emergency, but he'll talk to you later. He said to tell you he's very comfortable with Justin's condition."

The nurse lifted the baby from his bed. "You can use the rocking chair, or a straight one, whichever you find more comfortable."

Abby sat in the rocking chair and took Justin in her arms. She looked up at Nick, smiling. "He's so soft, Nick, and lovely to hold."

Nick pulled another chair close and sat. He gently stroked the baby's head. "Feed him, Mom. He's starving."

"Yes, sir!" Abby accepted a bottle from the nurse and offered it to Justin.

"Look at that!" Nick said loudly and colored. "Look," he repeated softly. "He knows to go after it." Justin's mouth was already securely fastened on the nipple. Nick put an arm around Abby's shoulders and stared down into the scrunched-up face. "I love you," he whispered. "Both of you."

Abby kissed the corner of his mouth quickly, then caught the nurse's eye. The other woman smiled before going to check her charges in the main nursery.

Nick was quiet for a long time. With the deftness of an expert, he tucked the receiving blanket securely around Justin's squirming arms and legs. When a minute hand worked free, Nick stroked it and spread the fingers, examining them.

Twenty minutes later, the bottle empty, Abby cuddled her son and felt the same protective urge she'd experienced when he was born. Her boy would be safe and free and have what he needed. He'd always be loved.

"We'd better get you to whatever room they want you in," Nick said. "If Michael gets back with your folks while we're here, there could be more explaining to do than you're ready for."

The new room was smaller than the first, but still bright and comfortable. Nick helped Abby get settled and was about to go home to change when Abby's mother burst into the room without knocking.

"Sweetheart, where is he?" Wilma Harris squeaked, rushing to bend over Abby and plant a kiss on each cheek. Her face was even more florid than usual, and her hair sagged slightly from its upswept puffs. "'Justin,' Michael said." She stood and crossed her hands, her chest rising and falling visibly. "Now where did you get a name like that? George Michael would have been perfect. You young people have such funny ideas about names.'' She gave no sign of having noticed Nick.

"Now, Wilma. Justin's a fine name.'' George Harris emerged from behind his wife and approached Abby uncertainly. He stopped beside her, an old tweed cap clasped in both hands. "How's my girl?'' His pale eyes were suspiciously filmed.

"I'm fine, Dad,'' Abby said and rubbed the fingers that turned his hat around and around. "You've got a neat little grandson. You'll have to teach him to make those prize-winning apple turnovers of yours.'' She truly loved this quiet man who'd always stayed in the background of her life, an anchor when needed, but never intrusive.

"Mike says the little one's got a bug of some kind, and he'll have to stay in the hospital,'' George commented. "Does John know about it?''

Abby shook her head.

Her father rocked on his heels. "He'll be back soon. Don't you worry, girl. And if you need help—money or anything—your mother and I will take care of things.''

Abby opened her mouth to breathe.

"Don't you worry about a thing,'' Wilma echoed. "I want you to come home with us until John gets back.''

"No,'' Abby began, instantly desperate, then she repeated "no'' with more control. "It's important for me to settle in my own place again. Everything's set there.'' It wasn't, but she wouldn't think of that now. Maybe the baby taking longer to come home was a blessing. She'd have time to get his equipment together.

"Well, if you say so.'' Wilma settled her head into her neck but kept a smile on her lips. "But I still think—''

"Abby knows what's best," George interrupted. He looked at Nick, not for the first time. Michael stood silently in the background. He must have forgotten to mention Nick to their parents, Abby decided.

Finally Wilma noticed Nick. She took him in from head to foot, finishing with a long stare at his unshaven face. "Are you a doctor?" she asked skeptically.

Michael came to life. "This is Nick Dorset, Mother," he said, moving to the center of the group. "I should have explained. Nick is Abby's neighbor, and he was kind enough to drive her to the hospital last night."

Abby watched her parents' expressions anxiously. Her father smiled politely and extended a hand for Nick to shake. Her mother's ample bosom swelled, and she crossed her hands over her stomach. "I don't remember you mentioning Mr. Dorset, Abby."

This was not going well, Abby decided.

"Nick, Mom," Michael interjected, "my friend Nick who bought the condominium next to Abby's. Remember, I mentioned it to you at the time. He's a flyer, too."

Reservation slowly faded from Wilma's eyes. "That's right, of course I remember. Thank you for helping Abby—Nick. I'm sure John would thank you if he was here." She looked more closely at Nick. "Did you wait here all night?"

Nick glanced at Abby before saying, "Yes. You kind of get swept along in these things. Once I was here, I stayed to find out if she had a boy or a girl. You know how it is, Mrs. Harris." He grinned conspiratorially.

Abby saw her mother's answering smile and silently blessed Nick's resourcefulness. "Michael, take Mom and Dad to see Justin. I'm a bit tired, or I'd go."

Michael ushered his parents out, winking broadly at Abby and Nick as he went.

"Thank you," Abby said simply.

Nick stared out the window. "I don't like lying."

"You didn't lie."

"I didn't tell the truth, and neither did you."

"I—I'm sorry I've involved you in all this."

He jammed his hands deeper into his pockets. "I want to be involved. But I'll be glad when everything's in the open."

Abby played with the sheet. "It soon will be. Once I'm on my feet, I'll explain. I want to get Justin settled in day care and find a job in my own field, so I can prove I'm coping. Then I'll tell Mom and Dad."

"I don't think you can put them off that long. And you don't have to rush back to work. A baby needs his mother around for a little while at least."

"I want to get on with my life. I've got to start over. And, Nick, being in charge of my future is going to feel so good." She did feel exhilarated. "I've made the right decisions."

He studied the toes of his shoes, then her face. "Let's talk about this later. Sleep now, sweetheart. You'd better rest while you can."

AT THE FIRST SOUND of footsteps on the stairs, Nick's mind went blank. Should he stay where he was, or go out and meet them?

Without giving his own question deeper thought, he hurried into the hall. He looked over the banister. Michael had paused between flights with Abby holding his arm tightly.

"Stay there!" Nick yelled. "Wait!" He leapt downward, two, three steps at a time, until he was beside them.

"Hi, Nick," Abby said, clearly out of breath. "I planned to run up, but I guess that'll take another hour or so."

They laughed, and he touched her face.

Michael coughed. "Why don't you take Abby's other arm, Nick. She may be skinny, but I wouldn't mind a little help."

Instead of her arm, Nick held Abby's waist. Then, without meeting Michael's eyes, he swept her into his arms and carried her the rest of the way. At her door, he waited for Michael to let them in and took her to the couch.

Abby scanned the room, her lips parting slightly. "What happened in here?"

Nick arranged a pillow behind her back. "You should take off your coat."

She slowly undid her buttons and let Nick pull the coat from beneath her. He spread the bright quilt he'd bought over her legs.

"Where did all this stuff come from?" Abby asked. "Nick, did you do this? How..." She chewed her fingernail. "You only had two days, and you spent most of the time at the hospital."

"Excuse me, folks," Michael broke in, giving a theatrical wave. "I hate to interrupt, but if you'll excuse me, I'll start bringing up the botanical display in my car."

"Thanks, Michael," Abby began, but he'd already ducked out.

"Can I make you some tea?" Nick asked, afraid to meet her eyes. He'd probably done all the wrong things in here.

"No, thanks," she replied. "Nick, I can't accept furniture from you. Or plants and pictures. I'm so embarrassed."

"You don't like them."

Her fingers closed on his wrist. "I love them," she said urgently, glancing from his face to the door, watching for Michael's return. "But I don't have any right to them. You've showered me with flowers until even my father has started making comments, and now this—all this. Filling up the empty spaces here must have cost a fortune."

"I saw John moving out, you know, Abby. I saw him taking your things."

Her fingers trembled on his wrist. "He took half of what we had. That was fair."

"It stunk," he hissed. "You're not living in a half-empty condo any longer, do you understand?"

She sank back, and he heard Michael whistle as he came in carrying several floral arrangements, as Abby's suitcase slipped steadily from under his arm. "Hey, Nick. Most of this lot is your fault. Give a man a hand, would you?"

Nick escaped gratefully to the cool parking lot and took his time gathering more plants and flowers. He had to handle Abby just right. She'd already let him know she wouldn't be manipulated by another man.

He passed Michael on the stairs. "She's all yours, Nick. I'm due at the airport." Michael checked his watch. "The folks are planning to come over at six. By my figuring that gives you about three hours to work with."

Nick watched Michael's back for an instant. "What's that supposed to mean?" he said.

Michael resumed his whistling then called over his shoulder "Whatever you want it to mean" before he slammed the outer door behind him.

When Nick tapped Abby's door, it swung open under his hand. "May I come in?" he asked tentatively.

He jumped when Abby stuck her head around the corner. "Yes. And quit the tiptoe bit. This isn't a hospital. It's a kept woman's quarters."

Nick recoiled. He *had* done everything wrong, and what he'd say in the next few minutes could make or break his future.

"Lie down, Abby," he said with more assurance than he felt. "It's too soon for you to be walking around."

"I'm not sick," she retorted. "I've had all the nursing I need. In the bush, women have their children and carry straight on with whatever they were doing."

"This isn't the bush." Her temper was rising. "And for the record, when a friend lends you a few things to make your life easier until you can get your own stuff, you aren't a kept woman."

"Would you like tea?" Abby said as if he hadn't spoken.

He opened and closed his mouth. "Yes," he said through his teeth. "And you're going to stop being pig-headed and at least sit down."

Abby lifted a hand, lowered it abruptly and sat on the closest chair—a rattan chair with brilliant tie-on cushions—one of the two he'd bought.

Nick pulled the matching chair close and took one of Abby's hands between both of his. "All morning I've felt like a kid waiting for Santa Claus. If you'd taken more than another minute to get here, I'd have been in the street hopping up and down."

"I'd like to have seen that. I was waiting to see you too, Nick. I . . . will you hold me?"

"It'll be a pleasure," he whispered, going to his knees beside her. He pulled her into his arms, at first carefully, then with a shaky force he couldn't quell. He could smell her perfume, light, faintly rose. "I'm never going to be able to stay away from you."

"Nick," Abby said quietly and played with the hair behind his ear, "I'm frightened."

He tilted his head against her hand. "Frightened of what, my darling? There's nothing to be frightened about."

She swallowed. "I can't believe you'll keep on wanting me."

"You think I could stop wanting you? Oh, Abby, I never will. Could we get married, do you think?" He'd promised himself he'd wait, damn it.

"Married?" Abby became still, her eyes wide. "Nick, do you know what you're saying?"

He held her face firmly, looked into her eyes and planted a kiss hard on her lips. He drew back. "I want you to be my wife. I want to help you bring up Justin. And I know exactly what I'm saying. Will you?"

"Get married," she whispered. "I don't know how to answer. I'm not sure what's right yet, for either of us. But I do love you."

"You don't have to answer now." He attempted a laugh that died too quickly. "I'll give you as long as you need—about two seconds."

She touched his chest, ran her fingers along his tensing muscles. "It's going to take longer, Nick."

He watched her eyes, her mouth, and waited.

"Can you see that?"

"I'll try to," Nick said.

At last she locked her wrists behind his neck and kissed him; a hundred tiny kisses rained over his eyes, his jaw, his neck. Firmly he stilled her face and pressed his lips to hers, ran his tongue lightly along her lower lip.

Abby reached between them and unbuttoned his shirt. She stopped, arching her neck to see his face. Her eyes shone dark and anxious before she slipped her hands beneath the shirt and bent her neck to put her mouth to his collarbone.

Nick's arousal unnerved him. She wasn't ready for more than gentle closeness. He eased her lips back to his before enfolding her against him and holding very still.

"We've got lots of time," he said and closed his eyes. "As much as it takes."

Chapter Thirteen

Streams of headlights, laser stripes through the restaurant's rain-spattered windows, wound along the Alaskan Way Viaduct. Elliott Bay lay beyond, polished obsidian in the faint glow from shore.

Abby pressed her shoulder to the glass and peered down from the sumptuous understated Penthouse Lounge on the cars speeding by below.

"You aren't eating." Nick's hand closed over hers on the table, but she continued to look outside. "Abby," he persisted, "is anything wrong?"

"No, Nick. Everything's right. I'm a bit afraid, that's all. You know, that old 'this is too good, so something's bound to go wrong' feeling?"

"It's not going to go wrong. Eat, sweetheart."

Abby smiled, kept her eyes down and managed some more of the delicious chateaubriand and béarnaise sauce. She felt Nick's still watchfulness. He was waiting, and they both knew why.

"You look lovely, Abby," he said softly. "The lady in gray. Your dress is the same color as your eyes."

The steak caught in her throat, and she coughed, reaching for her water glass. "Thank you," she said when she could speak. "It's an old dress. I haven't worn it for years.'' At least her red face could be passed off on the coughing fit. Compliments were something she'd never handled easily.

''I don't think many women could look as terrific as you do so soon after giving birth.''

This time she took a deep swallow of red wine. Her skin was hot and cold by turns. ''You aren't eating, Nick.''

''I've finished.'' He laughed and leaned across the table. ''You're shy because I said you look good. Look at me.'' He tilted up her chin. ''When we walked in here, every man in the room gave you the once-over. I didn't know whether to preen or punch them out.''

''Oh, Nick. You exaggerate. And there's nothing like a straight dress to hide a not-very-flat tummy. No man would be too thrilled by that, or stretch marks.'' She shook her head, hardly believing what she'd said.

Nick held his glass in front of his mouth while his eyes passed slowly over her. ''I'd be thrilled by every inch of you.''

''Nick, don't.''

''Don't what? Be honest? You know how I feel about you.''

Abby met his earnest eyes unwaveringly. Her body sent its own signals, and they only grew stronger. ''This is tough on me, too.'' Once she gave in to her desires, there'd be no turning back, and if it proved to be a mistake, she'd hurt them both.

Nick scooted his chair around to her side. ''It's been ten days since you came home from the hospital. I've asked you the same question every day, and every day you make some excuse not to answer.''

''We haven't had any normal time together, Nick. How can you know for sure what you want?''

His thigh touched hers. He stroked the soft fabric of her dress over her legs, then rested his hand on her knee. "What's normal? For months we've spent time together. This is our fourth date since Justin was born, and we've been together every other day or evening I've been in town. Abby, we've been closer than most men and women could hope to be before deciding they want to spend a lifetime together. What else is it going to take?"

Abby turned his hand over and touched her fingertips lightly to his. "Are you sure marriage is right for us?"

"I'm sure." He laced their fingers together and brought her hand to his lips. Gently he nipped the end of her forefinger. "Justin will be released in two days. You're pretty much ready for him at home. We could get married, and all you'll have to do is move next door."

She met his eyes, dark now; looked at his mouth, the white collar against his tanned neck. In the dark suit he wore, he resembled... Abby smiled, remembering Marie's comment: a male model.

"Let's dance," he said abruptly and slid an arm around her waist to guide her onto the floor.

When they faced each other, Abby stood still, gazing up at him. She tried to take a breath. Only part of her lungs expanded. "I'm not sure I remember how to dance," she said.

"It's like riding a horse, or swimming," Nick replied, taking her in his arms, moving smoothly to the music of a combo playing soft and easy. "It comes back to you."

He didn't allow any space between them. His hands, spread wide on her back, held her body tightly against his. The muscles in his chest moved against her breasts. His hips pressed into her belly, his thighs transmitted rhythm to hers—and longing.

Abby kissed the underside of his jaw and rested her cheek on his shoulder. The pulse in his throat beat hard. "I keep expecting to wake up," she said, "and find I've dreamed you. I'll go next door and ring the bell, and a stranger will stare out at me."

"I wish you'd try it, love. I'll be there all right, I promise you." His hand moved to the back of her neck, over her ear, rubbing lightly. "It'll be you and me—and Justin. Come, Abby, come."

He was whittling away her resistance steadily. Abby looked up at him.

Nick kept up the swaying motion but stopped moving around the floor. He framed her face, kissed the spot between her brows, her nose, each corner of her mouth. A slight thrust of his hips caused her eyes to fly wide open. His arousal sent a burning ache between her legs.

Abby tightened her own grip. Concentration took more willpower than he'd ever know. "Have you really thought what you'd be taking on if you married me? Not just a wife, but a baby who'd need a lot of my time?"

"My time, too." He grinned broadly and whirled her around. "I'm looking forward to it. I'm pretty good at the bottle and diaper bit. In fact, the nurse this afternoon said I performed like a pro."

Abby grimaced, tracing his shirt pocket. "I saw the way she looked at you. She'd have said what a good job you did if you'd diapered Justin's head by mistake."

"She would not," Nick retorted. "And it's not my fault if the only woman who doesn't find me devastating is the one I've fallen in love with. How about the way I gave him that sponge bath? Not bad, huh?"

"Not bad," Abby replied with difficulty. He did love her. And she loved him. Could she risk agreeing to marry him?

"You okay, sweetheart?" Nick bowed his head to meet her eyes. "You look faraway and sad."

"I was just thinking I'd like to be alone with you. Really alone. Somewhere we could talk."

He regarded her seriously. "Me, too. Let's get out of here."

He held her hand and hurried her back to their table.

"There's nowhere to go, Nick. We can't walk. It's raining."

"Trust me." He signaled the waiter and dropped a charge card on the bill.

They followed the man to the reception desk, and Nick signed the voucher before retrieving Abby's coat. "This thing has character," he said as he held up her black relic. "But I think my Christmas present to you is going to be something spectacular, maybe gray mohair."

Christmas. He was leaping ahead as if their future was a smooth trail. "I don't accept expensive gifts from men," she said and immediately turned her eyes to the ceiling, waiting for his comeback.

He was on cue. "I'm not *men* as you put it. Am I?"

"No, of course not."

In the elevator, which was deeply carpeted and surrounded them with soft music, she felt Nick's irritation. "I didn't mean to say the wrong thing. Sometimes I have a real flair for stupid comments. This coat is a rag. I'm surprised you put up with being seen with me in it."

He grunted. "I won't anymore. Tomorrow we'll shop for the mohair."

"Nick Dorset, you take advantage. I said I was sorry I was rude, not that I'd let you buy me a coat."

"Well, you will, anyway. And we have something else to buy, don't we? Something to seal a promise, I hope."

After the warmth of the fern-studded lobby, the night air was an icy breath-stealing blast. Abby didn't answer Nick's question.

The BMW was parked under the viaduct, but Nick, with Abby's hand firmly clamped between his body and elbow, headed directly for the waterfront.

"Where are we going?" Abby asked, shivering. "The car's back there."

"Have you ever taken the ferry anywhere?"

She tried to halt, but he kept walking, causing her to trot. "I have when I wanted to go somewhere."

"Want to go somewhere now?"

"It's after ten, Nick. Where would we go at this time of night?"

"Who knows?" They crossed railroad tracks to the water. Nick led the way into the brightly lit ferry terminal. At a ticket booth, he bent to see the clerk inside. "Where's that boat out there going?"

"Bremerton." The bald head didn't lift.

"Two, please," Nick said. "Round-trip."

The man took Nick's money, slapped down two tickets and some change and turned a page in the book he was reading.

"Nick, you're a nut," Abby said, stepping beside him while he walked, stuffing his wallet in a back pocket. "Bremerton? That's almost an hour's ride. And we're just going to go up there and turn around and come back?"

He glanced up, grinning broadly. "Unless you'd like to find a place to spend the night there."

She poked his side, and he doubled up, laughing. "Seriously," she insisted, "we'll be on the water for two hours at least. We won't be back till midnight."

"Hmm. Watch your step." They clattered down the metal gangway. "Two hours should be enough to get an answer out of you. If it's not, I'll just keep taking you back and forth until you do answer me."

Abby groaned, climbing ahead of him up a narrow stairway to the enclosed passenger lounges. The vessel was almost empty. Within minutes the aft doors where vehicles drove aboard clanked shut, and squealing winches hauled in the mooring lines. The huge ferryboat chugged from the terminal, rolling gently through the dark waters of Elliott Bay and Puget Sound.

Nick and Abby settled on a bench overlooking an aft deck. Rain slashed diagonally across the windows, and although the lounge was warm, Abby moved closer to Nick.

He hugged her. "Isn't this great?"

"I'm being kidnapped," she responded without conviction.

"Funny," Nick craned to get a clearer view of her. "You don't appear to be tied up or gagged. I thought kidnappers always restrained their victims."

"Unless they use sophisticated methods like brainwashing."

"Have I brainwashed you?"

She played with a button on her coat. "I think so."

"Did I do a good job?"

"I'm afraid you did." Abby pulled away and stood. "If we went just outside those doors, we wouldn't get too wet. There's an overhang from the upper deck, I think."

When she reached the doors, Nick blocked her path. "It's got to be freezing out there, Abby. Are you sure you want to go out?"

She dodged around him and pushed into the rain-laced wind. Nick followed. He undid his raincoat and wrapped her inside it. They leaned against the deckhousing, watching a luminous spume V out from the vessel and the red and green tinge of its running lights on the water. The scent of tar and oil hung heavy in the sodden air.

Abby turned inside Nick's coat, pushed her hands under his jacket and molded their bodies together. In the darkness, unspeaking, with the sound of the wind and the rotating radar scanner the only distractions, they kissed. The meetings of their mouths were wild, desperate attempts to assuage a deeper hunger.

Tentatively Nick unbuttoned Abby's coat. He touched her breasts carefully, bringing his thumbs to rest at their soft sides. She spread her palms over his flat belly, pressed down until she met hard resistance. The sound Nick made, deep, breaking, was lost on the wind before he held both of her wrists and put her arms around his neck. He kissed her again and again, forcing her mouth wide open, driving his tongue far into her mouth. His lips and face nudged, tipping her head back, until he could follow the soft skin of her neck down to the buttons closing her dress. Down, down, his lips and tongue moved, probing between the tops of her breasts until she moaned and urged his mouth back to hers. They must take this slower, much slower.

"I love you, love you," Nick said against her ear. "God, how I love you."

"You said all I'd have to do was move next door," Abby whispered breathlessly. "There'd be two of us, Nick."

He leaned away, his eyes glinting in the night. "Yes. So you've reminded me before. Then there'd be three. You, Justin and me. What do you say, Abby?"

"Yes. I say yes. If you're sure, Nick, so am I. Thank you, I'd like to marry you very much."

He laughed, the noise suspiciously cracked as he buried his face in her shoulder. "Thank you very much. Only you, my darling, would accept a marriage proposal that way. I thank *you* very much. How about doing it on Saturday?"

Now Abby laughed. "How about getting the baby home and giving me a day or two to let my family know what's happening? They probably deserve a few hours to take everything in, don't you think?"

"Michael already expects it. He'll stand up for me. I'm sure he will. Janet will have warned my folks."

"That's fine. But my mom and dad don't expect it. I suggest we plan on about four weeks from now, mid-January, for more reasons than one." She was grateful he couldn't see her blush.

Nick blew gently on her ear. "I do believe you're a very sexy woman, Abby soon-to-be-Dorset. I'd be happy to marry you tomorrow and just hold you for the next month. But—" he held up a hand to stop her protest "—we'll do it your way."

"Thanks," she said. "I also need to line up some job interviews. I had enough money to pay for the delivery, but I'll have a big bill still owing for Justin. And I owe Michael money now. I want to get to work as soon as I can."

Nick had turned his head away. He said nothing.

Abby's heart thudded. He mustn't think she expected him to take on debts she'd already incurred. "I will be able to deal with it all, Nick. You don't have to worry."

"I'm not worried," he responded, his voice muffled. He cleared his throat. "How about dropping by to see Justin on our way home? We could tell him our news."

"Oh, yes." She hugged him. "You always know what I want, Nick. I want to see him."

Nick pulled her coat together and fastened it. "I want to see him, too."

The rest of the trip to Bremerton and back seemed interminable. Nick bought hot cider and cinnamon rolls from the cafeteria, and they retreated to their quiet corner to watch the waves.

Finally the ferry docked in Seattle once more, and Nick hurried Abby to the car. The heater quickly warmed her cold nose and icy hands. When the hospital loomed ahead, she felt the odd jiggle of excitement in the pit of her stomach the thought of Justin always brought.

"Have you noticed how he watches your face when you feed him?" Abby asked while Nick swung the car into the parking garage.

"He follows movement, too," he said. "He's going to be a bright kid."

Abby laughed. "You sound like a proud father." She bowed her head and clasped her hands together.

"I feel like one," Nick said evenly. "And, after all, I'm going to get to share him."

The awkwardness evaporated. "I'm so lucky to have you, Nick."

He pulled on the emergency brake and leaned to kiss her cheek. "We're lucky to have each other. Now, let's go and see our boy."

"You don't think they'll mind us turning up so late?" Abby whispered when they left the elevator on the third floor of the hospital. "It's so quiet in here."

"We were told to come anytime, weren't we?"

She nodded as they turned the corner. Muted light from the nursery windows washed the opposite wall.

A man was standing there, his face framed by his hands and pressed to the glass.

"Oh, no," Abby whispered. Water seemed to replace the blood in her veins. She gripped Nick's forearm.

Nick glanced down into Abby's face and back to the man. For the first time in his life he knew what feeling *murderous* meant.

John Winston sensed their presence and straightened.

Chapter Fourteen

He approached them slowly while Nick's brain formed and rejected a dozen comments.

"Abby," John said when he stood in front of her. "How are you, baby?"

Nick's hands instantly curled into fists, but he held himself rigid. Abby's fingers dug into his arm.

"What are you doing here, John?" She began to shake.

John Winston ran a hand through his blond curls, looked at his feet, then beseechingly at Abby. "I couldn't stay away any longer. I wanted to see him—and you."

"Why? You didn't care before." Abby's voice sounded high. "You don't belong here."

"I got in from a trip this afternoon and tried to call you," John said. "When there was no answer, I called Michael. He told me the baby had been born." The man's blue eyes filled with tears, and Nick hated him for it. "I knew if I came here and waited long enough, you'd show."

"We should see Justin and get you home, Abby," Nick broke in, taking her past Winston. "It's late."

"I like the name Justin. Justin Winston is nice."

Abby stopped and turned back. "What else did Michael tell you, apart from Justin being born?"

"That you wouldn't want to see me. That I didn't have any right to come here. But I do, Abby. Justin's my son, too."

He had to keep hold of himself, Nick thought. He worked the muscles in his jaw and tried vainly to put his thoughts into neutral. *Don't hit the bastard, not here,* he ordered himself. And, his brain registered, Abby must deal with this in her own way. She wouldn't accept anything else.

"You didn't want him, John," she said clearly. "You didn't want him or me. I didn't ask for a divorce, you did, and it's final. We're strangers now. Please leave."

For the first time, John looked directly at Nick. "I understand you've been kind to Abby—Nick, is it? Thanks for that, buddy. She obviously trusts you. Maybe you can talk her into letting me see my boy just once— holding him just one time." A tear slid down his cheek.

Nick glanced away. "Abby makes her own decisions," he said, praying she'd tell the son of a bitch to get lost.

Her voice cracked when she said, "Cut the dramatics, John. They make me sick. Why don't you just get lost?"

"Please, Abby." Winston took a step toward her. "I made a mistake. I've been a bastard to you. I'm sorry."

Abby held her purse in front of her like a shield. "It's too late for 'sorry.' "

"I deserve this. But I hoped you'd understand a man needing to see his son." John covered his face.

When Abby touched the man's arm, Nick swallowed his rising nausea and rage. This creep, this manipulator who'd entertained himself by shouting at a lovely, gentle woman, by walking away when she needed him most, was working on her too-tender heart again.

Winston put a hand over Abby's on his arm, joining her to him. "If I can be with him—and you—for a few minutes, I'll go away. I promise.'

Abby looked at Nick and back to John. "Okay, a few minutes, but that's it," she said, dull distress in her eyes. "I'll do the talking to the staff. You're a friend, nothing more—understand?"

"Yes, of course." John Winston smiled a grateful little-boy smile that deliberately included Nick. With his blue, blue eyes he said *I'm wayward, and I know it, but I can be good if I'm given a chance.*

And Nick detested him.

Abby pushed open the nursery door. A nurse worked busily with a baby in an incubator. She glanced over her shoulder and raised her brows when she saw Abby and Nick had someone with them.

"This is a close friend," Abby said in a low voice. "He's just passing through town, and he wondered if he could see Justin."

The nurse hesitated, withdrawing her hands from the incubator sleeves. "Well," she said and smiled at Abby and Nick, "I suppose it's all right. Gown up, though, please. You know the routine."

After the woman left, Nick donned a gown and Abby did the same before handing one to John. He took off his heavy pea coat, and Nick was struck afresh by the man's massive build inside a dark blue turtleneck and jeans. A vital man. The kind women went for. Nick turned away and went to see Justin.

The child slept, his tiny fists curled beneath his chin. "Hi, fella," Nick whispered, touching a whitened knuckle. "How's it going?"

"Oh, Abby, he's a beaut."

John Winston stood on the other side of the baby's bed, staring at his son with an amazement that Nick doubted could be feigned, and it wouldn't have to be. Justin *was* beautiful.

"He was born a bit early," Abby said. "Then he got an infection, so he had to stay here for a couple of weeks."

"He's going to be all right?" John gripped the edge of the crib, glancing at the antibiotic drip.

"Justin's due to go home in two days," Nick interjected. The raw sensation closing his throat was foreign. Then he identified it: jealousy of this interloper, possessiveness toward Abby and Justin. He wanted John Winston gone.

Abby smoothed Justin's cheek, and the child's eyelids parted, closed, then opened fully. He stretched, and Abby bent over him, making the soft noises she always made when she was with him. She lifted him and rubbed her chin on his brow.

John went to her side, and Nick saw their eyes meet. Either he was dying or very very sick. He couldn't stand this. Abby smiled and placed Justin gently in John's arms. He held the bundle stiffly at first, slightly away from his body. Justin whimpered, and John looked startled before he smiled and relaxed, pushing a large forefinger into one miniature fist.

"He's perfect." John moved close to Abby where they could look together at their child.

Abby straightened the receiving blanket, her features soft. "He's strong, John. They say he'll do very well."

When John put an arm around her shoulders, Abby didn't seem to notice or mind. The couple stood, rocking gently, their baby between them.

Numb, Nick reached back to untie the neck of his gown. "Winston, do you have a car with you?" he asked. The pain in his throat was suffocating now.

The other man didn't look up. "Yes. It's in the garage."

"Could you give Abby a ride home?" Nick felt Abby's stare, the stiffening of her body. "I forgot I'm supposed to check in with the airline tonight." The excuse sounded pitiful in his own ear.

"Sure I can," John said quickly. "Be glad to."

I'll bet you will. Nick turned to Abby. "Hope you don't mind being abandoned. But I'm sure John will take good care of you. We'll touch base soon."

"Nick," she began, then nodded mutely, her eyes, shaded in the dim nursery, showing nothing—or everything. Nick didn't know anything anymore except he had to get out of here.

In the corridor he tossed his gown into a hamper and braced his arms against the wall, bowing his head and waiting for desperation to pass. Abby and John had appeared so natural together, holding their baby. He, Nick, was the interloper. On legs that seemed boneless, he passed the nursery without looking sideways.

Abby watched Nick go, every nerve within her jumping. Tears sprang to her eyes. His attempt at nonchalance before he walked out hadn't fooled her. Through no fault of hers he felt hurt, betrayed. Nick felt she had betrayed him simply by allowing John to hold Justin. And the excuse about having to call the airport office hadn't fooled her. He'd wanted to escape. Damn him. Damn him for doubting her. Panic clamored in her brain. She pulled her bottom lip between her teeth and bit hard.

"I must get home," she said abruptly. What counted was getting to Nick and making him see he'd overreacted to a situation she'd been unable to control.

John continued to hold Justin. He studied the baby closely. "He's got the shape of your face, but I think he'll be blond like me." He stroked the dark fuzz. "This comes out, doesn't it? I'm sure he'll end up blond."

Abby shifted restlessly. "It's hard to know yet. John, they don't like long visits." Not strictly true, but a necessary excuse to follow Nick as soon as possible.

"Okay. I hate putting him down, though." John replaced Justin in the plastic bed.

"Come on," Abby insisted, backing through the swinging doors and tearing off her gown at the same time. In the entry, she shifted from one foot to the other until John joined her and followed her example, disposing of the green gown and swinging his coat over one shoulder.

The clock in the hospital foyer showed 2:00 a.m. as they passed. Abby couldn't repress a shudder when the deepened cold of early morning drove into her. John put on his coat and pulled her against his side, shielding her while they crossed to the garage. The drawing together in Abby's belly was easily identifiable—revulsion. John's nearness alone was enough to sicken her now. The realization shocked Abby, and she shrugged away.

He drove a brown pickup she'd never seen before. In the cab he made much of making sure she was comfortable. Abby cringed at his touch. She calculated how long ago Nick had left. Too long. While John drove, he tried to make conversation. She hardly heard what he said. Nick mustn't, couldn't think she wanted to be with John.

Several blocks from her condo, John steered onto the shoulder of the road and turned off his engine.

"Why are we stopping?" Abby asked and moved closer to the door.

John let seconds click by before he answered, "We have to talk. You know that, Abby."

"I don't," she said, tears of frustration springing into her eyes. "Take me home, please."

"These past few months have taught me a lot."

She didn't want to know anything about what his life had been. "Just drive," she said.

"You never used to be so hard." He tried to hold her hand, but she crossed her arms. "We all make mistakes, baby. Even you, maybe. Would it be such a bad idea to give us another chance?"

A scream sounded deep in her head. But she hadn't really screamed, had she? "We were wrong for each other from the start," she said carefully.

"You never used to say that. Baby—"

"Don't call me baby. I'm not your baby. Will you take me home, or do I have to get out and walk?"

"Hell! I'm asking for a fresh start. What do I have to do, crawl?"

Abby bent over, rocking, the tears breaking loose.

"Justin's my child, too, remember that," John said harshly. "A father has rights these days. Rights just as strong as a mother's."

"You left me. You can't come back and...and..." She couldn't go on.

Keys jangled, and the engine turned over again. Abby felt the pickup swing back onto the road and kept her face bowed.

When the motion stopped once more, she peered up fearfully. Relief almost choked her. She was home.

John stopped her from opening the door. "I came on too strong, too fast back there," he said. "Tonight was more than I could handle. I didn't know it would be. Can you accept that?''

"Yes." She'd accept anything if he'd just let her go. She must get to Nick.

"Can I at least talk to you some more?"

"Not now, John. I've had it for tonight."

"Tomorrow, then?"

Strategy was what counted at this moment. "We'll see. Good night, John."

He removed his hand slowly. "I'll call you tomorrow."

Abby pushed open the door.

"Wait," John said urgently. "I brought this for you. I was going to get flowers, but it was too late."

She hardly looked at the envelope he pushed into her hands. Had John ever given her a card before? She didn't remember.

Leaving the pickup door swinging open, she ran through the parking lot and around to the back of the building. By the time she stood in the hall between her own door and Nick's, her breath came in gasps. She stood, her fingers an inch from his doorbell, willing her heart to slow.

She rang, waited, rang again. No footsteps sounded inside his condo. Abby pressed the button again, then knocked. Nothing.

Trembling, she let herself into her own rooms and dialed his number on the phone. He didn't answer. Tears started afresh, and she wiped at them disgustedly. She cried so easily these days. Nick wasn't the kind of man to ignore his doorbell or his phone.

An idea formed slowly, and with it, terror. What if he'd been hurt and never got home? She ran back downstairs to check for his car. The BMW wasn't in the lot.

Abby returned to her condo, trying to think. The first thing to do was call the police, or should she check the hospitals?

She had a key to his place. Nick had given her a key.

He's understand if she went in—just to check.

Minutes later she closed her own door behind her and went directly to the bedroom. Without removing her coat, she fell facedown onto the bed. She should be glad. Nick had returned home safely, his discarded suit proved that. But he'd left again, and God knew where he'd gone.

In one hand she still held John's card. She sat up and tore open the envelope. Her tears were bitter now. If Nick had truly loved and trusted her, he wouldn't have rushed away at the sight of John.

She pulled a folded sheet from the envelope. Money, bills in larger denominations than she'd seen often, slid into her lap.

"Abby," John's note read, "I never did know when I had it good. Leaving you was the biggest mistake of my life. Michael told me some of what you've been through since I went away. I can't take it all back, but I can say thank-you for the baby and ask you to try and forgive me." He signed, "Love, John."

"You never knew what love was," Abby muttered. She picked up the money and stuffed it back into the envelope with the note.

"YOU LOVE THE GUY." Marie chewed her fingernail and paced while she talked. "You're obviously crazy about him, or you wouldn't have said you'd get married."

Abby stretched full length on the couch and closed her eyes. "Yes, I love Nick." Why did Marie always show up at the least convenient times?

"So fight for him. Tell him he's all you want in the world. Don't let John spoil this chance for you."

"As I've already told you, Nick isn't here for me to tell him anything," Abby said patiently. Her head ached. Three or four hours of shallow sleep had done nothing for her health or the state of her mind. And Marie's hour-long interrogation since her uninvited appearance at nine had only increased the tension.

Marie picked up her purse and rummaged until she found a cigarette and some matches. "Where is he?"

"Like I told you when you arrived, I don't know. When did you start smoking again?"

"I never really gave it up. Nick saw you with John and took off?" She drew deeply on a cigarette, shaking out the match's flame. "He must have thought there was still something between you two. Is there?"

"There's nothing between John and me, damn it, Marie. You know that. But John's going to make it tough. I feel it in my bones. For some sick reason, he's going to try and stake a claim to Justin."

Marie whirled toward her, one elbow braced on the other forearm. "Why would John want Justin?"

Abby turned her face to the back of the couch. "How do I know? He never liked kids. Maybe he just wants what he can't have."

"And while he tries to get it, you'll let him ruin what you and Nick have?"

"I don't need this, Marie. I didn't sleep last night, or this morning. I'm scared of what John intends to do. And I miss Nick."

"He'll be back, and when he is, make sure he knows that nothing and no one matters to you as much as he does."

"What if he won't believe me?" Abby said miserably. "What if John keeps showing up on some pretext...saying he intends to see Justin? He could even try to get custody. Some of the things he said last night made it sound like he was thinking about it."

"Give him the baby."

"What!" Abby leapt to her feet. "What are you saying, Marie? After all that stuff about adoption I thought you'd know better than to make any more suggestions about giving up Justin."

Marie recoiled and sat with a thud on the edge of a chair. "Calm down and think." She ripped the tip of one nail completely off and glared at it. "How long do you think John would want to play house with a baby? If you gave him a few weeks at it, say until you and Nick are married, Justin would be back on your doorstep so fast your head would spin."

Abby couldn't believe what Marie had suggested. "My baby isn't a weapon," she said. "He isn't a thing to be used. Let John fight; he won't get him. And if Nick doesn't trust me enough to know I don't want John back, our marriage would be a mistake. One rotten marriage is enough, thank you."

"As long as you're free, John is likely to keep coming around."

"How do you know?" Abby was exasperated.

"I don't. But you're the one who said he's the type who wants what he thinks he can't have."

"'Thinks'? I— Darn, there goes the intercom. That had better not be John."

Marie got up, stubbed out her cigarette and grabbed her purse. "Don't let him in if it is."

Abby went to the speaker and heard Michael's voice before she could say anything. Relieved, she buzzed him into the building. Michael was exactly what she needed today.

She turned to Marie. "Michael's—"

"I know, I know. I'm going." Marie pulled on her coat. She'd grasped the front doorknob when Michael knocked.

Abby reached around her to let him in and suppressed a smile at her brother's strained expression on sighting Marie.

"Hi, Mike," Marie said brightly, edging past him. "I guess today is Abby's day for visits from beautiful people." She smiled winningly into his cool indigo eyes and trotted out of sight.

"You might try to be nice to Marie," Abby told Michael reprovingly. "She's really okay."

"I'm not interested in Marie," Michael cut in, marching past Abby. "What the hell happened between you and Nick?"

She turned instantly cold. "You've talked to him."

"Greg Schultz, another pilot, told me Nick took off from Seattle early this morning and that he's going to use Omaha as his home base for a while."

Abby closed her eyes. "Oh, Michael. What am I going to do?"

"Damned if I know. But you could start by giving me a hint of why he went, and why John Winston turned up at the folks this morning all sweetness and light and crowing about seeing Justin for the first time last night. Abby, for God's sake!"

She felt his arms around her before she knew she'd begun to faint. Michael helped her to the couch and sat beside her.

"Stay here," he said. "I'll get you some water. Or should I call a doctor?"

"Just water, please." John had been to her parents'. He intended to get back into her life. She wouldn't let him, but it didn't matter. Nick had gone.

A cold glass shoved into her hands made her glance up into Michael's troubled eyes. "Tell me what happened," he said. "Take it slowly and quit worrying. Whatever's happened, we'll work it out."

Yet again Abby stumbled through the events of the previous night and early morning. Each time she paused, Michael steered the glass to her mouth and rubbed her nape. When she'd finished her story, he sagged back beside her, expelling a long, low whistle.

"So Nick has limped off to lick his wounds. Idiot," he said finally. "If this is what love does to a guy, keep it away from me."

"Are the folks going to show up here, too?" Abby asked weakly. "I don't think I can face them today."

"No. From what they said, John made it sound as if the two of you needed a lot of time alone, so they intend to give it to you. I wouldn't be surprised if he'd try to see you."

She sighed. "He said he would, and I didn't have the smarts to put him off properly. Michael, all I want is Nick—and Justin. If John fights for custody of Justin and gets it, and I've lost Nick, too, I don't know...I just don't know. Tell me what to do, Michael."

"You won't lose either of them." He turned toward her. "Use your head, Abby, John wouldn't have a hope of getting his hands on Justin. And if he makes a nuisance of himself, I'll deal with him myself. Let's concentrate on Nick. You said you got along well with his sister."

"Janet, yes," Abby agreed.

"Call her."

"Call...oh, no, no, I couldn't."

"You can and you will—now." He went into the kitchen and returned with a telephone directory. "What's her last name? And her husband's first name? I'll call the operator."

"Crete Ross," Abby said faintly. "I don't think this is a good idea. Nick might not like it."

"You aren't going to call Nick. He can't tell you who you should talk to."

In what seemed to Abby like far too short a time, she heard Janet's voice on the phone and floundered into a series of confused remarks. She asked about Penny and about Janet's husband, the weather in Omaha, where they all intended to spend Christmas.

"Nick's at my parents'," Janet broke in quietly. "He got there this morning with some story about flying out of here for a while so he can spend Christmas with the family. What's wrong?"

Abby's heartbeat pounded in her throat. "He asked me to marry him."

After a brief silence, Janet said, "I'm glad. So why is he here?"

Once again, Abby explained John's unexpected appearance and Nick's reaction. When she'd finished, Janet launched into a short tirade about the immaturity of the male that brought a smile even to Abby's lips. By the time she hung up, she was almost sorry for Nick. If Janet delivered the lecture she'd said she intended for her brother, he'd come away minus most of his skin.

"She's on my side—Nick's and my side," Abby said distractedly.

"I gathered," Michael said. "She'll get through to him."

"If he'll listen."

ABBY TURNED JUSTIN on his tummy, patted his bottom and leaned to kiss the dark fuzz behind his ear. She closed her eyes, breathing in the clean scent of baby powder. Notes tinkled from the slowly twirling mobile attached to his crib. When she was sure he was asleep, she tiptoed into the kitchen, leaving his nursery door ajar.

Christmas night. Justin had been home a week, and she couldn't imagine the condo without him anymore.

In the kitchen she rinsed his bottle and poured a glass of wine. She went to sit at the dining table Nick had bought while she'd been still in the hospital. As soon as she could find a job and get Justin settled in day care, she'd start paying Nick back what she owed.

She left the lights off and nestled her chin on her crossed arms atop the glistening rosewood surface of the table. Outside, a dusting of snow sparkled on shrubs and outlined naked tree limbs. A Christmas Day had never been so lonely, or, at the same time, so special.

Tomorrow she was to visit her parents. Today, her mother had told her on the phone, should be Abby and John's first Christmas alone with their son. And Abby hadn't had the guts to set Wilma straight. So there had been no one but her tiny boy and the special magic he brought. No word from Nick. Michael hadn't called. And for the first time this week John hadn't turned up on the doorstep. For that, at least, she was grateful.

He'd refused to take back the money he'd given her. More had arrived by mail. He'd come at different times, bringing gifts for Justin, flowers and perfume for her, and champagne he'd insisted on sharing to celebrate their son's birth.

Abby opened the shades and rubbed at the condensation forming on the window. She didn't want to celebrate anything with John Winston.

What was Nick doing tonight? Laughing by the fire with his family? Evidently Janet hadn't managed to sway him. Abby compressed her lips. Nick wasn't any happier than she was. Suggesting, even out of anger and desperation, that he might be was immature. But he didn't trust her and wasn't about to be hurt any more badly.

A lone set of tires crackled in the street. She peered down, feeling the same rush of hope she'd felt a dozen times this week.

The vehicle that drew up to park half on the curb wasn't a silver BMW, but John's brown pickup. She drew back from the window, her first thought that she'd pretend not to be at home. But that wouldn't work. He'd know she was there.

When the buzzer sounded, Abby released the main door latch without talking into the speaker. Then she opened her front door and returned to sit by the window. She closed the shades.

"Merry Christmas, baby." John came in, bringing cool air with him. He stood, framed in the entrance to the living room, with a grocery sack in one arm, a pile of brightly wrapped packages in the other.

"Hi, John."

"Is that the best you can give a man bringing Christmas cheer?" He swayed slightly.

Abby held the edge of the table with both hands. He was drunk. "Shh, please. Justin's just gone to sleep."

"Shh," John echoed, rising to his toes and walking with exaggerated care into the room. "Shhh, Justin's sleeping. Good, 'cause that means his mommie and me can be all alone."

"I was just going to bed," Abby said and pursed her lips at the instant flash in his bloodshot eyes. "I think you should go, John. No, I want you to go."

He made it to the couch and flopped down, still holding his packages. "No, no, no." He shook his head repeatedly. "This is celebration time. We're going to celebrate."

Abby was afraid to move, afraid that he would reach for her. "Don't make this harder, John. You're drunk. Please get out of here."

"Nope." He stood and came toward her. From the bag he produced a bottle of bourbon, already open, and two bottles of pink champagne. The wrapped parcels slid to the floor, and he retrieved them clumsily, piling them on the table beside the liquor before he took off his coat.

Abby watched, horrified, while he worked his sweater over his head, unbuttoned his shirt and pulled the tails free of his jeans. He planted his hands on his hips, flexing the muscles in his chest beneath a heavy covering of blond hair.

"Just getting comfortable." His words slurred together. "I was surprised you hadn't told your mom and dad about the divorce. Why didn't you?"

"I'm not talking to you while you're like this." He'd struck another chord. Why hadn't he mentioned the divorce himself? "How come you felt so confident you could walk into my family's home when you must have expected them to know about the divorce?"

His eyes slid away. "I was ready to tell them what I've told you: I'm sorry about the divorce, and I don't want it anymore. Then I realized they didn't know, so I let it go. You don't want to stay apart, either, do you, Abby? You never wanted it, or you would have told them. We can get married again, and they never have to know we've been separated."

"Stop it," Abby said, getting to her feet. "It's over with us, John. If you think about it—soberly—you'll know you want it over, too."

"Oh, baby, you don't mean that." He clamped a hand on her shoulder, pulled her toward him. "We were always good together."

Even her mouth trembled. Her lips wouldn't stay together. If she shouted, no one would hear but Justin. "Either you go away and stay away," she said, drawing up to her full height, "or I'll call the police. Then I'll make sure you never get within a mile of my son again."

He stared into her eyes, his pupils widely dilated, then concentrated on her mouth. Slowly he drew her closer until she could smell the bourbon on his breath. She turned her head away, but he easily turned it back with a finger and thumb.

The instant before his lips would have met hers, Abby slapped him. With splayed fingers she hit the side of his face, baring her teeth as she did so and wrenching away.

John touched the reddening marks on his cheek and stepped back. "You bitch," he mumbled. "You make me go away tonight . . . you try to keep me from seeing Justin, and I'll find a way to get him. And that doesn't have to be through the courts."

Abby sat again, holding her head in her hands. Would he kidnap her baby if she didn't play his game? For some warped reason he wanted to get back in her life. She wouldn't take him. She couldn't take him. And she couldn't lose her baby.

John's hand on the back of her head brought a cry to her lips. She started to hit out, but he held her wrist until she went limp. He slackened his grip, turning the vise into a stroking action. And his hand on her head became the caress of a parent for a child.

"I'm sorry, Abby," he said quietly. "I was out of line, as usual. You're right: I'm drunk. It took me all day to get up the guts to come here and ask you to marry me again. And it took booze. I'm an ass. Forgive me?"

She couldn't form any words.

"Look," he said, backing away. "We can't talk now while I'm like this. But I can't drive any more either, baby. Let me sleep this off on the couch for a while, and I'll get out of your hair until we can talk rationally. Will you do that?"

If she refused, he might start shouting again, or try... He could force himself on her. As long as he was here, she wouldn't dare sleep, but she'd have to agree to his staying.

"You'll sleep it off, then leave?"

"I promise." He stripped his shirt all the way off and worked out of the soft Western boots he'd always favored. The socks followed. "Can I just look in on Justin?"

He didn't wait for her approval before going into the hall.

Abby stood in the middle of the room. She could call Michael for help. As she formed the idea, John reappeared, and at the same moment, her doorbell rang.

She hurried forward, only to be stopped by John's powerful arm across her breasts. He slipped his hand around her waist, holding her slightly behind him.

The doorbell rang again.

"Who would come at this time of night?" John asked. "You could be alone here. Never answer the door when you're alone."

"I won't. I won't."

He gave her a hard look and opened the door.

Nick had his back to the door while he stooped to pick up several packages. "Abby, I've been trying to get out of Omaha for two days." He rose, turning slowly, balancing his load, leaving his flight bag in a heap while he looked up. "Abby..."

Chapter Fifteen

"Little late for social calls, isn't it, buddy?"

Abby heard John's drawl but looked, stupefied, at Nick. He seemed to see only John.

"What can we do for you?" John moved farther in front of Abby, filling the doorway with his half-naked body.

"I came to see Abby," Nick said in a menacing voice. He met her eyes over John's shoulder. "We have things to discuss."

"Anything you have to say to Abby, you can say to me," John said, stepping back, sweeping wide his arm. "Come join our celebration. We always have a holiday drink for a neighbor, right, Abby?"

She shook her head. John was drunk, and Nick looked as if the packages he held were all that kept him from swinging his fists. They mustn't fight. She had to find a sane way out of this.

"John needed a place to spend the night, Nick," she said lamely. "You and I can talk in the morning."

Nick's mouth set in a hard line. "Good night, Abby." He managed to haul the flight bag over his shoulder without dropping the packages. With a last long stare at her, he turned away.

John shut the door an instant before Abby heard Nick's latch click sharply. He had come back. He'd said he'd been trying to get to her for two days. And now he thought he'd made a fool of himself, that she'd made a fool of him. What else could he think after seeing John dressed as he was, and hearing her admit she was allowing him to spend the night?

With her arms crossed, she dragged her leaden body into the living room. John followed, evidently finally at a loss for words. She glared at him and set about gathering his clothes.

"Put these on, John. And get out."

He spread is hands. "But you said I could stay."

"I've changed my mind."

"Because loverboy came back?" he sneered. "You want me out so you two can get together. I saw the way he looked at you at the hospital that night. And he was going to walk in here tonight like it was home, wasn't he? He must be used to coming home to you, Abby. Well, it isn't going to work anymore because I'm home now."

Abby shoved his shirt into his arms and waited, holding his sweater and socks in front of her. "Get dressed. And don't say another word about Nick."

"I'm not going anywhere."

"You are, unless you want me to scream. Nick's sober, John. This might be one fight you wouldn't win."

"Don't make me go." He crumpled to the arm of the couch, his shirt balled in one fist. "I'll go in the morning, like I said."

"If you ever want to see Justin again, you'll go now. *Now*, John, or I'll get a court restraining order to keep you away from us altogether."

He passed a jerky hand over his face. "I'll go. But I'll be back." The shirt went on, inside out, and she handed over his sweater. "You're going to be sorry, Abby. I need Justin, and I'm not going to give up."

"You're threatening me." Abby heard her voice waver. "What can you do to me? You were the one who left, not me."

"I can do plenty." He pulled on the sweater without tucking in his shirt and struggled into his socks and boots. "Keep a close eye on Justin, baby. Make sure you're always watching him."

Abby retreated to the nearest wall for support. He was talking about taking Justin, kidnapping him if she wouldn't play some warped game. "Get out," she whispered.

He stood and dragged on his coat, stumbled and held the back of the couch to steady himself before drawing himself upright. His skin had taken on a gray tinge. "I'll be back," he said, walking a ragged line to the door. "You'll see me again, real soon."

The bang of wood on wood reverberated in Abby's head. She covered her ears. She needed help.

As soon as John's pickup pulled away from the curb, she checked Justin and went to Nick's door. He answered her soft tap, still dressed in his white shirt and navy uniform pants, his tie hanging from beneath his collar. His brown eyes were expressionless.

"John's gone."

Nick braced his arms each side of the doorway. "You didn't have to chase him off on my account." He bowed his head.

"You said we had things to discuss."

He sighed deeply. "I guess I was wrong."

Abby touched his hand hesitantly. "I'm glad to see you, Nick. I've missed you."

When he raised his head, his eyes glistened. He turned his face away. "I missed you too, damn it. I wanted to get things straightened out between us. Janet told me you'd called."

"Come to my place and talk." Abby glanced over her shoulder. "Justin's asleep, but I don't like to leave him."

"Is he okay?"

"Yes," Abby said, smiling. "He's wonderful, Nick. Such a little sweetheart."

"I know."

"Will you come with me?"

He sighed again. "No, Abby. Not tonight."

Blood rushed to her cheeks. "Why?"

"You have to know why. John Winston was in your condo, getting ready to spend the night. I'm not saying there's any grand passion between you two. I don't know what's between you. But *you* don't know what you want for sure yet."

"I do know. I want you." She was begging and didn't care.

Nick stuffed his hands into his pockets, and she felt him struggle not to reach for her.

"Please, Nick. Give me a chance to explain what's been going on."

He hesitated, and for a moment she thought he'd give in. Then he straightened and met her gaze. "I'm not ready, Abby. And if you're honest with yourself, you'll admit you aren't, either. You have to decide what you want for sure. And I'm not convinced you're prepared to cut the ties with John. If you had been, you'd have told your family you were divorced instead of deceiving them."

"I didn't—"

"You did. And wasn't it because you hoped, deep down, that you and John would get back together? I wouldn't blame you. He was your husband. You must have felt something for the guy."

The thudding in Abby's chest hammered against her eardrums. Weakness clawed at her limbs once more. "I don't want John," she whispered. "I want you."

"Go back to Justin." Nick stroked her arm and let his hand fall away. Longing shone in his eyes. "I've got feelings, too, sweetheart. If you have any doubts, it can't work for us. If you come to me, it has to be whole. Give us time to think. A week. A couple of weeks. As long as it takes. Let's stay out of each other's way, and if we're meant to be together, we'll know."

Abby jammed her fist against her mouth, backing away. One more word, and she'd be in tears yet again. She heard Nick's door close before she'd shot home her own dead bolt.

"THEY TOOK IT even worse than I expected," Abby said. Justin in her arms, she stood beside Michael in the driveway outside her parents' house.

"Giving them the silent treatment for two weeks didn't help anything," Michael commented. "They've been expecting to see you since the day after Christmas. I'm amazed Dad managed to stop Mom from calling you."

"I should have called them," Abby said miserably.

Night had closed in, and she shivered while Michael helped her settle Justin in his car seat.

"It's late, sis," Michael said. He tucked a blanket securely around the baby and closed the door. "You'd better get home. And try to unwind, okay? You've got us all behind you—Nick, too, when he comes to his senses."

"I hope so," Abby said, crossing her arms tightly. "Mom called Nick a stranger. She didn't seem to understand at all."

"Give her time." Michael held Abby's door open and leaned on the window rim when she was inside the car. "You know what you have to do, don't you?"

Her head ached. She could hardly think. "Tell me, Michael. I need someone to tell me what to do, step by step."

"First you tell John to get lost." He straightened, balling his hands in his parka pockets and surveying a star-encrusted sky. "Don't worry about anything he might do. I can take care of John Winston. Only I won't have to with Nick around."

"Nick isn't around. I haven't seen him since Christmas night. I think he deliberately stays out of my way."

"He will be around, because when you've told John off for good, you'll go to Nick and threaten him with breach of promise proceedings if he doesn't marry you pronto."

Despite herself, Abby laughed. "Sure, Mike, sure." She sobered. "But you're right, brother of mine. That's what I have to do. That's what I will do."

She started the car, gave the belt around Justin's seat a last tug and drove off, waving to Michael. In the rear-view mirror she saw his tall figure in the driveway. He was still there as she turned the corner.

In her purse was a scrap of paper, the corner of an envelope, showing John's address. She'd torn it off and kept it without ever intending to write to him or go near his home.

With one hand on the wheel, she unzipped the purse and scrabbled in a side pocket until she found what she wanted. Keeping an eye on the road, she glanced back and forth at the address.

Instead of heading east and home, she turned toward Elliott Bay and found her way to an area of old houses perched on the side of a hill. Lower Queen Anne was a district inhabited by many singles and young married couples. Abby had little trouble locating the street and house she needed.

She parked against the steep curb and lifted the still sleeping Justin carefully from his seat. The clock in the car showed nine-thirty. Late, but what she had to do wouldn't wait.

A doorplate beside the leaded glass door showed three names, one of them John's. From his number, three, Abby decided he must have an apartment on the top floor of the three-story building.

No light showed from inside. Abby tried the handle and was surprised when it turned easily. Inside, the smell of cooked cabbage and something fried—fried a long time ago—assaulted her nose.

A door on her left showed an inked-on number one. Narrow stairs rose from the right side of the hall. Abby bowed her head over Justin, praying for enough strength to deal with John, and started up. She passed the second floor, each footstep sounding thunderous on the bare linoleum. Sweat broke out along her spine.

On the third floor, a short hall led to a door with a brass number three screwed to it.

For one moment, with her knuckles poised to knock, Abby thought she would lose her nerve and flee. Instead she rapped firmly.

Seconds passed. John didn't come to the door, but she heard movement inside. Narrowing her eyes and holding Justin more tightly, Abby knocked again.

Justin stirred and whimpered. She jiggled him. He needed a bottle. "John," she said aloud, "I'm not leaving until I see you." He wouldn't hear, but the sound of her own voice was reassuring.

This time she thudded on a door panel with the side of her fist and kept on banging until a shout came from inside.

"All right, all right. Hold it down, will ya?"

Abby kept thumping.

The lock clicked, and a slender wedge of raw yellow light outlined the small woman who stood before Abby. The long honey-blond hair was caught in trembling fingers as the woman pushed it back. The lush body inside a flimsy turquoise nightie didn't need any help from backlighting, but every curve was accentuated.

Only a strong, strong man would turn Marie Prince away on a cold night—or any night.

Chapter Sixteen

"Stop it! Hold still!"

Abby had reached the second flight of stairs when John caught her. He trapped her against the wall, covering her with his body until Justin struggled and cried.

She pushed at his chest with one forearm, trying to keep his weight from the baby. "Get away," she gasped. "Let us go. Get away! You're hurting Justin."

"God, oh, God," John muttered, pulling back, but placing himself below Abby. "I can't let you leave like this. We're going to talk. You'll understand everything if you just listen for once."

Abby closed her eyes and slid to sit on a step, her body curled over Justin. "I already understand, John. There's nothing else to be said." She looked up and met his eyes steadily in the ghastly half-light seeping down from his apartment. "Nothing, except goodbye and don't ever come near us again."

He jammed his fingers into his mussed curls. A T-shirt ended an inch above the jeans he hadn't had time to snap. "Up, Abby," he ordered. She heard each rasping breath he took. "You came to see me, and you're going to."

In one motion, he stooped and swept her to her feet, and holding her with one arm, propelled her upward.

Abby's mind cleared as they went, and the fear slipped away. The next minutes, or however long it took, would be tough, but she'd get through, and then John would be out of her life. Why wasn't she terrified? Abby didn't know why, but she was sure she and Justin would be safe.

John gripped her shoulders as they entered his apartment, clutching as if she were an animal trying to escape. She saw the dingy room that was his home: an unmade bed beneath the window, wallpaper that had once been sprigged with pink roses that were brown splotches now, pieces of furniture they'd once chosen and shared. A striped plastic curtain, pulled back and sagging free of several hooks, served as an enclosure for an ancient stove on legs and a free-standing sink. In one corner a door stood open to reveal a cramped bathroom.

"I'm sorry, Abby."

She jumped and glanced around. Marie, a long down coat wrapped over her nightgown, cowered behind John. Her lovely face, perfect even without makeup, shone unnaturally. Her green eyes seemed glued open and unblinking.

Abby shook her head. "You poor fool. He used me and used me. Did you think he wouldn't use you, too?"

Marie looked away. "I was alone. And John was alone. We both needed someone. I didn't go after him, Abby, honestly."

"Keep your mouth shut," John snapped and wrenched Marie from behind him, shoving her into a chair. "This is between Abby and me."

Fury burst inside Abby. "You're a bastard, John, a bullying bastard. I'll never know why you wanted me in the first place. I'm a bit bigger than most of the people you like to push around.

"You conned Marie, didn't you? You played on her loneliness, then put her to work keeping tabs on me. But you're right about one thing—I don't understand why."

"Listen," John began.

Abby waved for him to be quiet. "How long have you and John been together?" she asked Marie. "Why would you do this to me—all the visits, the suggestions I give Justin up for adoption or give him to John—why?"

Marie spoke through her splayed fingers. "I don't live here, Abby. We just . . . we just . . . I loved him," she finished, and the tears started, sliding noiselessly from her still wide-open eyes. "We were together before you two ever met, remember? Then he didn't want me anymore. But it was all right, Abby; I never blamed you. I got over him until he came to me after he left you. He told me what I already knew: that you two weren't making it, that your marriage was ending. I never meant this to happen, but it did. If I could change it, I would."

"Did you ever go to sea?" Abby asked John. "Or have you been here all this time, knowing how tough things have been with me and doing nothing?"

He made as if to touch her, then dropped his arm. "I went out on a couple of short trips."

"But you knew I'd had to leave my job and I was short of money?"

"I couldn't do a damn thing about it." Sweat gleamed on his unshaven face. "Look at this place. I'm not exactly rolling in green stuff. And with my mother . . ." He paused, bunching muscles in his jaw.

"What about your mother, John? She kept writing to my folks as if nothing was wrong, but her letters to us stopped. What did you tell her?"

He scowled. "I told her we'd moved and gave her this address. She thought I was doing okay, being a 'good boy.' And she kept on and on about 'when the baby's born' and how she could hardly wait to fly us all back there so she could see him.''

Justin whimpered again, and Abby rocked him. ''And that's what all this is about. Of course. If your mother finds out you left me—threw away your child—she may just cut off the little handouts you rely on. Why didn't I figure that out before?'' She gave a hollow laugh. ''I was going to ask where you got the money you've been throwing around for the past couple of weeks, but I don't have to. It's the money we were supposed to use for the trip to New York, isn't it?''

John didn't answer.

''You should have thought farther ahead,'' Abby continued. ''You should have known your mother would never understand how you could give up a child—her grandchild. Now you think if you can patch everything up between us she never has to find out. Too late. As of today, my folks know. Your mother will have to know, too. I don't want to hurt her, and if I can manage it, she'll see Justin, but there's no way to save her from this.''

''Don't tell her,'' John said urgently. ''If you do, I'll never see another penny from her. She'll change her will.''

Abby approached Marie. ''What was your angle on wanting me to give up Justin? If you knew John was going to need the baby to keep milking his mother for money, why would you push for that? The adoption, I mean.''

Marie hunched over, driving the heels of her hands into her eyes. ''The baby was the tie between you. I was afraid he would bring you back together. I never knew about John hoping to get money from his mother. All I wanted was to see you remarried and happy and make sure there'd never be a reason for you and John to see each other. I dreamed everything would come right, and we'd all be happy."

She dropped her hands between her knees and laughed. "I am a fool, and I'm no damned good. But we all know that, don't we? Only I do care about you, Abby. You'll laugh at that one, and I don't blame you, but it's true. All my life I've loved people who didn't give a . . . didn't love me. Why I believed it, I don't know, but this time I actually thought a man wanted me for myself, and I grabbed for the love with both hands. But I never wanted to lose your friendship. We know what the winner takes—what does that leave the loser?"

"You never did get over John, did you? I didn't realize how much he meant to you all those years ago." A shaft of pity pierced Abby. "I can't talk rationally about this now, Marie, but give it some time. I'm not a saint, but I understand loneliness." At a slight sound from John's throat, she turned to him. "Marie wasn't taking anything I wanted anymore, John. She was wrong. Lord, she was wrong, but she deserves better than you."

John didn't meet her eyes. He pulled Marie to her feet. "It's time you went home," he said, and his voice shook. "Abby and I have things to talk about."

"Wrong," Abby retorted. "You and I have nothing to talk about, ever. I'm going home."

"You're not going anywhere," John said, keeping his body between Abby and the door.

A steady trembling started in her belly and legs. "Back off, John. You've lost. Marie, get your things together, we're leaving."

"Not you, Abby," John said. "You and Justin stay with me, please."

There was no threat here. This big, usually confident man, was deflating before her eyes. "Forget it," Abby said, watching Marie gather her possessions and cram them into an overnight case. She pushed her bare feet into knee-high boots and zipped them.

John made no further attempt to make Abby stay. Her last impression of him was the defeated slope of his shoulders as he dropped to sit on the edge of the bed.

Within seconds, she stood on the sidewalk with Marie. "Where's your car?"

"Over there," Marie nodded across the street. "I don't know what to say, Abby."

"Nothing now. Give us time. And, Marie—" Abby gripped the other woman's hand briefly "—try thinking of yourself as worth something, will you? Stop believing you don't have anything to offer another human being."

Without a word, Marie hurried away, switching her case from one hand to the other, her boots scuffing.

"So long," Abby said, almost to herself, while she thought, *Goodbye, Marie.*

Chapter Seventeen

What if he didn't come? What if he did and he was furious to find her here? Abby walked back and forth in the living room. Nick would come. He would. He'd left his lights on, so he couldn't have intended to be out long. And if he didn't want to see her, she'd leave. Simple. She shuddered. There was nothing simple about any of this.

She'd come straight from John's and used her key to get into Nick's condo. Justin, propped in his car seat on the rug, sucked his fist loudly. Abby didn't want to be feeding him if Nick...when Nick got home. She moistened her dry lips. It was late. Where could he be this late?

She was standing in the hall when she heard a key rattle the lock. "Nick," she whispered, and silent dread swelled in her head, and longing. She must be calm and rational, and—

Nick came in, his head down, and slammed the door behind him.

Abby's heart began a slow drumroll. "Hi, Nick. We came."

He dropped his key and grabbed her in one steely arm. "Where have you been?" His grip was so tight she could hardly breathe. He repeatedly smoothed back her hair

while he searched her face. "Are you all right? Were you
at John's? I've been out of my mind with worry."

Abby couldn't move. "How? Michael talked to you.
He called you."

"I went to Michael's to talk. He told me you were upset. Then I came back here to wait for you. When you
didn't show, I started out to find John, only I forgot I
don't know where he lives. I was going to call Mike to
find out." He half dragged her into the living room and
pushed her onto the couch. "Are you all right? Did you
go to John's?"

She nodded. "It wasn't easy, but it is over, Nick.
Completely finished."

He gave her a long look before he turned away to
crouch over Justin. He lifted the baby and held him close.
"Your boy needs some attention."

Nick wore the bright blue running pants she'd tried so
often not to notice, and a baggy gray sweatshirt. Sitting
behind him now, Abby made no attempt not to study his
broad back, the way his shirt hung in folds at his slim
waist and rode across solidly muscled hips. Every sin-
uous line in the long, strong legs showed through the
clinging fabric of the pants.

He glanced around an instant before she could raise her
eyes. "You look great," he said, his voice barely audible.

Abby's cheeks heated. He knew she'd been assessing
him. "So do you, Nick. I've missed you."

Nick regarded her steadily.

Why, when she needed to say something profound, did
the air have to rush from her lungs and logical thought
flee?

He sat on the arm of the couch and ruffled her short
curls. "Whenever you feel like it, Abby—if you feel like

it—we'll talk." His tawny eyes, when they met hers, held his heart, and Abby felt a tightening low inside that was almost a blow.

"Is there anything to talk about, Nick?" she asked uncertainly. "You said all we'd have to do was move in next door, and we came. If you still want us."

"I still want you." Nick slid down beside her. "You know I'll never stop wanting you."

He brought his face close to hers, and she shut her eyes, waiting for the pressure of his lips. "Do you know I can see those gray eyes of yours whenever I try to sleep?" His mouth brushed hers. "And feel your hair? I've reached out my hand expecting to find you beside me." The next kiss was harder, and Nick's tongue met Abby's.

Justin wiggled between them and wailed. "Ahh," Nick sighed, and she felt his breath. "You did warn me about this moment. He needs changing and a bottle."

Before she could react, Nick strode to lay Justin on the rug. Deftly he found a waterproof sheet in the bag and slid it under the kicking legs. "Is there a bottle in here somewhere?"

Abby shed her coat and went to the kitchen to warm a bottle of formula. By the time she returned to the living room, Nick was crooning to Justin, holding him high and punctuating his hum with kisses to a face crumpled with fury. While she watched from across the room, he fed the baby, stopping the greedy sucking at intervals, coping as expertly as she ever could.

"I think you actually enjoy him," she said when the bottle was empty. "I wish..." She mustn't say it.

"You wish?

"Nothing."

"You were going to tell me something you wish, Abby We've been through too much together for you not to be able to tell me anything that comes into your head."

She turned her back. "I almost said I wished Justin was your son."

"He almost is, sweetheart, in a way. Didn't you tell me just now that you'd come to me, like you said you would? Didn't that mean we're going to be married?"

Her skin was cold, then fiery. "If you're still sure we should. You don't owe me anything, Nick. Just because we talked about—"

"Shhh. Can we put Justin down on a regular bed in my spare room? Would he roll off?"

"Not if we make bolsters out of towels or something."

"Look at me, Abby."

Slowly she turned to him.

"Will you stay with me tonight? Sleep with me? I only— No, I don't only want to hold you: you know what I want. But if you're not ready, I'll settle for just having you with me."

Words formed but came slowly. "I'll . . . I'll stay with you." She should tell him so much. "Nick, I've dreamed about you, too. And imagined you with me, beside me. I was afraid I'd lost you."

"You couldn't. I'm one of those pests who won't stay gone."

They settled Justin in a makeshift bed, surrounded him with fat rolls of towels, and within moments he fell into an exhausted sleep.

Nick held Abby's hand and started for the living room. She pulled him to a halt, tried a smile that didn't quite work, and walked backward, leading him to his bedroom.

When they stood at the foot of his bed, Nick asked, "Do you want to get some of your things?" and his voice broke.

"I don't need anything," Abby managed. "I came to you whole, the way you said I had to."

His gaze swept slowly over her, and she blushed.

"Oh, just a minute." Nick squeezed her hand before reaching to open a closet. "Remember the coat I said I wanted to buy you? I did buy it while I was in Omaha. I hope you like the thing. It can be changed if you don't." He was rushing now, filling the awkward moments for her. "I was going to give it to you when I got back, but—"

Abby caught both of his wrists. "Nick, you don't have to worry about me. This is where I want to be, with you, totally with you."

He looked at her, desire straining every feature tight. "God, I'm afraid to let go, Abby. I'm only a man, and I've wanted you for so long."

She ran her fingers into his hair, reached up, pressing close and kissing him with all the pent-up passion she'd suppressed for too long. Their mouths met again and again and with force. Tongues sought, breath became one breath, and it was Abby who grasped Nick's hips, clamping his hard body to hers.

He arched back, his eyes closed. "We've got to be careful, Abby. It's soon for you, maybe too soon."

She wanted to argue. Instead, she broke away and walked to the far side of the bed. Her eyes riveted on Nick's, she took off her sweater. Self-consciousness thickened her fingers as she unbuttoned the silvery silk blouse she wore.

"Is this too soon?" Nick asked. "We don't have to push." She heard him swallow. "Maybe I belong on the couch for a few nights."

Abby shook her head and undid the impossibly tiny buttons at her cuffs. When the blouse lay on a chair, she stood very still, aware of the rise and fall of her breasts. Reaching back, she undid her lace bra and let it fall.

"God, Abby," Nick said, "you're lovely. I knew you would be."

He pulled the sweatshirt over his head, and Abby felt the last vestige of air sucked from her lungs. His body showed the lean conditioning of an athlete. Broad shoulders, well-muscled chest, a dark shadow of hair fanning wide before it narrowed to a diminishing V at his waist.

Abby felt her breasts swell and flush. She unzipped her skirt, kicking aside her shoes, and slid off the rest of her clothes. Instinctively she covered her stomach, certain it must still carry the signs of pregnancy.

"Don't," Nick whispered. "Don't hide any part of you from me. You are so beautiful." He leaned on the bed to untie his shoes before stripping away the running pants.

Abby laid trembling fingers against her lips and waited until he stood inches from her. His back was straight, his stance unconscious and comfortable with the honest display of his desperate need for her. He kept his arms at his sides while she looked at him. She wanted to tell him it was he who was beautiful, he who was perfect. But speech was impossible.

"Sit by me," he said, throwing back the quilt and covers and sinking down. He smoothed the sheet beside him and offered his hand.

Abby lifted her hand, held it out until Nick threaded their fingers together. When she sat, she was half facing him, their hands still joined, her thigh pressed to his.

Nick tipped up his jaw, the tendons in his neck flexing, and she kissed him there, kissed the dip above his collarbone and followed unyielding muscle to touch her tongue to an instantly erect nipple.

"You must be tired, Abby," he said hoarsely. His chest rose and fell, and he turned her hand over his heart. Rapid thudding met her sensitive fingers. "Are you?"

Abby shook her head, smiling. "I've never been more wide-awake."

She pulled her knees onto the bed and moved behind him. "You're tense, my darling. You don't have to be. I'm not made of glass." Her fingertips found the bunched muscles in his shoulders and kneaded. And a kiss followed each delving pressure.

"Oh, Abby, you aren't going to be safe if you don't stop that," Nick murmured, bracing his weight on his hands.

Abby guided the back of his head against her neck, deliberately pressing her breasts into his shoulders until he groaned and twisted, pushing her onto her back. "Don't you understand what I'm asking you? Shouldn't we wait longer before we make love?" Bright color rose to his cheeks, and Abby couldn't hold back a grin.

"You're wonderful, Nick Dorset. I'm in perfect shape. The doctor says so. And if you keep this up, I'll think you don't want to."

His mouth on her breast made her back arch away from the bed. "I want to, ma'am. You don't know how much I want to. But I won't risk hurting you." His lips closed over first one nipple and then the other, and Abby's brain began to disconnect. She felt his teeth, his tongue, the rough texture of his chest hair, on every part of her body. The thigh that parted hers was rock hard, and the hands that caressed her were gentle.

The skin at his sides was smooth, and on his shoulder blades, where a thin film of sweat formed. His hair smelled clean and felt vibrant. "You're not going to hurt me. I'm ready for you," she whispered against his ear. "Now."

Nick supported his weight on his elbows, staring down into her face. He bowed his head to look at her breasts before he slid lower to kiss them, smooth them and pass his mouth over each rib until he kissed her belly repeatedly, making a line down, steadily down between her legs.

"No," Abby said, but faintly. He reached up to cover her breasts, rotated his palms slowly until she arched her pelvis against him. Her skin and flesh and blood were on fire. She heard a cry, her own, but distant and strange, before she thrust her hips helplessly up to meet the searing in her body and fell back, throbbing.

He lay unmoving for seconds, his cheek resting on her stomach, his hands clasping her hips. Then, slowly, he slid upward, retracing the kisses over her sensitive skin, until his mouth found her breasts again, and then her mouth.

"I love you, Nick," Abby managed at last.

Nick murmured something unintelligible. His breathing speeded, and he moved more urgently against her.

Closing her eyes tightly, Abby used all her strength to push him onto his back and slide her body on top of his. She reached to touch and stroke, missing no part of him until she caressed his most intimate places. "My turn," she said, and wondered at the sound of her own voice—the husky voice of a woman she didn't know.

"Oh, my sweet," Nick groaned when she sat astride his hips, "for a quiet lady, you're something."

Abby laughed softly as she joined them and moved them with an intense fervor she was powerless to stem. They turned onto their sides as one, rolling again. Abby wrapped her legs around Nick, looked up into his eyes and saw them glaze before all thought ceased.

When he slumped on top of her, she tasted damp salt on his skin, smelled the scent of their loving. "I love you, Nick," she heard herself say on a long breath. She sighed. "I keep saying that."

He shifted his weight and pulled her tightly into his arms. "You couldn't say it too often. And you couldn't love me as much as I love you. But I'll take as much as you've got. Did I hurt you? It was too fast, wasn't it?"

She laughed and cried, and clutched his flexing arms. "Yes, I can love you as much as you love me, and I'll give you everything I've got to give, and no, you didn't hurt me, and no, it wasn't too fast."

"Mmm." Nick peered into her eyes. "You'd better not be trying to fool me."

Abby stroked his tousled hair. "I wouldn't dare."

Abruptly Nick plumped up two pillows and sat against them, cross-legged. He maneuvered Abby's head onto his belly. "Let's get serious."

She kissed the taut skin beneath his navel. "I thought we were being very serious."

"You know what I mean. Justin's going to need a house with a yard. Plenty of room to run around in. We'd better start looking for a place."

"You want to discuss this *now*?" Abby peered disbelievingly up into his face. He gazed intently into the distance, and she groaned. "You do want to discuss it now.

Okay. But Justin can't even turn over properly yet. All he needs is a crib and food.''

"Kids grow up fast. We have to make plans."

"Of course," she agreed demurely. "But I'm going to have to get a job to help with a big expense like a house."

Nick frowned and looked away.

"What's the matter?" Abby sat up to face him. "Is something wrong, Nick?"

"I can't tell you what to do. Knowing you're going to be with me has to be enough."

"What aren't you saying?"

He kissed the corner of her mouth and stroked her cheek, pulling away to look acutely into her eyes. "Would it be so terrible to give Justin the time he needs with his mother—for a while, at least. I'm not suggesting you give up your career altogether, but a baby needs his own parents around as much as possible . . . I mean, his mother." He looked slightly confused.

"No," Abby said thoughtfully. "It wouldn't be at all terrible to stay with Justin. And if you feel awkward about behaving like one of his parents, don't. As far as I'm concerned, you are. You're taking us both on. But that doesn't mean I have to be a dead weight on you, financially."

"I can afford to keep a family, Abby. Later, if you want to go back to work—when our kids are older—fine."

"*Kids?*"

He smiled faintly and stroked her breast.

Abby felt an instant rekindling of desire. "I do want to have more children, Nick. How could I not with a man like you around to supervise?"

He rolled her tenderly onto her back and stretched beside her. "I want you to be happy, that's all. And I don't think you'd be happy if you left Justin too soon, okay?"

"Okay," she agreed slowly.

"So we'll take the work thing one day at a time?"

"One day at a time. Nick—"

"Yeah?"

"My folks know about you."

"What do they think?"

"Well, my mother wondered how I'd had a chance to fall in love with a stranger."

He laughed against her breast, nuzzled the sensitive skin and wrapped a heavy thigh over both of hers. He looked pensive.

Abby pulled a pillow under her arm and propped up her head. "What are you thinking about, Nick?"

He outlined the contours of her body. "I was thinking we'd better get married fast—like immediately."

"Why the hurry?"

Nick brought his lips close to hers. "Because I want your folks to see us legally hitched before they figure out I'm no stranger."

COMING NEXT MONTH

#197 SUMMER CHARADE by Karen Toller Whittenburg

Rebecca Whitaker's new antique trunk had to contain valuables because it was bringing her nothing but trouble. But *what* was the treasure? If she knew, she wouldn't be keeping company with Quinn Kinser, who was trouble personified. Just how far would Quinn be willing to go to get his hands on the trunk?

#198 SOAR AND SURRENDER by Maralys Wills

Finances unnerved her, aeronautics unhinged her, yet Jenny meant to keep the hang-gliding company she'd inherited. She had the dreams of an eagle, but co-owner Kirk had the instincts of an ostrich! When they're challenged to risk their lives for Jenny's dream, will Kirk be ready to carry her on wings of courage?

#199 WINTER'S END by Alysse Lemery

Chrys's young daughter loved everyone in the small Wisconsin town, and that included Eric McLean, who'd just returned. Chrys, though, had reservations, for she and Eric had once been lovers, a long time ago. A child's love is simple, but it's also magical for a man and a woman united after a long, harsh winter.

#200 FANTASIES AND MEMORIES by Muriel Jensen

Small wonder Destiny felt mutinous. Rafe turned a peaceful summer in Maine into sheer misery. No colas, spicy foods or work. Life would've been easier with Captain Bligh! Was it any wonder she'd jumped ship last time—would she again?

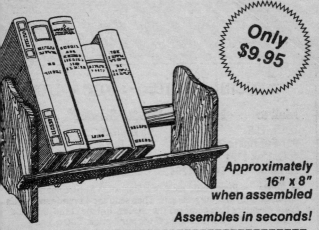

Take 4 best-sellin
love stories FREI
Plus get a FREE surprise gif

Special Limited-Time Offer

Mail to **Harlequin Reader Service®**

In the U.S.
901 Fuhrmann Blvd.
P.O. Box 1394
Buffalo, N.Y. 14240-1394

In Canada
P.O. Box 609
Fort Erie, Ontario
L2A 5X3

YES! Please send me 4 free Harlequin Superromance®
novels and my free surprise gift. Then send me 4 brand-new novels
every month as they come off the presses. Bill me at the low price
of $2.50 each*—a 9% saving off the retail price. There is no
minimum number of books I must purchase. I can always return a
shipment and cancel at any time. Even if I never buy another
book from Harlequin, the 4 free novels and the surprise gift are
mine to keep forever.   134 BPS BP7S

*Plus 49¢ postage and handling per shipment in Canada.

Name _____ (PLEASE PRINT)

Address _____ Apt. No. _____

City _____ State/Prov. _____ Zip/Postal Code _____

This offer is limited to one order per household and not valid to present
subscribers. Price is subject to change.   SR-SUB-1A